The Bad Sister

Rachael Stewart

DDP
DEEP DESIRES PRESS
Winnipeg, Canada

Copyright © 2019 by Rachael Stewart
Cover design copyright © 2019 by Story Perfect Dreamscape

All characters are age 18 and over.

This is a work of fiction. Names, characters, business, places, events, and incidents are either products of the author's imagination or used in a fictitious manner. Any resemblances to actual persons, living or dead, or actual events is purely coincidental.

No part of this book may be used or reproduced in any manner without written permission from the publisher. However, brief quotations may be reproduced in the context of reviews.

Published April 2019 by Deep Desires Press, an imprint of Story Perfect Inc.

Deep Desires Press
PO Box 51053 Tyndall Park
Winnipeg, Manitoba R2X 3B0
Canada

Visit http://www.deepdesirespress.com for more scorching hot erotica and erotic romance.

WIN FREE BOOKS!

Subscribe to our email newsletter to get notified of all our hot new releases, sales, and giveaways! Visit deepdesirespress.com/newsletter to sign up today!

This one is for my little bro, who will take great amusement in having a book entitled The Bad Sister *dedicated to him. Mike, this is for making me smile and laugh until I cry! You are one in a million! Loves ya! Rxx*

The Bad Sister

Prologue

Ten Years Ago

CARRIE PRESSED A CLAMMY HAND TO HER mouth and took a breath through her nose. She felt sick. Like at any moment, she would either vomit or buckle over and cry. And neither was an option.

This was it. Time to give the performance of a lifetime. A performance worthy of a veteran actress, not someone of her eighteen years and just starting out.

But if she could do this, then she could do anything. She would have no worries for what Hollywood had in store. She would take the acting world by storm, because hiding her true emotional state would take every ounce of her strength and skill.

Worst thing was, part of her hoped that Dan and her family would see the performance for what it was, because if they believed it to be real, they'd see her as a bitch. A cold, calculating, selfish bitch. And she wasn't. She really wasn't.

Doors started to slam; her father was on the move. It was now or never. She grabbed her suitcase from the bed and raced out of the bedroom. *You can do this. You will.*

"Dad, wait."

He was at the top of the stairs, his mouth a grim line, his eyes glazed as he looked to her. *Christ*, was she the only one to see how much pain he was in?

"You're not going without me."

He gave a shuddery sigh, his head shaking in refusal. "Don't be silly, sweetheart. You need to stay for Isla, she'll—"

The door to the master bedroom opened, cutting him off. Mum stepped out. She looked like hell too, but she'd had a say in this, she was partly to blame. They should have compromised, done anything but this.

"No, Isla has mum; I'm staying with you." Mum looked to her, and Carrie's heart broke just a little, her determination wavering. "I can't let Dad go alone, Mum. It's not fair..." *That's not going to convince them, you need to make it about you, no one else.* "...and it makes sense for me to go. You know it does. The acting opportunities are far greater in LA, and with Dad guiding me and his contacts as a producer, I'll get the career I dream of."

Mum nodded, but her smile was watery, and Carrie didn't dare blink, not until her own tears had receded. She couldn't back down. This was about more than any of those things. It was about Isla. Her twin, the person who mattered above all else and whose heart was breaking because of her. Because of her relationship with Dan.

Their twisted love triangle had to end.

She had to end it.

"It's okay, love. I know." Mum opened her arms and a betraying sob rose up in Carrie's throat.

She walked towards her. *Be strong. Do the right thing.*

Mum pulled her in and Carrie sucked in a breath; her scent, her comfort, her warmth—*Oh God, you need to move.*

"I'll call you soon," she forced out, giving her one last squeeze before stepping out of her hold.

Mum nodded with a strangled hum. Her fight to hold it all in as obvious and as painful as Carrie's own. And this wasn't even the worst of it. That was yet to come, when—

"Carrie, Dan's here!"

...*The worst was now.*

It was Isla calling from downstairs. Well, not really calling as such; her voice was mouse-like, shaken by the magnitude of what was happening. By Dad leaving, and now Carrie going too.

She took a deep breath and returned Mum's wet smile.

"Carrie, really, sweetheart," Dad said, behind her. "You don't need to come with me, I can source you roles from out there, I can help your career, I can—"

"Are you saying you don't want me to come?" Her words were purposefully hard as she looked to him over her shoulder.

His body slumped and he shook his head, that same broken move. "No, darling. I'd love you to come." And then he looked to Mum—fear, pain, guilt all striking in his glistening depths before he turned back to Carrie. "But it has to be because you want to come for *you*. No other reason."

"I do want to." No hesitation, no nothing. She had to go. She had to break out of the self-destructive love triangle and make a life without guilt, without forever worrying over Isla. And she didn't want Dad alone, pushed out because Mum couldn't handle Hollywood life and the absentee husband that came with it.

But he'd done his best; he really had. Why couldn't Mum see that? Why couldn't Isla?

"Carrie?"

It was Dan calling. It really was time to go. Time to give the final performance, the one that would truly prove her worthy of the Oscars.

She gave Mum one last look and then followed Dad down the stairs.

Isla had her arms crossed at the bottom, her eyes on the floor.

"Isla, sweetheart, I'm sorry it's come to this," Dad said, but she didn't even acknowledge him, and Carrie's heart broke that little bit more, fresh tears spiking. "If you want to visit, any time, you're more than welcome, I'd love—"

"Enough, Dad." She flicked her hand to cut him off. "Just go."

He hesitated before her. It was easy to see his desire to embrace his daughter, to bottle whatever he could of this goodbye, but Isla was having none of it. Anger sparked, heat rising in Carrie's gut, stinging at her eyes, and momentarily, she forgot Dan was standing in the doorway, no clue as to what was going on.

"Come on, Isla. You won't see Dad for a while, the least you can do is give him a proper goodbye."

She looked at Carrie, her eyes tinged with her own anger, her own tears. "It's okay for you. You're getting everything you could possibly want."

Carrie's mouth fell open. She couldn't quite believe Isla's words. *But it works for you, for the role you have to play. Go with it.*

"You'll have your name up in lights before you know it, sis. You'll forget all about us here in the UK, just like Dad does every time he swans off, leaving Mum to do all the work."

"It's not Dad's fault his career takes him away."

"No, but it's his fault we have to put up with the gossip columns dishing out the dirt, snapping him with this slapper and that, when he should be here, with us."

Carrie stilled, goosebumps prickling as ice ran through her. She couldn't believe her sister—*sweet, kind, good*—could sink that low. There was no truth to any of it, she was sure of it and her sister should know that too.

"*Isla.*" Dad's tone was loaded with warning. "I have never been unfaithful to your mother. *Never.* You three are my life. I would never jeopardise that."

Her sister simply scoffed. "Shame you put your career first then, Dad, living it up in Hollywood and all its two-faced glory, when you could be here, earning an honest living."

If Carrie's jaw could hit the floor, it would. She knew Isla took issue with Dad's career and her own dream to be an actress, she just hadn't realized she hated it *this* much. "Hey, seriously, sis, that's—"

"Don't you 'hey, sis' me, you're totally lost to that world too, leaving us—"

"Carrie?" Dan's confused voice cut over her, sending her heart into a downward spiral. He knew nothing of her plans. Not yet.

Isla turned to look at him. "Don't tell me you're surprised, Dan. Surely you of all people know this life isn't good enough for the superstar she is so determined to be. It's her dream after all."

Isla's voice dripped with sarcasm, and she got that it was because her sister was hurting, that it came from her pain over them leaving, but it didn't stop the words from cutting deep.

"*Isla.*" The warning came from Mum now standing at the top of the stairs, watching the scene unfold.

"*What?*" Isla snapped, but before Mum could say anything else she gave an incredulous laugh and walked towards the door. "I'm going out. Good luck to you, sis. I shouldn't really be surprised—you were always one to go after what you wanted, to hell with everyone else."

And then she was gone, barging past an open-mouthed Dan who now looked to Carrie, his gray eyes narrowing in confusion. "What's going on?"

A car horn sounded from outside.

"That'll be the cab, sweetheart." Her father turned to her. "I'll wait for you out there."

She nodded and watched him go. He was giving them privacy, she knew it and was grateful for it, even as her stomach twisted tighter, the lump in her throat swelling exponentially. *Be brave.*

She swallowed past the obstruction and nodded. Behind her, movement at the top of the stairs and a door closing told her that Mum had headed back to her room.

Dad passed by Dan with a nod and a grim smile. They weren't too dissimilar in that moment. Both losing their loved ones in some weird, messed-up way. And then Dan rushed forward, his hands taking hold of her hips. She could feel his body trembling through his fingers, hear the panic rising in his voice, "Carrie, why do you have a suitcase? What's Isla on about? Where's your dad going?"

She looked up into his eyes, gray pools always so full of love and desire, now awash with fear and desperation. This was it. Her moment. She had to be strong. But all she wanted to do was collapse against his tall frame, bury her head beneath his chin and let him hold her. Tell her she'd got it all wrong, that they could make this work without hurting Isla, that she didn't need to leave, that everything would be okay.

Isla's parting comment came back to her. *You were always one to go after what you wanted, to hell with everyone else.*

And there it was. Her resentment, her pain over Dan. The fact he chose Carrie over her coming to the fore. That's what Isla had meant. There was no getting away from it, no putting a stop to it, unless Carrie ended things with Dan. And she couldn't stay here and be strong enough to do it, to make that break permanent.

Dad leaving gave her the out she needed. And the strength. He needed her, too. Mum would have Isla. Dad would have Carrie. It was as good as they were ever going to get.

She stepped out of his hold, her eyes dropping to the floor. "I'm leaving, Dan. Dad's moving to LA and I'm going with him."

He gave a crazed laugh. "Don't be daft, your life is here."

"Not anymore."

"But Carrie…" He reached out for her chin and she turned her head away, stepping back to increase the distance between them. She needed to get away from his familiar scent, from the luring warmth of his body, the comfort she knew existed in his hold.

"Dad needs me."

"*I need you*…bloody hell, Carrie, *I love you*, you can't just up and leave."

"I have to." The words *I love you too* were on the tip of her tongue, desperate to come out, but to say them would ruin her fall-back position. The point she knew she had to get to. The one that would end it all, for good. "I *have* to go."

He took a shuddery breath, his fingers raking through his shaggy black hair, hair that she'd spent hours toying with, could feel on her fingers now if she put her mind to it.

"How long will you be gone?"

His question pulled her back, away from the bittersweet memory. "I don't know."

"What do you mean, you don't know?"

"I mean, I have no plans to return, Dan. I'm moving out there. I'm going after my dream—I'm going to be a star."

His eyes pierced her, wide, disbelieving. "This isn't you talking."

"I don't see anyone else here." She tightened her grip on the handle of her suitcase, on her heart. She needed to stick the boot in, bury his love forever and her own with it. "Look, Dan, the UK isn't for me. With Dad leaving..." She thought of Mum—of the heartbreak permeating the air not just between her and Dan, but her parents too—and hardened herself against it. To show any weakness would only drag out the inevitable. It would give him hope when there could be none, not while Isla loved him. "Dad leaving has given me the chance I need to break free, to get a better life...the life I deserve. I'm going to take Hollywood by storm."

She wanted to cringe, hating her words, hating herself even more as she threw them at him. But it was the right thing to do. *It was.*

"What about me?"

"What about you?"

He looked like she'd struck him. "You *love* me."

She couldn't deny it. The lie stuck in her throat, made her stomach lurch. "It's over."

"I don't believe you." He scanned her face, fiercely probing, his hands lifting to grip her upper arms. "What's really going on?"

"I've finally seen sense." She forced herself to hold his gaze as she brushed his hands away. "Staying here—being with you—it's only holding me back."

"Being with me?" His voice dropped, his eyes so pained and inside she was sobbing, great wracking waves. *You need to move, now.*

And then his eyes lit, a spark of hope coming from nowhere. "Look, if it's Hollywood you want, I get it. But I can get a job while I study, I can fly out, you can fly back, we can make this work."

She shook her head, trying to counteract the chaos inside. "No, you don't have time for it, you need to focus on your career too. Your degree."

"I don't give a shit about my degree, Carrie. I care about you, about our future. We can make it work. Long distance if we have to."

She gave a harsh laugh, honesty breaking out. "My parents have been together twenty years Dan, and not even they can make it work. It's two lives. Celebrity versus Ordinary." And now for the added lie, the kick in the teeth. "It's all or nothing, and I choose all. I choose Hollywood."

He scoffed, desperation vibrating through his body, his voice. "So, what's the last year been, you and me, a lie?"

No. God, no.

"I'm sorry, Dan." She said it so softly, it was almost inaudible. "It's been great while it lasted, but it's over now."

I can't be the bad sister, the one inflicting all the pain, not anymore.

"But, Carrie..." He broke off, his head shaking, his loss for words clear and giving her the push she needed to leave.

"Take care of Isla for me..." Her sister started the same hospitality course as him next month, a year behind him but the same university. So much in common. So much to draw them together.

Maybe he'll realize his mistake. Maybe he'll realize she's the better sister, the one worthy of his love. Maybe they'll finally be together.

The idea tore through her and she sucked in a breath, her conscience coming to her rescue—*But at least you won't be the one inflicting the pain then.*

She turned and headed for the open door, her legs dragging like lead.

You're nearly there, you can cry in the car, just—

"Isla's right," he said after her. "You really will do anything to get what you want, to hell with the rest of us."

She didn't turn. She didn't acknowledge his words. She focused on putting one leg before the other. Lugging her suitcase down the gravel path to the awaiting car. She could hear footsteps behind her, knew Dan followed.

"Good luck with your dream, Carrie," he bit out, his words cracking just a little. "You deserve whatever you've got coming to you."

Her heart split in two.

You have no idea, Dan.

Chapter One

Present Day

"I MEAN IT, MAX. IF YOU DON'T GET THAT BITCH off the premises, I swear to God I'll get one of the doormen to throw her out."

Carrie winced, falling back against the closed door that separated her from the man doing his damnedest to make sure she didn't get over the threshold. She'd hardly expected him to welcome her with open arms, but still, having Dan call her a bitch, it hurt. Really hurt.

She breathed through the unfamiliar pain in her chest, trying to ignore it. She'd shut down that side of herself ten years ago; she wasn't about to give into it now. Least of all when she had a goal to achieve. And her goal this second was to get Dan to help her—*No, not you, Isla.* To help Isla.

"Look, I get that you don't want to see her," came Max's response. "But she isn't taking no for an answer."

The sound of something hard striking a surface made her jump. "She never fucking did!"

On either side of her, the two overbearing thugs guarding the stairs that led out of the basement straightened up, their awareness of the escalating mood on the other side of the door clear.

She was close to being tossed out onto the street. She knew it. They knew it. But she refused to be bullied off course.

The hairs at the back of her neck prickled and she smoothed

them away. There was little she could do for the somersaults raging in her belly, though. It had been years since she'd been this on edge, but then the force of Dan's reaction had floored her. He was beyond mad at her arrival—she had expected that—but it was the underlying threat to his tone that had her wavering. The Dan she remembered wouldn't hurt a fly. And he certainly wouldn't be so bold as to turn her away.

She'd banked on him being the same dependable guy, the one who would have done anything for her, for Isla…

But that was before you broke his heart.

Before you broke your own and killed it off.

But if her heart was dead, why was she here now, quaking in her Louboutins?

Maybe this was the wrong call. Maybe she didn't need his help after all. Maybe she could do it without him.

There were plenty of resources at her disposal, what with her connections any one of them could help bring Isla's business back from the brink.

Yeah, but none of them know your sister like he does.

And she'd bet none of them knew the industry like he did, if the buzzing popularity of the exclusive nightclub in full swing above her head was anything to go by.

Plus, with him as her frontman, she wouldn't have to risk exposing her presence here to the world. And that made all manner of discomfort worth it.

"Seriously Dan, I don't think anyone would dare lay a finger on her," Max was saying. Then, speaking so quietly that she had to strain to hear over the music pounding through the ceiling, "I mean, it's Carrie Evans for Christ's sake."

Yes, she'd had to let her identity slip a little to get this far. There was no getting past the guards on the main club entrance without pulling the celebrity card. And the timely reminder of her elevated public stature had her body straightening, her shoulders squaring off.

Why was she letting his temper get the better of her anyway? In her line of work, dealing with heated outbursts was an occupational hazard.

"Don't you get all blasted star-struck on me," Dan snapped. "I'm warning you, if you don't get that bloody woman off these premises, I'm going to do something we all regret."

She could hear movement behind the door and sprang away from it, expecting it to swing open. Instead there came a rustling followed by a strung out, "Okay, okay, I'll sort it!"

What the hell? What was Max having to do? Restrain him?!

Panic taking hold anew, she filled her mind with the nineteen-year-old Dan of their youth; the sweet, kind and dependable Dan. She conjured up his lanky frame, not threatening by any means; his foppish good looks, perfectly harmless…

Holding firm, she faced the doorway and watched the handle shift. She sent a fleeting glance at the doormen. Would they descend on her as soon as the door opened? She wondered if she lost the wide brimmed hat and thick shades, would they all back off? Just as Max had suggested. He was right after all, no one stood in the way of her, not these days. Life had become one big obstacle-free ride since she had hit it big…obstacle-free and boring as fuck.

Parking her thoughts and the weird swell of emotion that was becoming far too familiar, she steeled herself to do battle, donning her perfect high-and-mighty persona and striding forward as soon as the door swung inwards.

A golden-haired Max gawped at her from his position on the other side of the door, his charming features contorted in surprise as he blustered over her intrusion.

"Apologies, I'm not one for waiting." She smiled sweetly, stepping around him as her eyes lifted to seek out her target.

She stilled, the air suddenly too thick to breathe. The deep red walls of the windowless room closed in around her, channelling her vision to the towering hunk of a man ahead.

She slipped off the shades that were hindering her view far too much and felt her lips part of their own accord, her pulse taking an appreciative leap.

This man couldn't be Dan. He just couldn't.

Steely gray eyes hit her, their chilling depths doing nothing to encourage her approach and yet failing cataclysmically to douse the burn igniting low in her gut.

It was just nerves, she told herself. Nerves and the abysmal start to her visit that had her insides freaking out.

He fisted his hands, planting them on the desk before him as he leaned forward to pin her with his gaze, his expression unwelcoming, broody and…and…

Nerves!

Who was she kidding? There was nothing nervous about the dryness to her mouth, her tripping heart rate and her sudden inability to speak.

If only he would actually address her, then maybe the spell would lift and he would become Dan again, because he sure as hell appeared anything but.

His shaggy black mane so far from foppish now, screamed *don't-give-a-fuck*, as it framed a chiselled facial structure that her Hollywood male co-stars would go under the knife to achieve. Gone was the fine smattering of facial hair and lips that curved easily into a smile. His dark, shadowed stubble, now outlined a mouth that even in its firm, tight line, spoke of its full, sensual, and utterly masculine appeal.

As for his body—his once tall, *athletic* physique—it was now unrecognisable in the tensed-up powerhouse before her, his black tee stretched taut over his broad, muscular chest, his exposed forearms straining as he continued to lean into his fists.

And Christ, is that a tattoo tracing up one arm, or just a trick of the light?

She was gawping, and she knew it, but the skill of pulling her jaw back up evaded her. Dan was so much more man than the boy of his youth and her body purred over the realization, her mind wrestling for control. Nineteen-year-old Dan she could handle. But twenty-nine-year-old Dan...her naivety hit her full force. How could she have been so stupid as to expect him to remain unchanged?

And why the hell hadn't Isla told her?

Ha, as if you don't know the answer to that one.

Given the history of their love triangle, there was no way her sister would have dished this dirt. Dan was and would forever be a taboo subject. As was the love they'd once shared: Isla for Dan, Dan for Carrie, Carrie for herself. It wasn't the whole truth—far from it—but that was the way it had gone down ten years ago, and that's the way it would stay.

Or should stay.

Only *this* Dan...she wet her lips. The transformation was as marked as heaven to hell, saint to sinner, sweetheart to playboy. Her insides quivered, unashamedly acknowledging that she'd have no trouble accommodating the last.

And what about your boyfriend stateside? What does that tell you about your recent relationship woes?

All you need to know, came the unequivocal response.

As for their messy love triangle, that was ancient history, surely?

Or maybe not...

And for fuck's sake, you're still gawping!

"I'm afraid, Miss Evans..." Max stepped into her line of sight, much to the annoyance of her libido, which hadn't quite had its fill of the new Dan yet. "...Mr. Stevenson has a lot to tend to at present, and can't see you."

She gave Max the holier-than-thou smile she had picked up in Hollywood. "I beg to differ. I think he *will* make time to see me."

Her tone and stance made it clear that nothing and no one would be moving her out of the way any time soon. Not unless they wanted to bear witness to a celebrity-bitch-style hissy fit.

As expected, he stilled, his eyes moving from her to look imploringly at Dan.

One man down…

The doormen crossed the threshold and immediately flanked Max, their gazes flicking between her and the big boss. Neither showed any inclination to come any further.

Three down.

Now for her true target…

She turned and locked her sights unwaveringly on Dan himself, praying he could be as easily tamed, her body sizzling over the very real possibility. *Your body should have nothing to do with it. You're here for Isla, not to get your end away. Jesus, Carrie.*

"Come now, don't tell me you're not even a little happy to see me." She gave him a perfect, teasing pout and slipped the wide brimmed hat from her head, shaking her long blonde waves free of their restraint.

She saw his knuckles whiten, saw his mouth clench further in its thin determined line. *If looks could kill…*

"Carrie."

Her name left his lips on a hiss of barely constrained contempt, but she refused to let it get to her. He couldn't hate her that much. Ten years was a lot of time to heal. *She* had…or so she'd thought.

And none of that matters. None of that fits with the reason you are here now, for Isla. For her club. Park your body and get on with it!

"They say absence makes the heart grow fonder," she purred, her outward composure still thankfully intact. "What's it been Dan? Nine…ten years?"

He scanned her silently, his slow, deliberate gaze, scathing enough to leave her feeling stripped and exposed. She shuddered. No one looked at her like that. Absolutely no one.

She felt her smile slip, and swiftly pulled it back. He was still Dan. Just Dan.

"Ten years this summer." His eyes finally slid back to her face. "And ten years too soon."

He stated the insult like a simple fact, its coldness rendering her speechless, which clearly delighted him if the glint in his eye was anything to go by.

"Don't tell me the great Carrie Evans, Oscar nominee, has lost her voice?" he mocked.

She swallowed, though it did nothing to loosen her throat, her vocal chords. Every word he spoke chimed within her, painful, acute.

He pushed himself away from the desk and walked around it, closing the distance between them with ease and sending her body on a dizzying spiral.

Just Dan, my arse!

The flutter in her belly became a full-on typhoon, every sense hitting high alert, alien uncertainty mixing with a raw desire that had her head struggling to produce anything rational.

He stopped an arm's reach away. "It's okay, Max," he said, freeing her gaze as he looked to the other man with a smile—an actual, genuine smile. He was still capable of those, at least. "She's in now, I'll come and find you shortly. The guys can go back to their post."

Max sent a brief look her way that only unsettled her further. Was it sympathy or the desire to protect her that had him grimacing like that?

But this was Dan; he wouldn't hurt her. The very idea was laughable. She felt the ridiculous urge to say as much, but then Max was gone, hightailing it out on the heels of the doormen. Probably relieved to be out of the firing line, she realized as Dan rounded on her and she became the target of his wrath once more.

He folded his arms across his chest, biceps bulging evocatively above his hands. It was no trick of the light—black lines of varying thickness swirled around one arm, the beginning of a design that extended how far, she hadn't a clue, but oh, how she'd love to find out…

He gave a harsh cough, calling her eyes to his face, and she felt color seep into her cheeks. There was no trace of that smile now, the hard set to his jaw accentuating the grim line of his mouth. His eyes were burning down into hers, and not with the kind of heat she was suffering. His was pure hatred, and she felt herself wilt beneath it.

You've really misjudged this one.

Dan pinned his hands beneath his upper arms, anything to keep from reaching out and grabbing her. Did she have to look so fucking good?

He took in her haughty demeanor, set off by her designer clothing: slim-fit trousers, a blouse that dipped low and shone around her curves, come-screw-me stilettos. Fuck, how he wanted to strip her. Not just of those, but her goddamn superiority complex too. She'd had one ten years ago, when she'd buggered off and left him; now she had it honed to perfection.

And he didn't *want* to want her. Not like this. He wanted to forget she ever existed. It was bad enough to have her taunting form splashed across the media, the billboards, the movie screens; why the hell did she have to come back in person and disrupt the status quo?

It was damn right vindictive, unjust, and…electrifying as fuck.

He watched with a spark of amusement as her eyes widened, darting from him to the doorway and back again. "What is it, Carrie? Concerned there aren't any witnesses?"

She gave an unnatural laugh. "Witnesses? To what?"

He didn't respond immediately, his mind off on a path that presented many possibilities, not that he knew which one he wanted more.

Liar. You know full well you want to crush her to the goddamn wall and do something about that heat in her gaze.

Fuck that. He wasn't giving her the satisfaction. Not after she walked out on him a decade ago.

What he *should* do is throw her waif-like body over his shoulder and fireman-lift her out onto the street, away from him.

She must have read the growing threat in his expression, her throat bobbing even as her smile remained steady. "Stand down, Dan, goodness. I think we both know nothing's going to happen that would require a witness."

"Is that so?" He raised his brow, his eyes locking onto the uncertainty he could read in hers, the balance of power inching ever higher in his favor. And Christ, did it feel good. To actually have the upper hand where she was concerned, even if it was a decade too late. "You sure about that?"

The Carrie he'd once known wouldn't break eye contact, not like the one doing so before him—although to be fair, her eyes didn't travel far, hitting his lips at about the same time as her cheeks flushed. It was a tell-tale gesture he could work with. Perhaps her appearance didn't have to be such a bind after all; maybe he ought to put the spark to the test. It could be rather enjoyable, now that he had the benefit of hindsight and there was no chance of her getting under his skin.

Again—you really want to give her that satisfaction?

"Look Carrie, it's great to see you back here." It was her turn to raise her brow, and his lips quirked as he changed tack. "Yeah fair enough, it's not great, but you really need to get to the point, I've a busy night to get back to."

He nodded in the direction of the booming ceiling, indicating he would be needed upstairs imminently. And he wasn't lying; they were short-staffed tonight, and in this particular establishment, he didn't believe in getting agency staff in last minute. Trust was paramount when people came here to have their deepest desires fulfilled, away from the general public and the relentless media spotlight.

Her smile was slow and steady; he could practically feel her gathering her wits together. "I'm impressed," she purred, her voice touched by an American twang that he found instantly irritating, if only because of the effect it had in his pants. *Like you need any added encouragement in that department.* "Your boss must be thrilled that you have such a new place doing so well already."

"My boss?" He couldn't hide his amusement. So she thought he had a superior, that he couldn't possibly own this place. Hell, he owned this and many others up and down the country. It's only that this one held a certain charm, a certain personal appeal that meant he kept his base here…

"Yes, your boss," she continued, waving her hand. "I mean, anyone who's anyone knows that this is the place to be a member of these days."

Was that why she was here? She wanted to be spotted in the hip new hangout? It wasn't about her needing to see him, *per se*. He ignored how the idea gripped his gut and considered the alternative: did she know about the darker side of the club, the side that only those truly in the know would be aware of? He looked at her uber-chic, once more composed exterior and immediately dismissed the idea.

"So, is that why you're here?" he pressed. "You want to join?"

"As great as I hear this place is…" She smiled at him, calm as you like—no edginess, no fear, just fully-controlled Carrie again—and it grated on him, her easy pace at total odds with the blood racing through his veins. "It's not the reason I've come."

"Then what is?" he bit out. "Because you have five minutes and then you're out on your arse, Hollywood entourage or not."

"Entourage?"

She smirked at him, seemingly unaffected by his obvious impatience as she moved away to leisurely walk about his office, her fingers gliding distractingly over the cabinets that lined the room. He didn't like how the sight of her caress over his furnishings had his body tingling with provoked memories. Memories of those young, innocent fingers tracing the planes of his body, teasing him as they'd fumbled around together in their teens, sharing a number of firsts.

"There is no entourage, Dan." Her voice penetrated his thoughts, her light tone provoking all manner of emotion, none of it conducive to keeping his cool. "I'm here on the quiet, and I have every intention of trying to keep it that way."

What? He couldn't help the laugh that erupted, his amusement going some way to douse the heat coursing through his veins. "*You're* here on the quiet?"

Her name was up in lights not two blocks away, and *she* was trying to stay out of the limelight. The woman who'd dumped him in her quest to be a fully-lit star of Hollywood.

"What's so funny?" She'd paused midstride, her sharp blue eyes narrowing, her lips quirking hesitantly as she seemed to work out whether to smile with him or not.

"You. Hiding out," he said easily, yet the bitter note was there. "The fame was all you craved once upon a time."

He saw a flash of guilt, or was it pity? His balls shrivelled. *Christ,* she could keep her pity. The last thing he needed was her thinking he harboured any lasting feelings towards her. Although the hatred, she could have that in spades. "I seem to remember it being one of the key reasons you couldn't stick around to be in a relationship with someone as insignificant as me."

She paled under the assault of his words. Good. At least she wasn't so insensitive as to not give a damn about her actions.

"It wasn't just about that." She nibbled anxiously at her lower lip, a hand combing through her hair. His eyes were caught between the pull of each action as unwelcome memories threatened ever more intense. "It was—"

"Forget it." He'd had enough of memory lane, enough of the weird turbulence she'd kickstarted inside. *You don't want to be the one nibbling at that delectable lip, you don't want to be the one with your*

hands running through those free-flowing strands, you want her gone…
"Just tell me what you're here for and then go, Carrie."

She looked hurt, and an instinctive pang of guilt pierced him. He straightened against it—*She's the callous bitch who left you for Hollywood, and you're no fool, not anymore.*

"Perhaps if I tell you that I'm here for Isla, you might stop looking at me as though you wished I were dead."

He gave a bark of a laugh. "I don't wish you were dead, Carrie, merely out of my life."

But mention of Isla, his friend, one of the few people he truly cared about, had got to him. Just as Carrie had known it would. Christ, *she* was the girl he should've fallen for. Not this torturing infamous replica. "What about Isla?"

She'd flinched at his dismissal of her but recovered swiftly, admirably even—*Admirable? Fuck that! She's a piece of work, and she deserves a taste of her own medicine.*

And oh, how he wanted to see that cool facade crack so completely…

"Come on, Carrie, don't tell me that my lack of membership to your fanbase is a crushing blow for you?"

She paled further. "It would just be nice if you could at least be civil."

"Civil? Oh, I can do civil alright." He smiled at her, his tone dark and suggestive. "Why don't you ask the people upstairs? They'll tell you just how *civil* I can be."

Her color returned, her eyes flashing wildly. "*Ha*, I'm beginning to question whether you still know the meaning of the word."

"Well, actions speak louder than words—wouldn't you agree, Princess?" He knew he was playing with fire, but he didn't care. Right now, he just wanted to wipe that prim and proper look off her face.

Yeah, that's totally all you want. You're not talking with another part of your anatomy at all. "You want me to show you just how civil I can be?"

He saw her swallow as she turned to face him head on, her brows drawn together. "And just how do you prop—"

He was across the room before she could even clock his intent, his body propelling her back against the cabinets as his lips silenced her, his hands snaking through her silken hair.

Ah, fuck, it was a bad move.

All hell broke loose inside him; Carrie's scent, her taste, her parting lips...if it was possible to drown in a kiss, he was already there, right on the seabed. Through the blood pounding in his ears, he heard her moan, a reciprocal growl erupting in his throat. He was supposed to be punishing her, so why did it feel like the total opposite? He kissed her harder, anger driving him to fever pitch. He *was* punishing her.

She moulded into him like putty, her hands coming up to claw at his back, clinging to him in total surrender, and that was when he knew he had to break it off, get the upper hand while he still could...

He thrust her away, just as swiftly as he'd instigated the kiss. Utilising every ounce of his hatred to regain control as he set her apart from him.

She blinked furiously, her eyes dazed and confused as she reached for him. It would be so easy to return to her, to give in and let his body have its way...

The realization had him stepping further back, his hands releasing her to fold his arms across his chest once more. Holding himself rigid to hide the way the air shuddered through his lungs and schooling his expression to give her the hate she deserved.

"Why did you do that?" She touched a shaky hand to her swollen lips and he had to tear his gaze from the contact, his eyes fixing with hers that were wide with unspent desire. Or was it the dawning realization that he'd been teaching her a lesson, nothing more?

"Because I can," he stated simply, years of fighting his way to the top, of showing no weakness, coming to his aid and burying the spark of guilt. "Don't be fooled into thinking I'm the same man I was ten years ago, Carrie. I take what I want, when I want, and no one stands in my way. Not even you."

Her eyes hardened, a tight smile forming as her hand fell away. "Did you honestly think that kiss meant anything to me?" She gave a short laugh. "Good Lord, Dan, I only let you do it because I felt bad for how I left things all those years ago."

He would have shared in her laugh at the blatant lie, if her words hadn't brought back the old pain. "So that was a pity kiss?"

"If that's what you want to call it," she agreed, smoothing out the crumpled fabric of her blouse. "But make no mistake, it will *never* happen again."

His mouth cocked to one side at the challenge she posed. "Never?"

She nodded, her eyes pinning him as she added, "Not that it means anything to you…but I'm spoken for."

The words bothered him more than he'd care to admit. As did the awkward manner in which she said them. But who the hell was this guy? She couldn't shit without some press article or other pouncing on it. The big news of her being *with* someone would have hit the tabloids. It would have hit his radar whether he'd wanted it to or not. Was she lying to him?

Hell, what did it matter either way? Not when she'd kissed him back like she had…

"Judging by your response to me just seconds ago, I don't think it means much to you either."

Her eyes turned wild and she swept forward, her hand gliding through the air to make contact with his right cheek. But he was quicker, softening her blow as he caught her wrist in his hand and yanking her against him.

The sweet pressure of her breasts crushed against his chest, her lower belly against his fierce hardness that refused to let up. He gazed down at her, her forehead in line with his chin, her upturned face screaming a barrage of different emotions.

"Don't you ever try to strike me again," he warned.

"You deserved it," she bit out. She was clearly trying to be forceful, but he could hear the tremble to her voice, could see the crumbling resolve in the bright blue depths of her eyes.

"Is that so?" He pondered her for a second as the air filled with the sound of their uneven breath, her undulating chest provoking him, testing his control. "Your eyes are telling me a different story, Princess. In fact, your entire body is telling me that you quite enjoy being treated badly."

She shoved against him, her eyes coming alive with fight as she tried to free herself.

"What is it? You scared I'm going to kiss you again?"

She stomped on his foot, an unladylike growl leaving her throat. "Let me go, Dan."

"Let you go where?" He spun her in his arms, one hand pressing against her lower belly to hold her tightly to him while the other came up to pull her hair over one shoulder, forcing her head to bend with it. She gave a sharp intake of breath, her anticipation palpable as he lowered his mouth to the sensitized, outstretched curve.

Her perfume filled his senses, the warmth that radiated off her luring him in as his mouth and tongue traced an expert path along the channel of her neck. She trembled and whimpered, the fight easing from her body as she surrendered to him and he smiled in his victory.

"You've always been so sensitive, just here," he murmured against her skin, his hands slipping up her front as he sought out those other sensitized parts of her body that would have her begging him for more.

How far would she let him go? Suddenly he wanted—*no, needed*—to find out. And it was this need that had his head raising, his brain clearing. "You should leave, Carrie."

She turned to face him, her cheeks an appealing shade of pink. Was it possible that ten years had only intensified her hold over his body? *Fuck that.*

"I told you…" she began, her wavering tone feeding his ego and mutinous cock. "I need to speak to you about Isla…it's important."

Christ. Isla. He couldn't even think about Isla when Carrie was this close, this distracting.

"*Please*, Dan."

Good God. Get with it. You owe it to Isla to hear her out.

"If you're here for Isla, then why isn't she with you?"

"She's in the States, taking a break while I…" She broke off, her lashes fluttering as her confidence slipped.

"While you?" He raised his brow. Now he was curious.

She shook out her hair and rolled her shoulders. "Look, her business is a mess and while I'm here, I want to sort it out. I want to help her, and for that I need you."

She had to be kidding. She was here on a selfless mission to help Isla. Will wonders never cease? Although he knew he wasn't getting the full story; he was sure she'd been about to say something else a moment ago.

But how can you turn her down?

He couldn't. Not if she was truly here for Isla.

It can wait, though. He needed time. Time to come to terms with her return and clear his head. And if he was entirely honest, he wasn't ready to roll over on demand; she could stand to sweat a little.

"And what makes you think Isla wants your help?"

"I don't. If I asked her to let me, she'd say no, so I'm not giving her a say."

"You mean you're doing this behind her back?" he scoffed. This was much more like the Carrie he knew. Doing what she wanted.

"You can scoff all you like, but if I make enough progress in the next few weeks, by the time she returns she'll be too pleased to resent it. She'll be happy again."

It was the last bit that was his undoing. How many times had he tried to help Isla over the years, but in her stubborn independence she'd refused to let him? Now he could do it with Carrie in the firing line. It was the perfect solution. And Isla *was* miserable, with her business under threat she'd lost her happy spark, she'd lost *herself*, and he'd hated watching that happen.

It didn't mean he had to roll over just yet, though.

"I'm busy this second." He strode towards the door and yanked it open before looking back to her. "My men will see you settled upstairs, and I'll find you when I'm finished for the evening."

She looked like she would refuse, her chin raising in defiance. "Very well, Dan, I'll wait...but only because this is for Isla."

She sauntered past him, slotting her hat back in place and donning her shades. He grinned in spite of himself. Did she not realize how ridiculous she looked?

"You don't need the disguise, Carrie."

"Like I told you..." She hesitated on the threshold. "I'm here on the quiet."

"And if you knew anything about this place, you would know no one gets into the actual club without signing a Non-Disclosure Agreement."

"So, where's mine?"

"I trust you."

What the actual fuck?

Her brow raised at his all-encompassing and ridiculously wild statement.

It's her situation that you trust, not her, you idiot.

"If you're on the quiet..." He forced his tone to remain neutral "...The last thing you're going to do is talk."

She gave a small nod, and he had to wonder if without the shades, he might have seen a hint of disappointment in those captivating blues.

What the fuck does that matter?

He watched her go and slammed the door shut far harder than he intended, but then everything about him was goddamn hard that second.

Painful, annoying, and frustratingly so.

Chapter Two

As much as it galled her to sit and wait, Carrie knew she had no choice. Not if she wanted Dan's help.

And boy, did she need it.

Yes, she could respond with bravado and use her notoriety to have everyone dance to her tune and help Isla's club. But that defeated the whole purpose of her visit here. To keep out of the limelight, to hide from the cameras, to get her head screwed on straight and decide what truly mattered.

Her tummy twisted over, her brain filling with the confused ramblings she'd been struggling with for weeks. She needed a drink.

Hell, you need several.

Thankfully, Butthead One had taken her straight to the bar and Butthead Two was getting her some Champagne. At least she'd have the company of the bar's finest while she waited.

And did what? Ignored what she should be thinking about and pondered what she wanted from Dan? Or more disturbingly, what her body wanted to do with him?

Both beat thinking on life back in LA and Brad's surprise marriage proposal—the true reason she'd legged it from the states. It had taken that "Will you marry me?" to realize she was treading a lonely path, one where she was destined to never feel that spark, that heat, that love…the kind she'd had for Dan.

If she'd been sensible, she would've steered clear of him—of the past—but the moment she'd taken a closer look at Isla's business, she'd known Dan was the person to call on, regardless of the added complication that gave.

At least, that had been her thought at the outset; now she'd seen him, now she'd felt the fireworks his mere presence had triggered, never mind his kiss…heat coursed through her veins, and with it a mixture of want and fear. Could she get through this unscathed? Help Isla with Dan's assistance, and return to LA like nothing had changed?

Not quite. You already know you can't marry Brad…if you're honest, you know you can't even be with him anymore.

But Dan…she swallowed down the thought and slid onto a stool tucked away at the edge of the bar. *Dan, nothing. Get him to help, and get out.*

She removed her hat and shades, adding them to the bar top with her bag. Behind her, Butthead One took up position, and she gave an eye roll.

"I don't need a sitter, you know?"

He cleared his throat, his eyes fixed on some point in the distance. "Apologies, Miss. I'll leave once you are settled with your drink. Should you require anything more, the bar staff will assist you."

Gah. Now she felt like crap. He was just doing his job and being polite, and she…well, she was being a bitch. She could blame it on jet-lag—she'd only been in the UK twenty-four hours—but it ran a whole lot deeper than that. A whole engagement ring deeper. She didn't want to hurt Brad. She knew he didn't love her, that his proposal had been born of convenience, but still…

"Of course. Thank you." She tried for a smile—not that he even looked at her—and was relieved when Butthead…*no, be nice*…Doorman Two approached, the barman in step with him on the other side of the bar. He delivered an ice bucket before her and proceeded to fill a flute with Champagne.

She beamed at him, genuinely grateful. "Thank you." And then, to the Doormen, "Thank you both, I promise to be on my best behavior."

She could have sworn their lips lifted a little as they met her eye.

"You're welcome, Miss," Doorman One said before looking to his buddy. "Best get back."

She watched them return the way they came, taking up her glass as she surveyed her surroundings. The place fit with his new look, she mused, not liking the way her body mutinously lit up over the thought. The dark furnishings screamed of a rugged, raw luxury. The soft lighting was perfectly distributed to provide privacy to the clientele, whether they were cosied up in the various enclosed booths, out on the floor occupying the small circular tables, or like her, seated at the bar trying to keep out of it.

She liked it. She liked *him*.

And speak of the devil—there he was, her body honing in on his presence even before she spied him. *Shit*.

Her fingers tightened around the stem of her flute as she lifted it to her lips, forcing her attention off him and onto the chilled liquid seeping down her throat. But even the Champagne's cooling influence couldn't take the heat out of the excitement rushing through her. Christ, when was the last time she'd felt such a thrill?

She actually couldn't remember. For all the excitement of her career, her success, even her comfortable relationship with Brad...none of it trumped this.

And she ached to satisfy it. Yes, she'd told him there'd be no repeat, even throwing her relationship status at him, but it was all front, designed to keep herself in check and deflect him from the truth: She wanted him.

There were several people at the bar waiting to be served and he disappeared behind them, emerging a moment later to converse with the barman who had served her. She watched his eyes flick in her direction, felt their hit like a direct charge to her clit, and then they were gone, fixed on anyone but her.

He took to serving, his movements efficient and effortless, his exposed muscles flexing provocatively as he delivered drink after drink. Her gaze was probably far more intent than it should be. She should have been playing it cool, should have been her usual aloof self. Instead, she couldn't look away.

What was it about him?

Why was she so hooked?

What did he have that Brad didn't?

Brad was intelligent and good-looking; he cared about people, cared about his family; he was great in bed. But the spark...it just wasn't there.

And you're looking at the cause right there, you fool.

Champagne caught in her throat as it hit home *You can't love Brad. You can't love anyone, not like that, because you never got over him. Over Dan.*

She pressed a hand to her stomach, trying to ease its churning. Seeing him again made it so bloody obvious. Brad just wasn't Dan.

It was so huge, so fundamental to what was wrong in her life, and the one person she wanted to tell, the one person she trusted, she couldn't. Her sister.

She hadn't even told Isla about Brad. The fact that he was away in Santorini filming for the next few weeks and had promised to give her radio silence while she considered his proposal had meant she could avoid the stress of explaining it. Her sister would never understand her hesitation—*Christ,* she was only just beginning to understand.

And with him away, their twin swap had been far easier to master, giving her the breathing space she'd really needed.

But what would her sister say if she knew? Not just that she'd been dating Brad, but that he'd actually proposed, and that it was his proposal that had sent her high-tailing it out of America and begging her sister to take on her life for three weeks?

She shook her head, felt the guilt, the angst, the worry all building.

She hated keeping such a huge secret. Especially when her sister was helping her out by pretending to be her, living out Carrie's own life stateside and keeping the press off her back while she hid out for a bit. But Brad wasn't just a movie-star; he'd been Isla's teenage celebrity crush. Just as Dan had been Isla's first love. And there was no way she wanted to add to that old wound, not when the relationship might not be heading anywhere.

Not heading anywhere?

Jesus, she'd got that wrong. From Brad's perspective at least, he'd been more than ready to commit. She could hardly believe it still.

And saying yes was the perfect next step in her career. The very idea should have filled her with excitement and yet, as it had when he'd pulled out the ring, she could feel a cold sweat breaking out across her neck and nausea tugging at her stomach. From that moment, she'd barely been able to kiss him, let alone say yes.

She remembered his confused frown as she'd made her request for time, his swift recovery and bold goodbye. He'd been so convinced…and maybe a year ago, she would have been too.

On paper, he was her ideal match, and the fact they both existed in the world of Hollywood gave them a much better chance than her parents had ever had. They understood the demands of their careers, the commitment required, the unrelenting press attention and the crap spouted by the gossip columns. They just got it. They got each other. It should have been, would have been, perfect.

But not anymore.

Somewhere along the line her priorities had shifted, and now she needed to get her head around what that meant. And perhaps doing that with Dan in the vicinity wasn't such a great idea.

Her eyes devoured him from across the bar, her body begging him to come closer no matter what her brain said.

Suddenly, she wished they hadn't given her a bottle, not when it meant she had no excuse to beckon him over to place another order.

Although, who's to say someone of her stature would want to pour their own drink? She could play that card well enough if it meant she'd gain Dan's attention.

She smiled and crossed her legs, leaning over the bar as she sipped at her glass. She wasn't about to neck it, but she'd work at catching his attention and be ready to make her request at a natural breaking point…

A natural breaking point, sure, she mentally scoffed thirty minutes later.

Her mouth was bone dry, her glass empty for going on twenty minutes, and not once had he caught her eye. His staff had, though, she was sure. She'd seen them send him a look, and he'd muttered a swift response before going back to serving, his smile enviable as he spoke to them. How she wanted to bask in the warmth of that smile, to strip away their difficult past and start afresh.

Fuck it—she was going to have to pour the bottle herself or look like an idiot. She felt heat flush her skin and thanked the soft lighting for its concealing effect. Taking hold of the neck of the bottle, she started to lift it just as a strong hold took over hers, easing it from her. "Allow me."

She looked up, her eyes colliding with blazing steel—*he must have moved quickly*—and her dried-up mouth failed her. She tried to moisten it up, her tongue sweeping over her lower lip before she managed a strangled, "Thank you."

He gave her a nod, his eyes lingering a second longer than necessary; then he was gone, his fleeting presence still resonating through her. Her fingers still tingled from his touch, her thighs clenching around the ache firing in her gut. If the merest contact, the merest look, could send her body into such a spin, heaven knew what *sex* would do.

And what about Brad? her conscience berated her. Yes, their relationship was a secret. Yes, it was over, or at least it would be very soon. But that didn't make it any less real. And she'd never considered herself a cheat before.

But is it cheating when your heart has always been here?

She didn't want that honesty; not when it came with a truckload of sadness, the foreign emotion coiling its way through her and driving her to take up her freshly poured glass for a large swig. At least she was starting to get answers…

"May I?"

She almost choked on her drink with a start. The request came from someone directly behind her, her distracted senses failing to detect their approach. She turned to look up at her unwanted guest, recognition sparking. A politician, maybe? Definitely someone she'd seen before, but she couldn't place the name, and she was pretty good with names.

He eyed the stool alongside her. "I'd like to see if I can bring a smile back to that pretty face of yours."

Oh God, really?

But at least his company would distract from the man determined to ignore her until he was ready.

And if he could make her wait, then… "Sure, why not."

He could say he was bothered because he knew the MP's reputation, and that even though there was no love lost between him and Carrie, she didn't deserve that.

But he knew jealousy.

More specifically, he knew what it felt like to be jealous over her, and it was that which had his body burning and his eyes constantly drawn to their corner of the bar while he counted down the seconds to closing.

He looked to them now and caught her eye; he could practically hear her little intake of breath as her eyes wavered and her lips parted, causing his own to lift into a one-sided grin. The obvious effect he had on her, the power of it, flooded his system with adrenalin, his cock twitching in its semi-hardened state.

"It's quieting down, boss. Why don't you get off?" Suzy, his bar manager, prompted. "We've got this."

He looked to her and wondered just how aware she was of his need to do just that, but she gave nothing away.

"Okay." He sent a swift look Carrie's way, noting how the MP was getting ever closer, everything about his demeanor speaking of his intent. "I'll just finish up this cocktail order," he ground out.

"You sure, boss? I can sort it."

"No, it's fine." He needed to get his temper in hand. He'd always prided himself on his self-restraint, for fuck's sake, so where the hell was it now? It really wouldn't do to deck the man tipped to be the future Prime Minister. And it's not like Carrie would appreciate his interference.

Maybe this was the way she rolled. Leaving her man stateside while she played around with those of an appropriate standing to parallel her own career. The MP certainly fit the bill.

And what were you then, back in your office? A momentary lapse?

He gritted his teeth and killed the thought dead.

Doesn't matter what you are, or whatever this craziness between you boils down to. She'll be back in the states soon enough, and life can return to normal.

He pulled together the order, determined not to look Carrie's way until the last glass was set before the customer and he'd updated their account, and then he turned and froze. The space the two had occupied was bare.

"She headed out," came Suzy's level comment as she reached across the bar to deliver a customer both his drink and a warm smile. "Mr. Donato is on her tail," she added.

Ah, shit.

He shouldn't care. He shouldn't.

But he did.

He rubbed the back of his neck with a scowl and bade Suzy goodnight, forcing his pulse and stride to calm as he made for the exit. He heard the ripple of Carrie's laugh before he'd even made it outside, and then his eyes lighted on her up against the wall, Donato's body fencing her in. Her sunglasses had been pushed back over her head, her hat and bag swung carelessly from her fingers as she let the man coo over her. *Fuck it.*

His brain screamed at him to walk away—to leave them to it, cut his losses before she reeled him in again. And still he found himself heading for her, his body tensed up, his teeth gritted—*what are you doing?*

"Sorry Donato, this one's spoken for." The words came out easily, like he had every right to stake his claim. And what the hell was that about?

The guy turned to him slowly, the set of his shoulders telling Dan he didn't appreciate the interruption. "You're right, she's w—" he broke off, his eyes widening. "*Dan.* Good God, man, you could have made that clearer sooner."

"What can I say, it's been a busy night."

"Still, she's a feisty one." He gave an awkward laugh as he pushed away from Carrie. "You might want to keep her on a tighter leash next time."

"Well, I…really…" Carrie blustered and Dan sent her a warning look. Yes, the guy deserved a fist, but it wasn't worth the trouble and it would only delay their conversation further. Not that words were on his mind right that second.

"Advice taken," he said tonelessly. "Now if you don't mind…"

"Of course. I'll leave you to it." Without sparing Carrie a backward glance he disappeared into the night, his security appearing out of the shadows almost immediately.

Carrie watched him go, her expression unreadable. "Pleased with yourself?"

"I could ask you the same thing."

She shot him a look. "I have no idea what you're talking about."

"No?" He wanted to laugh at her indignation; probably would have if his body wasn't urging him to kiss her until she forgot Donato ever existed, or any other man for that matter. "So, you weren't trying to make me jealous?"

He closed the gap between them and her eyes fell to his lips, her pupils dilating further in the dark.

"Don't be ridiculous."

"Ridiculous?" He gave a low chuckle, noting how she pressed her shoulders back against the wall, her breasts thrusting forward distractingly as she faced him off. Did she know she was doing it? Teasing him with her posture alone? "I don't think so."

"You can think what you like." She sounded breathless and her eyes were still fixated on his lips, telling him where her head was at, where her body was at.

He reached up to stroke his fingers down her neck, loving how her breath caught. "You weren't trying to convince me you're over our earlier episode?"

She raised her chin, her eyes colliding with his. "I can barely recall it."

"Barely?" This time his chuckle was so deep he wasn't even sure she'd heard it. "If that's the case, maybe I should give you a reminder?"

You're playing with fire, came the annoying warning again, but hell, it turned out fire was fun.

"What I want…" Her tongue flicked out to swipe her bottom lip, her throat bobbing as she swallowed. "…is for you to help me. Help Isla."

"And nothing more?" He cupped her jaw, his fingers coming to rest over her wildly beating pulse point.

"No," she breathed.

"So, you don't want me to kiss you right now?"

Her lashes fluttered, her mouth an open invitation that he was helpless to resist.

"How about we take this upstairs…" He bowed his head to brush the words against her lips, felt their yielding softness, her soft sigh sending the scent of Champagne, of her, his way. *Yes, Princess, don't deny me. Not now.* "And then you can tell me exactly what you need?"

"Upstairs?"

It was more a breathless statement than a question, and he nodded as he stroked at her neck, her head rolling into his touch as her lashes lowered. "To my flat."

"Your flat?"

"Are you going to repeat everything I say?"

She opened her eyes to scan his face, the strangest glint in their depths. "What happened to you?"

Me? His fingers stilled against her skin. "What do you mean?"

"You're different," she said softly. "Very. Different."

Yeah, he was different. And yeah, he knew the answer well enough, but there was no way in hell he'd give her the satisfaction of hearing it. "Are you complaining?"

She shook her head.

"Good." He stepped away, grabbing her hand just as the doors swung open to the front of the club, the drunken couple falling through them so engrossed in one another they could barely stay upright.

He pulled her past them to his own private side access and she came willingly, a fact that sent his blood racing anew and drowned out his brain's persistent warning that he was making a mistake, that he should send her packing before things got out of hand.

He nodded to his security detail, who opened the door for him and swept her inside.

Fuck it, the packing could come later.

Chapter Three

CARRIE LOOKED TO WHERE DAN'S HAND clutched her own, marvelling at how her body fizzed over at the contact and left her barely aware of her legs moving after him.

Her every sense was in overdrive; it was exhilarating, all-consuming, and she was scared. Scared that if she couldn't keep this in her control, then she wouldn't be able to keep her heart in check either.

Control was part of her makeup. She depended on it. But from the second she'd heard his voice in the basement her control had been slipping, and now it had gone the way of her common sense. Because common sense said that going upstairs with him meant one thing. One thing that she shouldn't do, no matter how much she had teased herself with the idea. That was before she'd truly realized just how vulnerable she was to his touch, his presence, *his* control.

And he confused the hell out of her.

She knew he wanted her; he couldn't fake that. But he also hated her, he'd made that clear enough.

So what the hell are you doing going upstairs with him?

Her feet faltered, and he looked to her over his shoulder. "You okay?"

Okay. It wasn't the word she'd use. But did she really want to stop this?

"I'm fine."

A second's hesitation and then he was pulling her into him, his mouth crushing hers and forcing out her sanity. Her taste buds coming alive on his wicked scent, his expert tongue invading her mouth, rough and demanding. Her fingers shot to his hair, forking through the thick mass so achingly familiar as she clutched him to her. His own fingers fierce in their exploration of her body, her back, her arse as his need pressed into her belly, feeding the heat already dispersing like wildfire through her limbs.

There were voices, strangers talking nearby and breaking through the periphery of her awareness. They weren't alone, not fully, not yet.

She pulled back, her hands staying hooked around his head. "Lead the way."

He grinned and pulled her deeper into the darkened corridor. The voices were close, but they came from the other side of the doors they were passing. Separate rooms in the club, she supposed. The place had to be huge. Impressive. Just like the man she was tailing.

They hit a stairwell, the light thankfully less gloomy so she could navigate the incline without landing face first. Still, a lift would have been preferable. "Don't you have an elevator?"

"Not in here, Princess." He looked to her over his shoulder. "Don't tell me you're tired already."

"Of course not."

He chuckled, the sound teasing at her spine. "It's only a few flights."

She continued after him, her nerves making a resurgence. This was a bad idea. *He doesn't even like you, doesn't even want you around, and here you are, following him to do what exactly?*

By the time she got to the top, her breathing was erratic, but it wasn't through exertion.

He released her hand to extract his key, and headed down a corridor housing one door at the end.

His door.

His flat.

She heard him push the key into the lock, followed by the click of it twisting open, and her heart fluttered. "Maybe we should save this conversation for the morning, it's late and I…"

"Conversation?" He looked to her as he pushed the door wide. "Conversation wasn't the first thing I had in mind."

No, it wasn't, was it…you silly, silly woman.

And now she was looking into those gray eyes, so familiar and yet so disturbingly not, and she was forgetting her mind all over again.

"You coming in?"

Her feet were rooted, her teeth gnawing at her lower lip. Something told her if she crossed that threshold her entire world would tip on its axis.

He held the door open with his body, his arms crossing his middle, muscles bulging provocatively. "So, the great Carrie Evans isn't as confident as she would make out?"

His words hit a nerve. But it wasn't that which had her heart kickstarting, her cheeks burning, her body striding forward, it was the smile he gave her. The easy grin that had old-Dan jumping to the fore and the banter they used to share…*the love.* She tossed her hat and bag to the ground, freeing her hands to thrust him back against the interior wall of his flat.

Better, much better…

She heard the door thud closed behind her, a growl erupting in his throat as she devored his mouth, the submissive sound tugging at her heart, her clit, his need as obvious as her own. She angled her head, seeking to go deeper, to tangle with his tongue, to graze against his teeth. It wasn't enough. She needed more. So much more.

He grabbed her arse, lifting her against his rigid length as her own hands explored his chest, raising his T-shirt to travel brazenly over the hot, hard surface. His muscles rippled beneath her fingers, his breath ragged from her hungry assault on his mouth.

She'd never been so desperate, so caught-up, so lost in someone. *No, you have, with him. Always with him.* "I can't believe how much I want you."

He spun her back against the wall, his mouth dropping to her neck, hot on her skin. "You and me both, Princess."

His words rolled with his attentions, firing her desire. She arched her back, her fingers scrabbling to pull his shirt over his head. He came to her aid, tugging the rest of it up and over, and for a second, time halted. She was used to men in all shapes and sizes, but they were nothing compared to him. A strange sense of possession, of belonging coming over her as she trailed her fingers over his skin. His chiselled hardness was so surprising, so different to how he'd once been; and then there was the tattoo that filled the right side of his body, the intricate black Celtic pattern that was so menacing, so fucking sexy as it dipped into his waistband and left her wanting to unveil more.

"You like it?"

Like didn't come close. But she couldn't speak. Words clogged up with desire as she raked her nails down the pattern, and watched his body flex beneath her touch, his stomach contracting as her hand came to rest above his waistband. She hooked her fingers inside and tugged him forward, hard.

He fell against her, his weight crushing her to the wall, the heat of his bare chest searing her through the thin fabric of her top. She moaned, her mouth seeking out his but he evaded her, his fingers forcing her head to the side and exposing the sensitized path from her ear to her collarbone. His teeth nipped at her skin, his tongue lapped, his hands still rough as he pulled at her blouse. He ripped it over her head, sending her expensive shades falling to the ground with it. Not that she cared. He could toss a thousand of the damn things and break them all, if he'd just fulfil the promise building.

And then his palms were on her breasts, and her brain emptied on the surge of heat racing to greet them. He teased her through the veil of lace, her nipples prickling against the fabric, desperate, needy. She whimpered, the sound so alien to her ears. Was that really her, so wanton, so natural? No acting, no thinking, just her?

"Dan?"

It came out like a question, almost fearful. Is this the real him? Would he do this if he hated her? Could she do it if he did?

"Yes, Carrie?"

His mouth hit the valley between her breasts; the brush of his lips interwoven with the sweep of his tongue as he continued to cup her, to grope. He was driving her crazy. Enough to see off the question she couldn't bring herself to ask: Do you hate me? It was caged in a ball of fear that she didn't want to examine. Scared of his answer; scared of her response.

"Hmmm?" he murmured as he moved to trace the swell of one aching breast.

She shook her head. "This is insane."

"Insane, but so fucking good."

He closed over one hard peak, his teeth biting through her bra and making her cry out. He did it again, and again. It was merciless, unrelenting, and just when she thought she could take it no more, he started on the other. She was dizzy with it. Her legs buckling beneath her, and he took her weight, lifting her legs around him, thrusting his clothed hardness just where she needed him .

The pleasure magnified, her clit joyous on the contact it so craved, and she moaned as she rode herself over him, her fingers hunting out her bra clasp to rid herself of the frustrating barrier. She tossed it aside and he rewarded her with a groan, his appreciative gaze raking over her before bowing to take in one pleading nub. He sucked it into the hot, wet cavern of his mouth, his tongue rolling over it. Dizzying. Hypnotic. Playful. And then he released her through his teeth, harsh, brutal, a sudden hit of pleasure-pain.

"*Fuck, yes.*"

Now she got it, the whole heaven is a place on earth. It's where she was, her entire body flooded with a carnal heat. She arched back into the wall, giving herself over to his ministrations. Riding him. Mindless to her actions. Caring about one thing only, the promise of release. *This* release.

Shamelessly tightening her legs around him, she ran her fingers through his hair, urging him from one breast to the other. "Yes, God, yes, like that…like that…"

Watching him, his tongue, his mouth, his teeth attack her, doing everything she wanted was as erotic as feeling it. His willing, almost crazed appreciation, so mutual to how she felt inside, pushed her higher, compounding the bolts of ecstasy tearing straight to her clit at every nip, every suckle, every flick of his tongue.

She started to pant, her hands dropping to his shoulders, her nails biting into the hard expanse of muscle. Her limbs started to tighten, her body pulling her taut, she was coming, she was hitting the edge and suddenly, he backed away.

She looked at him through her haze, pleading, confused. He reached into his back pocket and pulled out his wallet, followed by a condom packet, and she bit into her lip, a surge of relief and anticipation making her dizzy.

He nodded to her. "Lose the trousers."

His command was rough, and her fingers trembled as she dutifully undid the fastening, sliding off her shoes and stepping out of each leg as he unzipped his jeans. She dropped her gaze, desperate to feast on what she had felt. What she knew to be just as impressive as the rest of him. He pulled himself out, pumped his hand over the magnitude of hard flesh, and she heard herself whimper. Christ, she wanted to lick him, taste him, bury him within her.

"Touch yourself."

His instruction seared her brain. It was hot, it was naughty, and it was a first for her in front of someone. But she wanted it; her clit needed it.

Tentatively, she trailed her fingers down her belly, down to the stretch of lace and further still. She cupped herself, could feel her wetness seeping through the fabric into her palm.

"Take them off."

A shiver ran through her, her power over him vibrating through every tight word he uttered. She took her time, shimmying the delicate fabric down her thighs, her calves, her ankles before daintily kicking them off.

"Spread your legs."

Oh God. Desire choked her. She'd never been instructed like this. *Never.*

She stepped wide and his jaw pulsed, his cock seeping in his fist as he pumped himself harder.

"Now touch yourself."

Oh fuck.

She smoothed her palm over her mound, letting her index finger sink in deep before pulling it back to circle over the sensitized nub of nerve endings and work her body back to the brink. She moaned, her movement slow and savouring, and he tensed before her, his fist stilling at the base of his cock, knuckles white as he gripped himself steady. His eyes burning into her, driving her on.

She picked up her tempo, her need to come taking hold. She fixed her gaze in his, refusing to miss a second of his response to her, the tension now thrumming off his entire being—and then he shifted, his fingers tearing open the packet to take out the condom. Her thighs clenched with anticipation, and she tried to control her breathing, to stave off her release, to wait for him.

He gritted his teeth as he rolled the condom down his girth, his control visibly hanging in the balance. Still she wanted to push him, to tease him more. She brought her free hand up to cup her breast, her palm moving desperately against the ache beneath, her fingers pinching at her nipple almost painfully.

"*Fuck, Carrie.*"

She was drunk on him now. Wild even. Her hands serving to satisfy her every need as her eyes drowned in the sight of him losing it over her, and then he was crossing the room, his stride fierce, the growl emanating from his throat animalistic.

He crushed her to the wall, his mouth claiming hers in a hard assault, his cock pressing wildly between them. Christ, she needed him. Now. Her orgasm was still there, coiling tight in her belly.

She took hold of him, riding her hand over the latex covered length and he hissed into her mouth, grabbing at her wrist to pull her away. He dropped his hand to the back of her thigh, lifting her leg to wrap it around him, and she did the same with her other, enclosing him in her legs. Taking his hardness in hand, he slipped himself between her legs. His eyes watched where their bodies joined, but she could only watch his face, his desire, his lust for her. She craved it. She needed it.

The heavenly presence of his cock met with her entrance and he paused, a split second, his eyes connecting with her own, before he thrust himself forward, his jaw clamped tight. His size stretched her wide, her slickness sending him straight to the hilt and making her scream out with the erotic intensity.

He stilled, searching her eyes. Was he worried he'd hurt her?

She clung to him in response, her mouth finding his in desperation, telling him with her actions that she was so close—*don't stop*. And then he was pumping, hard and fast, their pace so frantic, their need so desperate, their mouths not once disconnecting.

They exploded in seconds, their bodies undulating with the force of each wave. And she wanted to draw it out—she didn't want the aftershocks to pass, didn't want his body to leave her, to empty her. She didn't want reality to return; his hate, his dislike…

Tears came from nowhere, pricking at the backs of her eyes. She closed them tight, her head burrowing into the crook of his neck. She listened to their breathing, the atmosphere slowly shifting with each steadying breath. As he lowered her against him, she sought something to say. Anything that wouldn't betray the fear mounting inside her.

What the fuck was her body playing at?

She didn't crave, didn't want, didn't *need* someone else.

And yet, she'd needed him in that moment. Still needed him. And it wasn't for Isla. It was for her.

Was this some weird payback?

Was karma trying to kick her arse for what happened a decade ago?

She was so lost in her thoughts that she hadn't noticed him looking down at her again, those piercing grays stealing inside her soul and surely seeing too much.

Fuck.

She looked scared. *Shit.* He tensed up, shocked still. And it wasn't just her sudden fear, it was the realization that he was well and truly fucked.

He'd lost it. So completely and utterly. Orgasmed so hard his sense had been wiped out, as had the last decade—the pain, the anger, the lesson he'd learned. Now, as he stared into her worried blue depths, he didn't know what to think.

Carrie didn't do fear. She was the strongest woman he'd ever known. But it wasn't the first time he'd glimpsed it that evening.

Was it some weird mind trick? Was she trying to manipulate him, adopting her award-winning skills to get it done? His stomach twisted. It was the only answer that made sense. Because if she truly was scared, then that would show another side to her, a side that would make him care, and that just wasn't happening. Not again.

He pulled back abruptly, forcing a neutral expression, the kind he reserved for *his* line of work, screw her acting skills. He wouldn't let her see she'd gotten to him—he wouldn't give her that power.

"Some reunion, wouldn't you say?"

She blinked. Once. Twice. And then the shutter came down, all hint of emotion gone. *Good.*

Stepping to the side, she moved out of his reach and elegantly lowered herself to the floor to pick up her bra.

He watched her; he couldn't help it. Her composure, her grace...they goaded him to make her crack all over again.

"Quite." She fastened the bra around her and slipped her breasts inside the cups, the move making his sated cock twitch and prompting him to sort himself out.

He averted his gaze, slipping off the condom and righting his jeans. "I'm gonna get cleaned up. Why don't you head on through to the lounge, and we can talk."

He nodded in the opposite direction of where he was heading, and without waiting for her response, walked away before his cock had other ideas. Shoving open the door to his toilet, he tossed the evidence of what he'd let happen into the bin and turned to face himself off in the mirror.

His reflection glared back at him, every muscle thrumming with tension as he gripped the edge of the sink.

What the fuck are you playing at?

His knuckles whitened, his jaw flexed, but he had no good answer. He'd given into his basest urge, the kind that had led him down the road to heartache all those years ago. And he was about to do it all again, if he wasn't careful.

He pushed himself away and slammed on the tap, throwing water over his face and praying for the effect of a cold shower. Not that showers had worked before—why would now be any different?

Because you're not the same. You're not the lovesick fool you were then. You're bigger than that now. Bigger than her. Bigger than this thing that seems determined to resurface. And you have your pick of women. You don't need her.

He shut off the tap and towelled himself off. One last determined look in the mirror and then he went to join her, collecting his shirt on the way and throwing it on.

He found her perusing his selection of drinks at the bar, her fingers closing around a bottle of whisky.

"Whisky? Really?"

"The perfect post-orgasm drink, wouldn't you say?" She cocked an eyebrow at him, all confident and clothed now. Had he imagined the fear he'd glimpsed? *No, it just proved it was an act.* "You going to join me?"

Her prompt brought him back. What did it matter if he'd imagined it or not, fake or real, he just needed this over with? Then, he could get rid of her and get his life back on track.

"I'll pass."

He didn't need the alcohol to weaken him any further than she already had.

"Suit yourself." She turned back to his bar and poured a healthy measure.

"There's ice in the freezer below."

"Neat's fine."

He turned away and headed to the glass doors that lead out onto the roof terrace. The boom of music was just audible through the glass and the sound-proofed floors, a reminder that it was still early in some parts of his club and that his clientele were sure to be enjoying similar delights to what the two of them had just shared. *Against your better judgement.*

She was so quiet, he didn't hear her come up behind him until she spoke. "You must have quite the view from here."

He instinctively stepped away, his eyes still on the dark outdoors and the twinkling lights of the city, the revellers and the few cars. "It has its appeal."

It did. If he felt inclined, he'd tell her where the sun came up, where he liked to sit with his morning coffee and take it all in. His perfect moment of peace before the day kicked off in earnest. But he didn't say any of it. It was too personal. Too like old times.

Instead, he walked away and pulled a Becks Blue from the fridge. At least it would taste like beer and it would give him something to do with his hands, which seemed determined to reach for her.

"So, you're really here to help Isla?" He didn't bother to hide his disbelief as he took a slug of his beer and eyed her.

"*Christ*, do you have to sound so stunned?" Her cheeks flushed angrily, and all he could think about was the other reason they'd flushed that same shade not fifteen minutes ago. He clamped his jaw shut and forced the memory out, but his body's reaction was harder to douse. "She's my sister, of course I want to help. And her club is facing bankruptcy—you must know it's not in a good place?"

He *did* know. It didn't change the fact that Isla had never wanted his help. "And where do I fit into this?"

She looked frustrated, the heat in her cheeks still blazing. "Isn't it obvious? I want you to help me save it. You're clearly experienced in the way clubs work, you must have contacts…ideas…expertise that I can tap into."

He shook his head. "No can do."

His words caught her mid-sip of her drink and she coughed over it, her eyes watering. "What do you mean *no can do*?"

"Exactly what I said."

"Look…" She coughed again, her eyes blinking past the obvious sting of whisky. "I know there's no l-love lost between me and you."

His eyes narrowed over her obvious stumble and his fingers flexed around the neck of his beer bottle.

"But don't let that affect things with Isla," she continued, pushing on. "I know you guys have a good friendship, mum told me. I know you care about her, I know—"

"I'm already a silent partner in her club, Carrie."

It was her turn to pause, her turn to narrow her gaze. "You are?"

"Yes, I have been since day one, but Isla has been determined to go this alone."

"What? That makes no sense, she never said you were involved with it."

"Did you ever ask?" He said it under his breath, the retort one born of the past, but he couldn't help it. What was it about Carrie that brought out his worst?

Besides the fact she broke your heart.

Besides the fact you still want to fuck her senseless.

"There's no need to be so nasty about it."

"If I was being nasty, I'd go a whole lot worse, believe me."

Her mouth parted and closed again, whatever she was about to say going without airing. She looked to the window and took a contemplative sip of her drink. One second passed. Two seconds. Three…

He started to think she was going to leave, was preparing himself for that when she looked back to him. "Please, can we park this between us and just think about Isla? I know that together we can do something to pull her club back from the brink."

"Surely, with your name, you can pretty much do that alone?"

"It's not that simple. Despite what you think, I really am here on the quiet. I don't want it getting out that I'm in the UK, but I don't want that to stop me from helping her. That's why I need you—a frontman so to speak, someone that can co-ordinate the efforts and also help advise on what should be done."

"You're asking me to lead this little Samaritan project?"

She righted her stance. Her eyes locked solidly with his own, their depths pleading for his agreement. "Yes, I guess I am. I know that together we can do this."

Together, him and Carrie, for the foreseeable future?

No fucking way.

"For Isla," she pressed.

Isla. Fuck. Guilt nagged, but hell, he'd already tried to help Isla, numerous times over, and she had refused. Why should now be any different?

Because this time you can blame Carrie for the interference.

He could do what he'd always wanted and help her, but it would be Carrie that could take the credit or the fallout.

It all sounded so reasonable, so perfect.

Only it wasn't. Not if he wanted to put distance back between him and Carrie.

"It's admirable that you want to help your sister..." He bent to place his bottle on a low side table, shoving his hands into his pockets as he straightened again to look at her. "But she's made her feelings clear, and she doesn't want my aid."

"She's not asking. *I* am."

He laughed then, but there was no humour in it. "And you think that makes all the difference." He shook his head. "You haven't changed one bit."

"Dan, *please*..."

"Look, it's late, and as much as this has been fun..." He gestured to the hallway—to the location of their little tryst—as if it hadn't turned him inside out. "I'd like you to leave. Do you have a driver outside, or do you need me to call you a cab?"

"Come on, Dan, this is for Isla." She strode towards him, eyes desperate, her free hand reaching out to rest upon his arm and searing his skin. "I have to help her, I have to make things up to her, don't you see?"

See? He saw alright. He could see the guilt in her face. The desperation. But her guilt wasn't his problem. *She* was. Carrie. He couldn't help her and keep his distance. He couldn't be around her and keep this in his control.

He lifted her hand away and took the glass from her unresisting fingers. "You should go."

"*Please, Dan?*"

He shook his head. "Do you need a car?"

She stared at him a moment longer and then her shoulders sank as she dropped her gaze. "No, I have a car waiting for me."

She walked away, dipping to collect her things from the floor where she'd abandoned them. He was slow to follow, careful to keep his distance.

"If you should change your mind," she said, pausing at the door, "you can reach me on Isla's mobile."

And then she was gone, the door closing softly behind her. He let go of a jagged breath, the impulse to go after her burning through him. Instead, he lifted out his mobile and called down to his doormen, asking that they keep an eye out and ensure she got away safely.

Then he headed to the bar and downed the rest of Carrie's drink, topping it up for another and throwing it back.

Let her go. You can't help her and protect yourself.
Just forget it.
Forget her.

Chapter Four

CARRIE LOOKED AROUND HER, TAKING IN THE boxes, the stacked furniture, and the dust—Isla's future plans for the club, all laid out in her purchases and a listed building that was as visually stunning as it was a money pit.

She could see the appeal, see why Isla had fallen in love with the place. The few areas her sister had successfully completed and already utilised were impressive, the character of the nineteenth-century sandstone building lending a unique charm. But that wasn't the problem. It was the investment it clearly still needed to get it fully open—the amount of man hours, building work, TLC...

She perched on the edge of a corner couch, something her sister must have grabbed from some second-hand sale or other, and sighed. Where did she even begin? Maybe it was madness. Maybe she should just accept defeat and make things up to her sister in some other way.

"Oh honey, don't look so defeated." Her mum bustled over, a box in her arms. "I only agreed to help because you seemed so determined to do this for Isla—if it's going to get you down then I say we pack it in right now."

She gave her mother a small smile. "It's a lot of work, and I don't even know where to start..." She shrugged. "Maybe Isla won't even appreciate my interference. Dan certainly seemed to suggest as much."

"That's different. Dan isn't family and there's history there. Your sister didn't want his charity or his pity."

"No, she just wanted him to love her."

Her mother set the box down, her expression sombre. "She did, yes, but that's all in the past. Dragging it up now helps no one."

The past—she scrubbed at the dust gathering over the toe of her suede heels, keeping her eyes off her mother's perceptive ones—*yup, all in the past*. And yet, she still felt that uneasy guilt over it all. Guilt at how much her and Dan had hurt Isla. Guilt at how she'd behaved less than twenty-four hours ago under Dan's roof.

And then there was the crushing fact, he'd just dismissed her and her request for help like it meant nothing; like *she* meant nothing.

"Hey, come on, sweetheart." Her mother sat down beside her. "It's lovely that you want to help her, and I'll do all I can to support you."

"I know, Mum, thanks."

"And Dan might still change his mind, you know."

Carrie gave a noncommittal snort.

"Maybe he's been in touch already. Have you checked your phone?"

She hadn't. But she doubted it. She pulled her bag up off the floor and looked inside for her phone. "Bugger."

"What's up?"

"I must have left it at home." It was so unlike her to travel without it. But then it wasn't her phone, it was Isla's, all part of their switch, her escape.

"Ah well, never mind. We can check when we get back later." Her mother patted her leg reassuringly. "Look, why don't I go get us some drinks from the cafe across the road. We can have a brainstorming session and get a plan brewing?"

"Sounds good, thanks."

Her mother sprang up, clearly energized with her mission. "I'll be back in five."

Carrie watched her go, marvelling at her mother's ability to keep upbeat even in the face of her crazy scheme. But then, she wasn't blind to the fact her mother was just happy to have her home. She'd probably still be smiling if Carrie suggested burning the place down and starting again.

She smoothed her fingers over her hair and shook out her ponytail, half-expecting a spider to fall out and shuddering at the thought. At least they could start with cleaning the place. Although a fat lot of good that would do if they then had to get the builders in. And what if the place wasn't even sound? What if—

Just quit it, and breathe!

You're doing this for Isla, just focus on a plan, not the what ifs.

First things first, she needed to raid Isla's office for documents, plans, the works. Find out what she was dealing with. She could then put those what ifs to bed and focus on what needed addressing. She sprang to her feet just as the door pushed open.

"That was quick, Mu—"

It wasn't mum.

"Dan." She frowned, her eyes far too stunned and hungry in her swift appraisal of him: white T, ripped blue jeans…face just as grim…just as hot. "What are you doing here?"

She tried to keep the heat out of her voice, but it was no use, it came through like she was a buzzing hive of need and it pissed her the hell off. She was a prized actress, for fuck's sake; why couldn't she perform in front of him?

He looked around the room, his hands sinking into his pockets. "I've changed my mind."

Relief washed over her. Had she really heard him right? "Come again?"

He didn't look at her as he shrugged his shoulders. "I've decided to help."

Oh my God. The helpless feeling of seconds before lifted. She could do this with him on board. She just knew it.

When his eyes finally landed on her, her relief died. He didn't look like he'd changed his mind. In fact, he might as well have had a gun held to his head for all he looked pleased to be there.

And then came the realization yet again that despite all they'd shared, nothing had changed. He still hated her. And it *hurt*.

She raised her chin, the desire to tell him to leave, to tell him she didn't need his help, warring with the fact that she did. *Isla* did. "Good."

"Good?"

"Yes, good, what else do you want me to say?"

He shook his head but his eyes sparked with amusement, his lips quirking at the corners and setting off butterflies deep in her gut. Hot off the back of his displeasure, the simple lift in his mood was as effective as his touch, his kiss…

"Thank you," he suggested, his smile widening and poking at the fire spreading inside. "You're my savior…I owe you big time…"

"Thank you. You're my savior. I owe you big time," she rushed out, feeling the burn in her cheeks and wishing it gone, praying he didn't notice. "Now, can we get started?"

He chuckled, the deep resonating sound torching the butterflies and leaving her breathless as he strode into the room. "No time like the present."

"Right, I've got two—*oh*." Her mother halted in the doorway, two cups and a paper bag in hand. "Dan, how good it is to see you."

Her eyes swept from him to Carrie and back again. "If I'd known you were coming I would have brought another…tell you what, no bother, you take mine and I'll leave you two to catch up. There are some things I can get done at home. "

"Don't be silly, Mum," Carrie assured her, panic swelling at the idea of being alone with Dan again. Her mother's sudden presence had been reassuring, calming to her nerves, her libido even; if she stuck around, nothing bad could happen. *Nothing bad*, her conscience laughed at her. "You should stay. Dan's here to help—he can hopefully give us some direction and we can get stuff underway."

"Absolutely, Mrs. Evans. I'm not taking your drink."

Carrie could practically feel her own anxiety mirrored in his voice. He didn't like the idea either; had probably seen her mother's presence as a blessing too.

"It's Helen, Dan, and I will only be in the way. You guys can put me to work when you have a plan of action."

She walked into the room and set the cups down on the box she had deposited earlier. "Now they're fully loaded so best enjoyed with the lids off, but I'm stealing one of the muffins."

She extracted one and deposited the bag back on the side with a flourish. "See you later, kids."

And with that, she was gone, the two of them watching her go in a stretched silence.

This wasn't awkward at all. Not even a bit.

"What do you think she meant when she said it was fully loaded?" Dan asked.

Fully loaded?

Oh, the drink!

"I've no idea, a coffee's a coffee in my book." Grateful for the distraction, she crouched down to extract the lids, the scent of cocoa hitting her immediately and her smile lifting out of long-forgotten habit. "Bloody hell, Mum."

"Funny looking coffee."

"Seems Mum thought a sugar hit more appropriate," she murmured, lifting both cups and passing one to him. "You've not escaped."

"I'll pass."

"Just because we're older, it doesn't mean she won't give you shit for wasting it—do I have to remind you of the rollickings she would deliver when we were younger?"

He laughed, his face lighting up and re-igniting the flutter within. "You have a point."

He took the cup from her, his hand brushing over her own, and everything around her fell away. She looked into his eyes, to the humour in them, and she couldn't breathe.

"Thank you," he said, but he didn't move, didn't break her gaze.

Stop it, you're getting carried away…again.

"Nothing to do with me, this is all Mum."

She turned her back on him, unable to control the unsettling rate of her pulse, her thoughts, and took a sip of the heady drink. Wow, it was good. The creamy topping, the teeny marshmallows, the rich sweetness.

"That good, hey."

She snapped her gaze to his, to his teasing expression, and realized she'd hummed her appreciation. Her cheeks flushed and she nodded, averting her eyes once more and taking an even bigger sip. But she didn't need a heady drink right now, not when his presence was going to her head enough.

"Sounds like you need it."

"I've not had one of these in years," she mused. In fact, how long had it been? She'd been on a permanent diet for at least twelve, which meant it was at least that long. "And it is good, you should try it."

He eyed the drink before he took a sip, his head nodding in appreciation. "You're right, that's delicious."

She swiped her tongue over her lip, feeling the remnants of cream sitting there and spying the same clinging to his stubble. She smiled; it was funny to see such an innocent thing mar his dark good looks. Especially when his eyes had honed in on her mouth and were projecting thoughts that were far from innocent.

"Why do I feel like you're laughing at me?" His tone was distracted, laced with heat, and she wondered just how far they were from a repeat of the other night. Even though he hated her; even though she was going back to LA in a few weeks; even though they had more important things to be getting on with…

"Carrie?" It was a warning now. "You going to tell me what has you grinning like a fool, or am I going to have to work it out of you like the old days?"

Her tummy contracted. The old days—the way he would tickle her until she wailed with laughter, wriggling uncontrollably in his arms. She swallowed, hard. "You have a white moustache."

"A white…?"

She swiped her tongue over her upper lip to spell it out and his eyes traced the move again, burning into her with such desire that the contrast with his creamy addition had her erupting on a giggle and shocking him out of his trance. He swiped the back of his hand over his mouth and shook his head, his hair moving hypnotically with the gesture.

"Having watched you with that delightful white blob on the tip of your nose for the last minute, I should have guessed."

"*What.*" She scrubbed at her nose, her embarrassment heating her through, and then he laughed—a real, belly laugh.

"Got you."

He'd duped her. Played her for a fool.

Without thinking, she grabbed at the bag containing the muffin and went to lob it at him. He got there first, his hand closing around her wrist, holding back the makeshift weapon. "That's the second time in forty-eight hours I've had to stop you from assaulting me. You have quite the temper."

She flustered, the heat of his hold driving her crazy with a multitude of desires, none of which were about helping Isla or keeping her sanity intact…

As soon as his hand closed around her, he regretted it; the memory of pulling her against him in his office had his body urging him to do so again.

Christ, all you had to do was come in, agree to help, delegate, and leave.

Now look at you…

"You deserved it," she blurted. "You were laughing at me."

He frowned, something in her sincerity catching at him. "From where I'm standing we were laughing *with* one another."

She tugged her hand out of his hold and backed away. The moment was over. He should be glad. But he wasn't.

Was she really upset that he'd laughed? Or was she backing away from the crazy attraction so determined to pull them together? The camaraderie that they'd once shared so easy to spark?

"Well, enough laughing." She took a swig of her drink and increased the distance between them. He had a feeling she was doing it mentally too.

You should be glad, his brain repeated, *get over it.*

Help her get the job done and get out.

Then she'll be gone, and you can forget about her.

Yeah, because you did that so well the last time.

"So, if you're going to help, perhaps you can tell me what you know, because I…" She turned to look at him, now all business-like and giving nothing away. "I know nothing about this place. I was about to hit the office and go through the paperwork, hopefully get an idea of why she closed the doors on the space that was completed, and dig out her vision for the rest." She waved a hand about her helplessly. "Because from what I can see she was doing a great job."

At least she was focused on the end game; he could be grateful for that, even if her ability to rise above the pull between them bugged the hell out of him.

"Okay. On all that I can help."

"You can?" Her eyes widened, hope alive in their brightened depths. "Really?"

Christ, now he felt like her savior, and even that pissed him off. "Yeah."

Her brow furrowed, and he knew she'd caught the annoyance in his tone. *Way to go keeping yourself in control.*

"Sure." He forced a lightness into his tone, relieved to hear it pay off. "Come on, let's take this to the office and I'll lay it all out for you."

She started at his choice of words and he couldn't blame her. He would have kicked himself if not for the color sweeping her cheeks, telling him she was still as vulnerable to him, as he was to her.

Not that it helps you get the job done.

He ignored the taunt and headed for the private stairwell that led to Isla's office. He sensed her following in his path, and realized too late that taking this to the closed-in room wasn't such a bright idea. But it was where all the documents were, where Isla's drawings would be; it made the most sense.

Three hours later, he was full-on cursing the decision.

Having gone through the basics, the financial situation, the structural reports, and the listed building restrictions, they were now onto Isla's designs. And rather than look at one sheet at a time, Carrie had insisted on spreading them over the floor, taking them in as a whole. Not only that, she was now on all fours and leaning across them, the black sweater she wore hanging forward and offering up teasing glimpses of the scarlet lace beneath.

Move. Stand behind her.

"Wow. Look at this. It's amazing. Her use of color, the variety of textures, light fixtures…it's stunning…"

Yes, look at the drawings, not at her. Anywhere but her.

He walked to stand behind her. That had to be easier, right?

Wrong.

Now he was faced with her petite round behind, thrusting up at him in tight-fitting black denim. Christ. Replace one delight with another. Way to go.

"Seriously, Dan, how could you not have forced her into accepting your help? This is sure to bring in the money."

"It's not as simple as a great venue." *Focus on the job, focus on the business.* "It's the location too; a club like this requires feeder pubs, restaurants, places for people to go where they can come here after."

"Yes, I get that, but from what I see the recent developments in the area have brought all that."

She was right; the problem was, some of those recent developments meant competition, and that competition had gotten there first, taking trade from Isla when she really needed the income to put back into the club. She hadn't wanted his 'charity' as she deemed it, regardless of his silent partner status; she saw the money he was pouring in as too risky on his part. He'd had faith—she just hadn't listened.

And now Carrie had that faith too, and as much as he didn't want to acknowledge it, he admired her for caring, admired her for wanting to do this, just as much as he admired her arse still thrust up at him. He shouldn't be thinking of anything but the club and their plan to fix it. Instead his palms itched with the memory of tracing those soft, pliable curves; the moans she made when he gripped her against him; rode his—

"So long term, this project has legs, yes?"

"Hmm?" His cock pulsed against his jeans, contending with his brain, which had to rewind to work out what she had asked.

"Dan?" She looked to him over her shoulder, her passion for her sister's project blazing in her gaze. She was so tenacious. So passionate. He could feel it re-energising his own lost enthusiasm…as well as fuelling another, less helpful urge.

Stay on task, for fuck's sake. "Yes."

"Then when can we get started?" She smiled up at him, her cheeks flushing, her eyes ever brighter. The desire to swoop down and kiss her stole his voice and she frowned. "Don't worry, I won't lean on you too much, I promise. I can—"

Ah, hell. Guilt surged, the words with it. "I'm not worried about that. I have contacts I can call on, and if we bring people in under

NDAs you'll be able to oversee things onsite without fear of your identity getting out."

Her smile was back, and God help him, he loved it. "That would be amazing."

She looked so happy, so relieved—like a weight had been lifted off her shoulders—that his insides lifted, his heart doing an unsettling dance. *You need to leave. Now.*

"I reckon so."

She hopped to her feet, so swift he almost back-stepped, and then her arms were around him and squeezing tight. "Thank you, Dan. I can't tell you how grateful I am, especially after…"

She broke away, her head lifting to meet his eyes, the heat of her body still pressed up against his own.

She swallowed, her eyes wavering, her body turning rigid. "Look, maybe we can forget—"

His head dropped before he even realized what he was doing, his mouth closing over hers and his pent-up need bursting free. She moaned into his groan, her body turning into putty against him as she kissed him back.

Oh God, she tasted good. She tasted like she belonged to him. She behaved like she belonged to him. The great Carrie Evans—

You fucking fool.

He thrust her away, holding her at arm's length, his breathing ragged as he shook his head at her. "I'm sorry. It wasn't my intention…I didn't come here for this."

She took a step towards him, her hand raising to rest her fingers over her lips. "You don't need to apologize. I'm not sorry."

What did that mean? That she wanted more? She wanted him to take more?

"You should be," he said, turning away and rubbing the back of his neck, unease sending ice through his veins. He couldn't do this again—he couldn't go there with her and have her walk away. Hating her was just…*easier.*

"Why should I? We're grown adults, why shouldn't we enjoy one another while we can?"

While we can…a reminder that this was temporary, short term, a bit of fun…no strings.

He'd indulged in that plenty over the years. Just not with her.

And that was the problem; it would never just be fun with her.

"I have to go. I'll be in touch when I have the contractors lined up."

And then he left, his mind made up: it was time to hit the club and make use of its benefits. He'd clear her out of his system, and then he could return and get things in motion. With a clear head and an unloaded dick, his brain back in the driver's seat.

It was a great plan. In theory.

But a few hours later, even he was forced to admit, the reality fucking sucked.

He was sat in the observatory wing of his club, and…nothing. Not even a twitch.

He watched the group entwined on the other side of the glass, listened to their sensual moans, tried to feed off their excitement as they licked, teased, fucked their way to orgasm. It was the perfect voyeuristic offering, a sure-fire way to get himself off, but…nothing.

He raised his hand, unseeingly waving his waitress over.

"Sir?"

"Whisky, on the rocks."

Her scent swept over him, a sweet, almost sickly mix. It hadn't bothered him before, but it did now, because it wasn't the scent he wanted. It wasn't *hers*. It wasn't Carrie's. She had a subtle twist of something exotic and he couldn't get it out of his damn head. That, or the way she had felt coming apart around his cock.

Now his dick twitched, the damn thing as disobedient as his brain.

The fact that she'd offered herself to him only a few hours ago, had in fact offered up *fun* for the duration of her stay, taunted him.

Every time he closed his eyes, she was there asking "why shouldn't we?", her words upping in their plead-like quality the more his twisted brain replayed it. Coaxing him. Urging him to reconsider. To take…

"Here you go, sir." The waitress dipped alongside him, placing the drink on his side table and offering him an extended view of her cleavage as she did so. Her offer was clear too, but she wasn't the one he craved. She was complication free and all he wanted was trouble.

He gave her a brief nod. "Thanks."

She smiled, but he could see the disappointment in her eyes—*Hell*, *he* was disappointed. There was no getting away from it. He wanted *her*. *Carrie*. Screw the fucking consequences.

And he wanted her *now*.

What would she say if he called her here? Introduced her to this side of his club? Would she freak out? Or would she get off on it, just as he did…when he wasn't distracted by thoughts of her?

He'd mentally accused her of not having the balls for it, but now he wasn't so sure…

Curiosity had him pulling out his phone, his brain backing up the move: bringing her here took emotion out of the equation. This was a place of sex. Nothing more. It would push her to her limits while keeping all else in check.

Who knew what the composed Carrie Evans, the one the public knew so well, would make of this hidden, hedonistic world? He was ready to find out.

He looked up Isla's number and opened the message screen:

My club, now. Will send a car.

It wasn't soft or polite. It was short and demanding. Exactly how he wanted it.

It was how she would have treated him a decade ago—how would she take it coming from him now?

He slotted the phone back in his pocket and took up his drink, a smile forming. She would come. He knew it.

And the fun they could then have…

He looked to the center table, the four bodies entwined in various stages of arousal, and felt his cock protest against his zipper, his phone buzzing in unison. He pulled out the device and the screen lit around her message:

OK. I'm at Mum's.

His smile grew as he brought the glass to his lips, his eyes returning to the sexual display before him. Everything appealed now…

Chapter Five

CARRIE LOOKED TO HER PHONE. THERE WAS something about Dan's bluntness that told her he'd reconsidered—not on the help front, but the sex—and her response had been immediate; instinctive. But was it right?

She'd left Isla's club late, not wanting to return home with Dan's rejection still hanging over her. Her mum was too perceptive, and she wasn't ready to face her questions. Mum was already grilling her enough about the real reason she'd returned to the UK, and Carrie didn't want to add her messed-up feelings over Dan into the mix.

But it turned out she needn't have worried; her mum's first concern had been to thrust her phone at her and tell her to call Isla. Apparently, her sister had been trying to reach her all afternoon, and when she'd listened to Isla's voicemails they had escalated in their heated plea to call her back. She was worried.

And even though her mother had spoken to Isla and assured her she seemed fine, Carrie wasn't convinced .

The last thing she'd expected when she'd finally called her back was to be cut off with a text that said Isla would call back in ten.

That was nine minutes ago, and now she was sitting here riddled with guilt over the thrill at seeing Dan when something was clearly amiss stateside. Not that she could imagine what.

Unless…

Was it to do with the goings on here? Did she know something about her and Dan? Had mum said something? Did Isla still harbour some feelings for him? Was that why she'd kept his transformation so under wraps?

No, it had to be her guilt talking.

She looked around her bedroom, memories of laying on her bed, stressing over their love triangle, making her feel sick.

It was ten years ago and they'd all grown up since then; surely her sister no longer felt anything for him.

What, like you *don't?*

The phone came alive, signalling a video call from her own number. Anxiety pulled at Carrie's brow and she swiped the call to answer. "Isla, you okay?"

"What do you think?" Her sister barked back at her, skin flushed red, a towel around her head and body that told of a recent shower or bath. Maybe the water could explain the skin color too.

Yeah right, and you're going to blame that for the angry tone as well.

"Have you just boiled yourself in the shower?" she asked, trying to keep a lid on her rising panic and wrinkling her nose in distaste. "You look like a lobster. It's really not a good look."

"Yes, I've taken a shower," Isla snapped, her eyes flaring. *Shit.* "But believe me, the color of my skin has sod all to do with your water temperature, and everything to do with the heat of your sex life."

Oh fuck. "I don't know what you're talking about."

"Don't lie to me, Carrie! How could you think not to tell me?"

"How did you find out?" She could feel the color creeping into her cheeks; the guilt, the shame… "Did mum say something?"

"Mum?" Isla returned. "You mean mum knew and still you didn't think to tell me? Christ, Carrie! The guy turned up in my—I mean, *your* bed…while I was in it…asleep!"

Wait. What.

She doesn't mean Dan.

She doesn't…

Oh no, Brad.

Carrie's mouth fell open as the truth hit, the visual Isla had created sinking in.

"Oh my God, Isla! I am so sorry!" she hurried out. "He wasn't supposed to be back for another month or so. I didn't think to tell you because I didn't think you needed to know."

"So, you didn't think your sister should know that you are in a relationship," she threw back at her. "And not with just anyone—*with him*? We're supposed to tell each other everything, I should have been the first person you told!"

Oh God, oh God, oh God. Isla was right but Christ, she hadn't wanted to tell her. Why would she tell her something that would only play on the inferiority complex she knew her sister held?

"I didn't feel comfortable telling you," she said, desperately seeking the right words to explain herself and not make the situation any worse. "Not when I wasn't sure where it was heading." She swept a shaky hand over her face, trying for honesty. "It felt like rubbing your nose in it unnecessarily."

Isla shook her head down the screen. "So, instead I have to find out by waking up to a stranger in the same bed?" she screeched. "I kicked him in the nuts, Carrie! His *naked* nuts! Do you know how humiliating that was?"

Oh God. The visual just got worse.

"Never mind the fact that I've been unable to avoid the intimacy your relationship demands," she continued, "the guy is on heat I sw—"

"You haven't!"

Her sister froze, her confusion, anger, and pain all staring back at Carrie.

Oh God, they've slept together.

She didn't need to hear the words; she could see it written in her sister's distraught expression. And it was all her fault. She'd put her in this position; she'd created this mess. How the hell did she fix it?

By calming Isla down for starters. Which meant *she* needed to be calm…

She took a breath and nodded slowly. "I see."

"You see?" her sister repeated dumbly, her eyes falling away. They were harrowed with guilt, shaming Carrie through. *You're the one who should be suffering. You're the one who's guilty.*

But hell, both of them wallowing wasn't going to make this situation any better.

"Yes, I do," she said calmly. Her mind might have been racing, but she wasn't going to let Isla see it. The damage was done. It didn't mean she should lose sight of her goal to help Isla. All she needed was enough time to get the club in a decent state, and then she could at least give her sister something good to come home to. After that, she could let Brad down gently. It was the best possible result. A win-win. Almost.

Isla just stared back at her, wide eyed and speechless.

"Well I can't say I'm surprised," she continued with what she hoped to be an easy shrug. "I mean, what else could you do in that situation?"

*Err, tell the truth…*her brain annoyingly supplied, and she promptly ignored it as Isla flushed even deeper, her eyes sparking. "You mind telling me why you're so goddamn cool about this?"

"I'm not cool." She waved a hand about her for emphasis as she added, "I'm just accepting it as a fait accompli."

Isla snorted in disbelief. "A fait accompli?"

"Absolutely!" She *needed* Isla on board with this—had to make her see it this way. What was the alternative? Bringing an end to their switch? Or worse, confessing to Brad? No way. Not without her being there to pick up the pieces and take the flak. "It's not like you had the advantage of advance warning, and I know first-hand how hard he is to resist."

Crap. She shouldn't have said that last bit. Isla instantly paled; she looked fit to vomit. And then her shoulders slumped, her next words coming out quiet and defeated. "So, you'll understand if I end this charade then, sis?"

She stilled—*Oh Christ, no.*

"I can't pretend," Isla continued resolutely. "Not to him."

Carrie shook her head, her composure slipping. "Please, you have to! I *need* people to believe you are me."

"I'm not saying I won't keep up the pretense in public," her sister said softly. "There's no reason for all and sundry to know I'm not you, but he is your…he is your partner, he should know."

Her sister was the voice of reason, she knew it, but it didn't matter. She wasn't ready to deal with Brad. She couldn't. Not yet.

"It's not that simple."

"It really is, Carrie."

Isla *would* think that though. She didn't know about the proposal, the true extent of Carrie's reason for escaping LA. But it wasn't as if Carrie could tell her that now—not after Isla had slept with Brad.

But what if he says something? What if he already has?

"Look, it's hard for him to trust women as it is…" She tried not to cringe as she said it. It was all wrong. Wrong, wrong, wrong. Brad didn't deserve this. But what was the alternative? Have Isla face the music alone, come home early and ruin her plans for the club? She had to push back, make her sister realize it was for the good of all concerned. "I don't want him knowing that we came up with this idea. He'll hate the falsity of it all."

"Are you shitting me?" her sister blurted, her sudden fierceness surprising Carrie and yet not. She knew how bad she sounded—hated herself for it even. She'd put them in this position. "You live in a world that feeds on lies and deceit, it's second nature, surely!"

She winced. "Well, that's a bit harsh."

And bang on the money if you consider your behavior right now.

"You know my feelings on Hollywood, Carrie, it shouldn't be a surprise to you."

"Yes." She knew well enough how much her sister hated her world. It had started as an excuse, a reason to give for the numerous arguments they'd endured as teenagers when Mum and Dad had thought they were out of earshot. But it hadn't been Hollywood's fault, or Dad's career, not really. It had been the side effect of it. The lack of home time for Dad, how much Mum had missed him, her perceived single parent status for most of the time, the constant aggravation of the press…it had been hard…but it wasn't all Dad's fault. It wasn't Hollywood's. Carrie had been able to see that, why couldn't Isla? Instead her sister blamed it, *and* Dad, for tearing their family apart, and no matter how many times they'd had it out over the years, Isla wouldn't back down . But right now, it helped no one.

"And," she continued levelly, "I still stand by what I said, you're being unfair…"

You sure about that? Really? Aren't you pushing her to lie, to deceive, to continue their pretence? All for the sake of your life in Hollywood.

But it's for the good of Isla *too*. Carrie's plans *here*.

She sighed, confusion and guilt weighing heavy on her chest as she lowered her gaze. Maybe she should just tell her the truth, tell her everything—*And where will that leave you?*

She didn't know, but it had to be better than this.

"I don't want to argue about this with you," she said. "I'm sorry I didn't tell you everything, but life has gotten really complicated of late and I've been struggling to think straight. I know it's no excuse, but I never meant to upset you."

"I don't get you, Carrie. I tell you I've slept with your bloke and you hardly react, I tell you I'm pissed at you and that I hate the world you live in and you fold."

"Like I said, it's complicated." She could feel the confession building, had to work out a way to say it that wouldn't make this situation a thousand times worse. *Just be honest. Start with something she'll understand.* "Part of me wanting to come back here was about seeing past the glitz and glamor of Hollywood life, to try and get a handle on what's truly important to me. To work out what it is I really want."

"Okay, I get that," her sister acknowledged, her eyes softening with understanding. "But why does that mean I have to lie to him? Surely he will understand if you just explain like you have done me?"

"No, I can't," Carrie stressed, desperate for her to see. "It'll cause more problems than it's worth right now."

"So, what exactly are you suggesting I do then?" Isla asked, incredulous. "Roll around in the sack with him until you get back and hope that our sexual nuances don't give me…*us*…away?"

Carrie flinched. "There's no need to be so graphic about it."

"There's every reason," Isla said firmly. "You should know full well how high his sex drive is, you want to tell me how I go about rebuking him without landing you and your relationship in it?"

Now her cheeks blazed. She didn't want to think about them rolling around in any manner—not with the deceit hanging over them, over Brad. "Just avoid him. At least, until I get back. He has a rammed schedule, so I can't imagine he will be sticking around for long, just make excuses—"

"You mean, more lies?"

"I know, Isla, but I need the space, space without him in it right now."

"This is crazy! I can't avoid him. In fact, I'm committed to going out with him this evening, his mother has organized a party for his sister Amy, and—"

"She's done what?" Carrie thought she must have misheard her; there was no way his mother would do such a thing. Amy was too fragile, her recent drug rehab making a party the last thing the girl needed. Brad would be going out of his mind.

"Bradley said it was for her birthday," her sister stated, clearly startled by her outburst. "But apparently Amy is stressing that their mother will get carried away with the planning so he volunteered me…you…to help."

"What the hell is Marie playing at?"

Isla shrugged. "I thought a birthday party was a nice thing to do for someone."

"Yes, it's nice when it's something they will enjoy," Carrie agreed, her brows knitted together. "But when the guest of honor is a recovering druggy with a fear of relapsing so powerful that she collapsed at her last social event, it's plain thoughtless."

Her sister gasped. "Oh my God, poor girl!"

"And poor Brad," Carrie acknowledged, her reasons for keeping him in the dark growing exponentially. "This is going to be killing him."

"Well, it's just another good reason to end this charade now," her sister hurried out. "At least where he is concerned, he has enough to deal with."

"I can't." She *really* couldn't now.

"What do you mean you can't?"

"It's complicated."

"You're going to have to go one better than 'it's complicated', sis."

"It just is, Isla, please take my word for it. Right now, Brad is going to need me there to support him, but I can't be there." *…But Isla could be…* "And I can't give away where I am without telling him stuff that I need to explain to him in person."

"Then call him and speak to him directly," Isla encouraged. "You can tell him you can't make this evening and that you are going back home for a bit, sending me in your place to keep the press off you. It's not the complete truth, but it's better than telling him it's me he's been…been…" Her sister couldn't finish the sentence, her cheeks blazing with the unspoken.

"I can't." Her voice shook with her mounting anxiety. "I'm not ready for that conversation."

"Ready for what conversation? You just tell him you're taking some time out to evaluate your life. What's so difficult about that?"

Their gazes locked via the phone screen, their role reversal not lost on her—Isla all steely composure while Carrie was brimming with angst, her teeth grinding as her tummy churned.

"Tell me what's really going on," Isla said eventually, her tone so soft with concern that Carrie could feel herself cracking. "Look, I know you, and I know that there is more to this than what you are telling me."

She was right. She was so right. Carrie let out a gust of air, her cheeks puffing out as her shoulders sagged.

"Christ, it must be bad if you feel capable of pulling that face."

Carrie was barely aware of her sister's teasing; she was too focused on the next words out of her mouth, her body leaning forward as she whispered, "He proposed."

There. She'd done it. It was out. And it actually felt good to be honest.

"Seriously, Isla," Carrie stressed into the silence. "He proposed, and I didn't know what to do."

Her sister was still, her face unreadable.

"Did you hear me, Isla?"

"I heard you," she said eventually, her voice eerily quiet. "I'm just struggling to process it."

"I'm sorry, I know I should have told you," Carrie hurried out, her words tumbling one after another. "But in truth, it was a huge shock when it happened and on paper it's perfect, how could I tell you and expect you to understand my hesitancy?"

"Hesitancy?"

"Yes, you won't get it," she continued, desperate to make her understand. "After all, he's a successful actor-cum-director-cum-production company owner. He has the power to let me be whoever I want to be, for as long as I want to do it. And he is a great man too. Trustworthy. Gorgeous. Amazing in bed—"

"Yes, you're right, on paper it's the perfect match for you," Isla cut in bitterly.

"But..." she began and then paused, her sister staring daggers at her and cutting off her voice. She wasn't understanding it at all; she was looking at it in black and white, and drawing her own conclusions. "See, you're doing it now! You're judging me!"

"You don't need me to judge you, Carrie, I think you're doing a pretty good job of that yourself."

"You don't understand, Isla."

"I understand perfectly. You bewitched him, he fell in love, he proposed, and you ran."

"No."

"Yes! You gave me this crap about it being a good idea for me to get away with my business folding and gave me the sob story about how you needed a break from the public eye, but all the time you wanted to escape another love-crazed buffoon."

"Isla, stop it!" Carrie snapped. Now her sister was spouting nonsense—and that reference to Dan wasn't lost on her. "He is no buffoon. And he is *not* in love with me."

"Of course he is."

She wanted to laugh in hysteria; Isla had it so wrong. "No, if you let me finish, I will explain."

"I can't talk about this any more right now." Her sister's voice shook as she said it, and Carrie wished they were in the same room so that she could put her arms around her and convince her how wrong she was.

"Isla, please, if I explain then hopefully you will under—"

"Save it, Carrie."

She wanted to grab the phone, do something to keep her there; she knew Isla was about to hang up. "Please."

"I'll call you when I'm ready to talk."

Tears welled in Carrie's eyes, her hand reaching out for the phone on instinct. "Wait!"

Isla stilled. "What?"

"Please," Carrie whispered, focusing on the one thing that she needed right now. "Promise me you won't tell him, not yet. Just help him get through the party and I promise I will get my head together."

"Don't worry, I have no desire to tell a man that the woman he loves has legged it and left him with her second-rate sister."

No, no, no. She was about to fight back when her mother's voice reached her from downstairs. "Carrie? Dan's driver is here."

No. Not now.

She looked away from the screen, composing her voice enough to call back. "Tell him I'll be down in five minutes."

When she looked back to the phone, Isla was frowning at her. "What was that all about?'

She felt her cheeks flush all over again. "Just mum."

Isla nodded. "I make it eight in the evening your way, who's the guy that needs you at this time of night?"

No more lies. "It's Dan."

Her sister's eyes pierced her, something akin to hatred glowing in their depths. Just like Dan had looked when she'd turned up at his club. Ice washed over her, her skin pricking. *Hell*, she didn't need their hate, she had plenty enough for herself right now.

"So," her sister said bitterly, "all day out with him, and now all night too? I can really see how you are using your time well to work out your relationship issues."

She was transported back a decade, in this same room, amidst a row that wasn't too dissimilar. "Isla—"

"Bye, sis."

And then her sister was gone, and Carrie had no idea what to do. She'd played it wrong. The whole entire thing. But she'd felt trapped in a lie of her own making, and now she was making her sister walk that lie with her, which wasn't fair. Isla didn't lie—she'd only agreed to the swap because it hadn't involved deceiving the people that they knew up close. Only the media, really.

But now, it wasn't just the media.

It was one thing for Carrie to live a lie—hell, her whole life was a lie as she lived cleaner-than-clean for the purposes of good PR. And yes, she felt suffocated by it. But Isla…

"Carrie, are you coming?" her mother called. "The poor guy has his engine running."

Jesus, what was she doing? She shouldn't go. Not if Isla's remarks regarding Dan masked deeper feelings for him. It wasn't like her sister had mentioned any other love interests over the years to put her mind at rest.

Or had Isla just been feeling protective, defensive even, over Brad? Maybe the idea that Carrie might be messing around behind Brad's back is what had upset her? It was possible.

But what if she'd got it wrong; what if Dan just wanted to talk about the club renovations? Or heaven forbid, wanted to back out of helping?

She thought back to the kiss they'd shared. It had been explosive, right up until the point he'd ended it and high-tailed it out when she'd pushed for more.

No, she had to go. She had to find out what he wanted.

"Carrie!"

"Coming, Mum."

And if it was sex, then she would just have to put him straight…just like she had ten years ago.

She was stronger now; older and wiser.

So why did it feel like she was asking the impossible of herself?

Because you are.

Chapter Six

LOOKING UP AT THE DOORMAN FROM THE other night, Carrie felt her tummy twist. She was nervous. Really, freakishly nervous.

Whether it was a lack of trust in herself to resist Dan's possible advances, a hangover from her conversation with Isla, the resurrection of the past, or panic that he may have called to pull out all together—she was a mess.

She forced a smile. "Dan sent for me?"

It came out like a question, like she was unsure, and she shook her hair out, righting her shoulders. It wouldn't do to be weak.

He gave her a brisk nod, maybe even a smile if the slight twitch to his lips could be interpreted as such. "This way, Miss."

She followed him through the same access she had entered when she'd agreed to going upstairs with Dan the other night. But instead of turning to the stairs, he opened one of the doors she'd heard voices through on that last occasion.

It opened into a bar area, a smaller version of the one next door and far more intimate. The background music was low and sultry, the accented lighting providing a subtle privacy to the various sofas and table arrangements. There appeared to be no staff, just clientele wrapped up in their companions and the sensual atmosphere.

She passed a threesome to her right: two men and a woman, the latter very much in charge as she exposed both men to her eager hands. She averted her surprised gaze, an intense hunger surging through her belly and eating at her nerves. What was this place?

Discretely, she scanned the room from beneath her lashes. There were maybe ten, fifteen others, all at ease in their varying states of undress. *Fuck me, is that guy royalty?* She'd swear he was…the man's eyes swept to hers, interest burning in his gaze, and she snapped her eyes back to the rear of the doorman, her mind tripping over the various ideas forming.

What had Dan said about NDAs? That no one would dare speak her name outside these walls—is that what this was? An exclusive club catering to the elite, to the tastes that no amount of fear at being caught could lessen? *Christ*, she'd hungered for this kind of excitement for years but hadn't dared enquire, hadn't dared to trigger suspicion and the press interest that would then ensue.

But Dan? *Really?*

She couldn't think it of him…*no, that's a lie.*

She couldn't think it of Dan as the boy he once was.

As for the man…

"He's just through here, Miss." The doorman pushed open a heavy wooden door and used his arm to keep it open. He made no attempt to enter, his intention clear: she was to step inside, and he would vanish.

Heart in mouth, nerves bubbling away, she quickly surveyed her outfit: a classic chiffon blouse, hint of black bra, black leather pants, and heels to suit. She felt decidedly underdressed…or overdressed, if what she'd seen on the way in was to greet her on the other side.

And would it?

The heat that had sparked the second she'd crossed the threshold, spread through her limbs, the dregs of hope she'd had at behaving herself burned to smithereens.

She wanted what they had in the room behind her. She wanted that with the man that had summoned her.

Unless he'd brought her here as some kind of tease...he'd hardly wanted more from her at the club that day.

Her feet felt heavy, rooted to the spot, when the doorman gestured to her. "Mr. Stevenson awaits."

Yes, he does.

She gave him a short nod, straightening her spine and setting her legs into motion. Whatever was to greet her, she would deal with it when—

She couldn't see a thing. As she entered the room, the light dipped further, her eyes slow to adjust. Behind her, the door closed and she saw movement in the shadows along one wall.

"I'm glad you came."

His voice rumbled through her, sounding louder than it was when she couldn't actually make him out; then he appeared, stepping into the low light cast by the floor to ceiling glass that ran along the opposite wall. He was back in black, his T-shirt far too taut, his black jeans fitting his frame to perfection and sending desire climbing up her throat. She swallowed it back, finding her voice.

"I was curious as to why you summoned me." She looked to the glass, to the various plush sofas arranged before it, and her brain went into overdrive. What was this room?

"Here." He offered her a glass—whisky, no ice, just as she'd chosen to drink it two nights ago.

"That's a bit presumptuous, don't you think?" She smiled at him beneath her lashes, accepting the drink regardless and taking a slow sip.

His eyes fell to her mouth, their intensity stoking at the fire inside her. "Which bit? The drink—" he lifted his gaze to lock with her own, "—or the orgasm that comes before it?"

Her lips parted on a rush, her deepest, darkest desires sparking off the back of what she had witnessed, what this strange room inspired, and the lust that laced his words.

Remember Isla, her conscience tried.

"Come, I want to show you something." He reached out to take her hand, his touch sending heat whirring through her veins and pushing out her good intentions with an instant hit of lust. She looked to his hold, his fingers laced through hers, and desire bubbled up her throat. *She was screwed*.

"Come." He repeated, the word loaded with meaning and sending an excited shudder rippling through her. He spied the telltale tremor, his lips curving softly. "I think you'll enjoy this."

He turned to move away, and she followed, her brow furrowed, her heart beating wildly—*This? What's this?*

He paused at the end of the room, his hand rising to a unit on the wall. The glass to their left started to change, the light level shifting, and suddenly all became clear. The air filled with the sound of moaning; real, orgasm-induced moans. *What the fuck?*

She turned to look back through the glass. A large circular bed filled a central platform on the other side, occupied by three women and a man. She felt her lips part; her fingers pulsing around her drink as her hold tightened and she strove to control the salacious rush that consumed her.

She shouldn't be looking…she shouldn't…but she couldn't tear her eyes away.

The man lay on his back, his head buried between the legs of a redhead crouching over him, her naked body undulating with every moan she made as her cheeks flushed with impending climax.

At his waist lay a blonde woman, her lips wrapped tightly around his cock, her cheeks hollowed out as she sucked him back, her eyes fixed on where he licked out her friend, her own body rocking as a raven-haired beauty drove into her with a strap-on—*fuck*. Carrie's tummy contacted, her clit throbbing, the wetness between her legs instant and shameful. Shameful because not only was she watching, but she was *enjoying* it.

She'd told herself there would be no more of this with Dan—no more sex, no more hurting her sister. And still her clit panged, incessant and needy.

"What is this?" she whispered, scared they would hear her, scared they would catch her staring. "Can they see me?"

"Only if you want them to."

He moved behind her, his fingers closing around her glass to extract it and place it on a small side table at her thigh. Christ, she shouldn't be looking. She shouldn't. "They know we're here though? That they're being watched?"

"That's why they chose this room," he explained softly. "It's to fulfil that fantasy."

The redhead lost it, her body spasming, her moan morphing into a heady wail of bliss and Carrie gasped, the force of the girl's reaction delivering an emphatic one of her own.

"You like?" He murmured the question against her neck, his lips brushing her skin.

Like? Her body was an aching, craving, mutinous bundle of need. She wanted to come, and she wanted it now. Screw all her good intentions. She swallowed, trying for words, not daring to admit…

"I recognize the guy." She did; she was sure of it. Even with his face buried in the redhead's pussy, she was sure she'd seen him before.

Dan nipped at her skin and an electric jolt struck at her core. "You'll probably recognize some of the others if you look hard enough."

"But…how?" His hands curved around her hips as his body closed the gap between them, all hard and warm and inviting. She was struggling to form the question she wanted to ask, the cloud of lust descending too heavy, too thick…*just once more, let go once more and then the good intentions can take over…but is it safe?* She needed to get that question out before she lost herself in the scene before her; in his presence, his hand, his mouth… "What if it gets out? What about their reputations?"

"I told you, no one gets in without signing on the dotted line;

everyone is safe." He tugged at her blouse, pulling it out of her waistband. *This is so wrong…you should stop him, you should—*

His fingers slipped beneath her top, their heat setting her skin on fire as he traced upwards.

"You trust a bit of paper?" Her voice was breathless, disbelieving even.

"Everyone is here for the same reason. To let go in private."

"And what if they change their mind?"

"Trust me, no one goes against the rules of my club."

My club. It sounded so possessive. And the power in that simple statement—it made her shiver.

"Do you trust me?" he pressed.

Yes. She did. There was no denying it. And it terrified her. She felt so safe in his arms, so secure, like nothing could get to her, nothing could hurt her. And yet…he had the power to do all that. He could break her, all over again, and she couldn't give him that. She couldn't admit it.

His hands found the button of her trousers, working it undone. Each brush of his fingers against her skin had her tummy clutching tight.

"Do you trust me, Carrie?" he whispered into her ear, his fingers sliding her zipper down. *Oh God yes…*

Her head fell back against him, her body like molten liquid under his attentions.

"Tell me you trust me." His fingers hovered just above the lace band of her thong, his other hand tracing up her belly. "Carrie?"

"I…I…I don't know you anymore."

He tensed, but only for a second, and then she felt him smile against her ear. "Let's fix that."

His fingers dipped lower and she bit into her lower lip, scared of moaning, scared of letting go…

"Would you like them to know you're here watching? Would you like them to see what I'm doing to you?" She shook her head against him; no, she wasn't ready for that, no matter how much the closeted exhibitionist in her wanted it.

But she would watch *them*; her eyes fixed on their erotic display as Dan's fingers slipped between her folds, her clit pleading for the imminent contact.

"So wet for me, baby," he murmured approvingly, dipping in deep and then pulling back, his fingers slick with her need as they traced around her clit. She rolled her hips against him, savouring his invasion and wanting him closer, harder, faster.

The group switched position behind the glass, the man maneuvering himself to the rear of the raven-haired woman. He planted his palm on her lower back, stilling her rocking motion into the blonde as he slid the tip of his cock between her arse cheeks, his face tense with desire and feeding Carrie's own. He eased forward at the same time Dan hit upon Carrie's clit, his fingers expertly working her as her ears rang with the moans from beyond the glass. She was being driven by sight, sound, touch and it was taking her to the brink; swift, forceful and like nothing she'd ever known.

The man rode into the raven-haired girl, driving her pleasure higher and Carrie's with it. Something about the movement—the steadiness, the tension—told her it was her arse he was fucking, the realization sending heat raging through Carrie's limbs.

And then the blonde shifted, turning herself to kneel before the girl, her fingers dipping beneath the strap-on she wore to slip inside. And hungrily, the girl took them both, her moans wild, contagious, the sight so fucking erotic Carrie writhed wildly against Dan, her own climax building with force.

"That's it. Go with it, Princess." He picked up his tempo, his free arm holding her fast against him. And she was; she was losing herself in the whole carnal scene.

And suddenly she wanted it—she wanted them to see her, to hear her; she wanted it all. "Let them see," she rasped. "I want...I want..."

But it was too late, she was crashing, wave after wave wracking her body, blissful heat flooding her veins. Dan pressed his hand against her, letting her ride it out, his teeth nipping at her neck and arm tight at her waist, holding her upright.

"*Fuck.*" The curse was out without her even thinking it. In fact, she was hardly aware of anything but the pleasure rippling through her, the hard expanse of Dan's body behind her, the scent of sex, the very real fact that she wasn't yet sated.

She wanted more. More of him, more of his world…

You came for Isla, to help her, and now you're just helping yourself to what you want.

She squeezed her eyes tight against the unwelcome reproach, more coming hot on its tail: *it's always what you want…to hell with everyone else.* The same words flung at her over a decade ago, by her sister and Dan alike, now thrown by her own conscience.

But it wasn't like that. Not then.

Now, though…now she should know better.

"I have a proposition for you, Princess." He murmured the words in her ear, his arm slackening as he felt her regain her footing.

"What's that?"

He caught an edge to her voice—was she suddenly self-conscious? Nervous? Regretful?

He hoped not. The proposition he had brewing depended on her being completely wrapped up in this.

He brushed a kiss to her cheek, inhaling her scent and ignoring the warning that sparked in his blood. He wanted this. For however long he could have it. "Turn around."

She did so slowly, her lashes raising to look up at him as her hip brushed against his erection. He gritted his teeth against the heat that surged to meet her, his hands easing inside her trousers and cupping her arse against him. Her skin was so warm and yielding beneath his palm and he flexed his fingers against her, loving how she bit into her lip, a whimper choking up her throat.

To hell with words. He crushed her to him, his mouth claiming hers with such ferocity that they fell back against the glass. He fumbled with his trouser fastening, cursing his inefficiency and she came to his rescue, yanking at his zipper. His cock sprung free in its commando state and she gave a small gasp, the delighted sound swallowed by his mouth as he tongued her deep.

He couldn't get enough of this. Of her. Her taste, her heated response to everything he did. He rode his body against her and she pressed a hand between them to grip him tight, pump him hard, her fingers slipping with the pre-cum already seeping free. *Fuck.* He was going to come, like some sex-starved fool.

His pride had him taking hold of her wrist, pulling her away, and she whimpered her complaint. The sound as evocative as her wanton expression and he grinned. *Fuck.* He could get used to seeing her this out of control, this desperate…*no, there's no getting used to anything. This was a short-term deal, and this time you're in control.*

The reminder had him stepping back. *Take control.*

She looked to him in silent question.

"You want me?" He gripped the base of his cock and moved his other hand over himself, watching her follow the movement as she gave a slight yet definite nod. "How much?"

She cocked her head, her eyes drunk on passion. "So much."

"Prove it."

She reached for him and he shook his head. "On your knees."

Her eyes flashed. "My knees?"

The Carrie he knew would never…not in a million years. "Yes, your knees. Show me how hungry you are."

Her mouth parted, her eyes flicking back to the clear glass, where the guy beyond now had two women showing him just that. "Yes, Princess, just like that."

Her eyes widened further, her tongue leaving a wet trail over her lips as she looked back to him, her cheeks a delicious shade of pink.

Was she going to refuse? Had he pushed her too far?

"Just…like…that." She said it slow, her movements sultry as she lowered herself to her knees.

Fuck yeah. He couldn't breathe, didn't dare move as she slipped her fingers beneath his, nudging him away.

"Whatever you say…" she whispered over his tip, her eyes fixed with his as she held him tight.

Christ. He could get used to hearing her say that, too.

Slowly, she moved her hand up and over him, her lips parting ever wider, so close but not close enough. "How would you like it?"

Her breath teased over the freshly beaded pre-cum and he stiffened—anything to stave off the heat spreading through his limbs. He wanted to savour this. Wanted to draw out every last second… *How would he like it?*

She touched the base of his cock with her tongue, the contact barely there, and his cock strained within her hold.

"Yes," he hissed between his teeth, calling her eyes to his and locking on. She trailed her tongue along his length. "All the way…*yes, just like that.*"

Her tongue circled around the head while her hand worked him slow and steady. He was engraving the sight in his brain, gritting his teeth, holding his breath, doing everything he could to prolong it. Carrie. *His* Carrie. On her knees, devouring him.

She tucked her free hand into his jeans, her nails grazing his skin as she brought the tight fabric down his thighs. The cool air of the room swept over his exposed skin, followed by the heat of her fingers as she cupped his balls. "*Fuck.*"

"You like that?"

His thighs quivered and he fisted his hands, lust clouding his brain. "Suck them." He whispered the order, his fingers unfolding to comb through her hair, encouraging her to do as he commanded. He was going to get his fill, load up his memory bank with every last thing they dared do together.

She ducked her head as her tongue replaced her fingers, her mouth coming next. She sucked him in, first one, then the other, the heat of her mouth encasing him, her hum of approval reverberating around them, through them and singing through his cock. The head swelled into her pumping hand, his toes curling in his shoes as his climax built.

Christ, he could come like this, was ready to, his body rocking into her hold and his contracting balls surrounded by her heat. He'd make a mess of her. The great Carrie Evans, covered in his cum. Hollywood polish forgotten, and all for him. "*Fuck.*"

She released him, backing up to eye his throbbing length, her lips parted teasingly. The idea of ramming hard into that delicious pink mouth ripped through him, nearly robbing him of his control.

But not yet.

This was too good.

He took hold of himself and slowly traced her glossy lips with the tip of his cock. "You want this?"

She flicked her tongue out, probing at his slit, scooping up the escaping pre-cum on her dainty pink tip before swallowing it down and nodding, her mouth rubbing against him.

"Here." He pressed his head between her parted lips, watching with fascination as she sucked him with a pop. Her tongue flicked out, calling him back, and he slid in further, pulling out just as she started to take him deeper. It became a game—her wanting more and him resisting, his cock swelling ever harder as the ache in his gut built out of his control. She moaned around him, begging him for more.

"What is it, Princess? You want it all?"

She nodded as he thrust forward and rammed himself inside, catching the back of her throat and losing himself in the sounds she made.

"That's it," he murmured tightly. "Take it."

Her mouth slid over him; its heat, its wetness, the vibration of her moan surrounding him. Halfway in, he felt the back of her throat again. Her lips closed tight around him and then she sucked back, his body spasming with the motion.

He dropped his hands to her hair, forking through the strands as he gripped her seeking to go deeper. "More. That filthy mouth of yours can take it all."

She moaned around him as she took him deeper doing as he commanded, her breath rasping, her movements fast and hard. Each time, she took that little bit more, until she had him at her throat. Then she pulled back, taking a breath through her nose before sinking him deep, her throat clamping and squeezing him tight. He was gone, heat exploding through his body as he came, his cry guttural and contending with her eager hum as she took his all.

Fuck. Fuck. Fuck.

He dropped forward, his hand hitting the glass to hold himself upright as his knees weakened. He took in Carrie's form, her head still slowly moving over him as she drank down everything he spilled, her eyes lighting on his with such lust, such need. She'd never been more beautiful, and his chest tightened.

"I think you're done," he whispered eventually, shivering as she slipped her mouth over his sensitized head.

She smiled as she let him go, pressing a soft kiss to his tip. "I like to be thorough."

Her words teased him anew, his cock twitching despite its release, and he reached down for her, pulling her up. "You always did."

It was out before he could think better of it, and he felt the instant the past came between them.

Carrie wiped her fingers over her mouth and he reached out automatically to stroke away the remnants, loving that he'd done that to her and wanting to do it all again.

There was no stopping this. He couldn't work with her and keep it in check. Screw the past and the pain. It would be a damn sight easier if they just accepted it and enjoyed whatever this was for the time they had left. It would never be love—he couldn't go there again. He wouldn't.

But sex...*that* he could handle.

Her lashes fluttered, her eyes suddenly hesitant as she moved to right her clothing and he felt something inside him soften, weaken.

No, don't. Not again. This is sex. Just sex.

"I should go," she said softly.

"Not before you hear my proposition." He pulled her up against him, beating back emotion with the far baser need to have her close to him. He scanned her face, taking in her flushed skin, the brights of her eyes, her infinite appeal. "I say, we work together to help Isla."

"Yes...we've established that."

"You haven't let me finish."

She was eyeing him funny. An edginess, a need, that same fear?

As with her sudden hesitation, the emotion caught at him. There was something familiar there, something that chimed too close to home, too close to how he felt. "There's no need to look scared."

She gave a short laugh. "I'm not."

"No?"

"No."

"Good." He paused, trying to read her, ready to gauge her reaction as he added, "Because I'd like this to continue."

"This?" Her eyes flared over the word. "You mean us." She wet her lips. "Sex?"

He smiled softly, relieved to see hunger pushing out the fear. "Yes."

He stroked back the hair that had fallen over her face, his thumb brushing over her lower lip as he did, and she quivered, her eyes ablaze. *Oh yes,* this arrangement had so much potential; there were so many avenues to explore together. "I want you in my bed...my club...any time, any place."

Her brow furrowed, at total odds with the need simmering beneath the surface. "I can't."

"Can't?" He cupped her jaw, his eyes burning into her own. He could have guessed at a variety of responses, but *I can't* wasn't one of them. "I think we've just proved otherwise."

"I'm sorry, Dan." She shook her head, freeing herself from his hold, her eyes lowering and shutting him out. "I shouldn't have let things go this far as it is. I can't do this again, not to Isla."

He froze. "What's Isla got to do with us having some fun?"

"I hurt her ten years ago by being with you—I won't do it again."

It was his turn to frown. "What the hell are you talking about? There's nothing between Isla and I."

"Yes…" Her eyes speared him with their sudden pain, "But not because she doesn't want it."

"*Want it?*" he said incredulously. "Isla wants nothing of the sort, she hasn't for a long time."

"You sure about that?"

Was he? He reckoned so. Christ, they'd cleared the air years ago. Why would Carrie think otherwise? And why would she let it get in the way now? "Yes, I'm sure. And why the hell would that bother you? You didn't let it stop us all those years ago. Why now?"

She reacted as though she'd been slapped, her golden skin and the low light not enough to hide her sudden pallor.

"I have to go."

"What?" He straightened as she moved away from him, and he had to work hard to ignore the sudden chill she left in her wake. "Seriously Carrie, you've got this so wrong."

She wasn't listening to him. She was too busy getting her clothing straightened out, and then she was gone, heading out the door and leaving him stranded, just like she had ten years ago. Only this time, he wasn't calling her back. He wasn't begging. If she wanted to go, she could bloody well go.

Chapter Seven

ONE DAY HAD BEEN AND GONE.
One whole day without seeing him.
One day without the exhilarating hit of adrenalin that always accompanied his presence, and Carrie felt like she was in some weird state of withdrawal.

She couldn't sit still; she couldn't focus. And she couldn't regain her cool—that's what bothered her the most. Carrie Evans was cool. It was a given. But apparently that wasn't the case anymore and what the hell was she supposed to do with that?

She'd even taken to leaving her sister's phone lying around, her fear that Isla would ring and read far too much into her harried state making her avoid it at all costs. Not that she could do that forever. They needed to talk and get a plan in motion. But she couldn't trust herself not to make matters worse; it wasn't like their last conversation had gone well.

No, first she needed to get Isla's club resurrection underway, and then she could worry about the situation stateside. After that, maybe she could work out the mess her head was in over Dan.

Your head—don't you mean your heart?

"Will you please stop pacing, Carrie?" Her mother looked at her over the plans Dan had sent over and sighed. "He has it in hand. Just look at this, it's brilliant."

Carrie paused in front of the mirror behind Isla's main bar area and re-checked her hair. "I know, Mum, he's definitely come through for us."

That isn't the problem, she complained inwardly. *The problem is the man himself, and keeping a safe distance.*

You walked away, though, she reminded herself. *You put an end to the sex. Now you just have to keep it that way.*

So why the hell are you preening like a goddamn peacock?

She let go of a pent-up breath and rechecked her watch.

"Stop worrying. If Dan said he'll be here with his team, he'll be here."

She wasn't worrying about him not turning up; she was worrying about her own reaction when he did. And her time was up—the sound of the door opening in the lobby had them both looking in its direction.

"See?" her mother beamed, placing the papers on the bar and walking off to greet Dan. Carrie shook herself out of her daze and followed close on her heel. At least mum was here, and a stack of contractors; an audience big enough to ensure a purely platonic reunion and no going back on her plans. *Perfect.*

"Dan," her mother cooed as she met him in the lobby, Carrie in her shadow.

"Mrs. Ev—Helen."

His voice sent her pulse tripping out, the memory of the carnal orders falling from those same lips not two nights ago shaking her up inside, and she stumbled in her heels.

"Hey easy." He reached out to clutch her elbow, his touch setting her skin alight. She looked to his hand, his arm, that distracting tattoo, right up to his face, and nearly died as heat flooding her cheeks. *Did he have to look so good? Smell so good even?*

He frowned down at her, his gray eyes deep with concern and hypnotic in their intensity, their closeness. "Are you okay?"

"Fine. I'm *fine*."

Christ, she sounded like she'd been gulping bloody helium!

His brow furrowed even further, his hand still gripping her elbow as his other moved to cup her other one. "You sure?"

Yes, I'm bloody sure, she wanted to scream at him—at herself.

No, her heart wasn't rapping against her tonsils over his proximity.

No, she didn't feel like she needed his continued touch and a whole lot more.

She shook her head as if it would somehow shake out the ridiculous rant, and stepped around him, out of his hold. "Right, let's get down to business, shall we?"

She took in their audience: at least a dozen hard-hat contractors stood to attention, observing their little encounter, and then there was her mum, taking it all in with an expression far too easy to read.

She looked away from that knowing look before the heat of her embarrassment, her dogged need, broke through her foundation layer. "So, who do we have here?"

Thankfully, Dan fell into step, taking her through introductions and delegating out the tasks at hand before sending each man on his way. She stood back during the latter part, watching him in motion and wishing she hadn't as her swelling admiration only served to up the dogged attraction she felt.

Even in what must be his laidback loungewear, she wanted to strip him bare. Those sweatpants that skimmed over his backside and barely concealed the bulge that she knew grew exponentially in size. That gray tee that showed off his pecs far more than was decent, teasing her with the memory of how it felt to trace her fingers over their taut expanse…*fuck*. Her clit pulsed.

She needed to make an excuse to get out of his company, just for a moment—anything to stop her reconsidering her decision and getting herself in any deeper. No amount of saving Isla's business would make up for stealing her guy a second time round.

"Tea anyone?" Her voice rang out in the high-ceilinged room and had several people in the near vicinity jumping. *Oh dear.* She hadn't meant to be quite so loud. But then, she hadn't *meant* to behave like a besotted teen, either.

She started for the kitchen, her mind made up; they were having tea regardless.

"Oh, good idea, darling," her mum called after her. "I'll get that sorted. I think Dan needs your opinion on the light fittings next door?"

No, Mum. She continued into the kitchen area, purposefully ignoring her mother. She wasn't about to have her escape plan hijacked, no matter how well-meaning her mother's intentions were .

"I said I'll do that, love." Her mother bustled in, reaching around her for the kettle before Carrie could take it up. "Dan needs you."

Not in the way I need him right now, came her mind's frustrating response. "He has it covered."

"No, he doesn't. He needs your eye for this one."

"My eye?"

"Yes, your eye, now off you go."

Carrie wavered, her weight shifting from one foot to the other. Her mother halted at the sink, her eyes narrowing. "Is there something you want to talk about?"

"Nope," Carrie blurted. *Absolutely not.* "Everything's fine. I'll go find Dan."

"You sure?"

She grinned with false bravado, knowing she probably appeared mental, but it beat *that* conversation. "Absolutely."

Her mum raised her chin. Her eyes were still probing, but Carrie sensed she was letting it go…for now. "Fair enough, love, you know where I am if you change your mind."

"Sure do."

"You want a tea?"

"How about something stronger?"

Her mother's brow hit the roof and Carrie cursed her instinctive response. *You were in the clear, for fuck's sake.* "What's going on, Carrie?"

"Nothing, Mum, I'm fine." *But it wouldn't hurt to tell her a little of the truth...* "I just want this to work. I owe it to Isla."

Her mother put the kettle down and placed a hand on Carrie's shoulder, her fingers gentle as she gave it a reassuring squeeze. "You don't owe her, love. Why would you say that?"

Because Dan chose me. Because I left when she needed me the most. Because I have the career I dreamed of, and she has nothing but this. Because I want her man all over again. Because. Because. Because. "Because I'm her sister, and I want the best for her."

It was simpler, less messy to say, and those words didn't get stuck in her throat.

"You and me both, darling," she said softly. "And I have faith. This is going to work, I can feel it in my bones."

Carrie gave a small laugh, her mum's age-old saying tickling her. "You and your bones Mum, thank heaven for them."

"Carrie?" It was Dan calling from the other room, his voice taking her from tickled to on fire in an instant. "Can I borrow you?"

Anytime, her body returned. "Black coffee, please, Mum."

Her mother nodded and turned away, leaving Carrie to go it alone, save for the dispersed contractors. Not that she really saw them as she re-entered the room—all her senses had honed in on the man filling the doorway across from her.

Right. Business, Carrie—stick to business and all will be well.

She headed towards him, a smile pasted to her face.

"How can I help?" She paused a few strides away, keeping a safe distance. Her eyes lifted to his just in time to catch a sudden flash, his jaw flexing.

"Do you want the work-based answer?"

She swallowed her instinctive reply, cursing his ability to flirt so easily, to pull her down the path that she was fighting so hard to stay clear of. "Yes...*please*..."

His eyes wavered, arms crossing over his chest in that way that sent her eyes to the flexing muscles of his forearms and had her mouth drying up, and then he turned away. *Phew.* "Follow me."

She let out a gust of air, thankfully one that was masked by the incessant drilling already starting up in the room they were entering. At least she'd passed that test, getting his focus back on work. She just had to keep on doing that, and all would be fine.

They walked across the wooden floor, her step wary with the cables strewn everywhere. She made a mental note to pull out a pair of trainers for her next visit; heels did not belong on a building site.

"Now," Dan said, stepping up onto the raised dance floor and gesturing to the high ceiling. "See this—"

His voice broke off as her mother came rushing in, a phone in her outstretched hand. *Oh no.*

"Carrie, you left this in the kitchen." Her mum held the phone out to her, her brow raised. "Since when have you been so bad at keeping your phone on you?"

Since you've been running scared from your next conversation with Isla. "Since I'm supposed to be on holiday, Mum," she said, taking it from her.

"Well, I thought I best bring it out. Isla's been calling."

Crap. "Thanks, I'll call her back shortly."

"Make sure you do," her mother said easily, thankfully oblivious. "I'll get back to those teas."

She turned and headed back out, the air tightening in her wake. Mention of Isla brought with it their argument from the other night, and it stretched through the silence, Dan's stillness telling Carrie she wasn't alone in thinking on it.

But thinking on it wasn't getting the job done.

She slipped the phone into the pocket of her skinny jeans, determined to get back to business.

"You should call her back." His tone was low, distracted even. "This can wait."

"No," she said firmly, schooling her features to suit. "I'll ring her back later." *When you're not around.*

"It could be important."

Yup, she was fairly certain it was going to be important. But he had no idea just how important.

"I'll do it in a bit."

"You sure?"

"Positive." She looked up to the ceiling, making it clear she wanted to press on; if she could park Isla for now, so could he.

He hesitated a moment longer, and then to her relief, spoke up. "It's Isla's plans for this area…I'm concerned the lighting isn't going to work—not with the angles we're dealing with."

He passed her some drawings and pointed to the corner of the room where the light fittings lay, ready and waiting to go up. "You see, with the balcony just there, and then the drop of the lights here, it's not going to give enough light, or at least, not the kind of light you would want."

She studied the drawings. Anything to keep her attention off those arms, which were too close for comfort.

"If you're not sure," he said, "I can see if I can pull some strings, get the interior design company I use to come on board. It's last minute but I'm su—"

"No," she blurted, hating his lack of confidence in her. Christ, it wasn't her lack of skill in the interior design department that had her silent—look and feel was her thing. It was him—his presence, his voice, his scent, just *him*—disengaging her bloody brain. "I've got this, it's something I can actually bring to the table."

"Fair enough."

Whether he'd thought her upset or not, she didn't care. It had been the slap she needed to focus on what mattered. She scanned the room and the drawings.

"Okay," she said eventually, a plan brewing. "If we take these lights…" she started walking, her eyes on the plans as she got swept up in the idea that was forming, "and swap them with the ones we have chosen for the chill out room next d—*whoa.*"

Her heel caught in a mess of cables, sending her off balance. She sailed through the air, sending papers flying up around her, then felt Dan's arms sweep around her middle and spin her into his body. "Hey, steady."

Steady. Like hell could she be steady with the shock-like current ripping through her. She was pressed up against him, both palms flat against his chest, his scent invading her senses, his protective hold tight around her. One second passed, two, three. They didn't move. They didn't speak.

"Carrie?" His prompt was soft, his arms easing, encouraging her to look up and she did. She read the heat blazing back at her, saw the lust, need, desire…*something more?*

And then his mouth was upon her, pushing away their surroundings, the club, the workers, the reasons they shouldn't do this.

All she could hear was the beat of her heart in her ears, the thrum of heat in her veins; all she could feel was his lips against hers, his hands as they stroked down her body and cupped her against him.

"Dan?" His name was a whisper as she broke away just a little; she wasn't even sure why she'd said it, but she felt lost, incapable of stopping. She needed reassurance, clarity, something that said this was okay. And then he stilled, and beneath his touch she felt the vibration of her phone tucked inside her pocket. *Isla.*

She thrust him away, the clarity she'd been desperately seeking hitting with force.

He blinked at her, the haze of his desire lifting as he swiped his palm over his face. "You should get it."

Of course, you should get it. Look at where your good intentions are getting you? Face the music…you deserve it.

She yanked the phone out of her pocket, her glare fixed on him but entirely directed at herself as she answered and lifted it to her ear in one swift motion. "Isla! So sorry, I'm here."

She strained to listen down the line, struggling to make anything out above the incessant drilling in the room. "Can you hear me?"

"I can," she heard her say. "Just about, where are you?"

Where am I? Good question. One she couldn't answer without giving the game away. She stared at Dan, her cheeks heating—*just be creative with the truth.* "Out with Dan." *Oh God, like that's going to help Isla's sanity.* "It's a long story," she blustered on. "What's going on? Are you okay? I am so relieved you've called, after our last conversation you had me so worried."

"You can forget our last conversation, Carrie." She was still straining to hear her sister, yet the edge to Isla's voice was unmistakable. "Things have moved on since then."

*Oh God. H*er tummy sank. "In what way?"

She listened hard, but there was nothing. She started to fear the worst. "Isla? Are you okay? You don't sound okay?"

Sound? She wasn't even bloody talking…

"No, I'm not," she eventually heard Isla say, tears obvious in her pitched tone. *Oh God.*

"Hang on, let me get somewhere more quiet."

She looked to Dan, her hand over the speaker of the phone. "I need to take this call somewhere quiet; it's important—Isla doesn't sound good."

"Okay," he said, his expression unreadable. "Use the office."

She nodded and backtracked into the other room, weaving through the contractors and the mess as she headed upstairs. The whole way, her mind was doing overtime trying to work out what could have happened and burying all thoughts of Dan.

She was beside herself by the time she entered the office and closed the door. Ultimately, it didn't matter what had happened to make Isla so distressed, because whatever it was, there was one thing she knew for sure…

It's all your fault.

Chapter Eight

DAN WATCHED HER GO, FORCING HIMSELF TO stay put.
Hell, stay put?
He should be leaving.

He was supposed to be two hundred miles away scoping out a new club location in the North, not here taking an active role in Carrie's Guilt Project. The contractors he'd brought in were capable enough; they'd take Carrie's direction, keep her identity quiet, and stick to the two and a half week timeframe she'd dictated. It was ambitious, but they could get two thirds of the place up and ready for the relaunch. The rest could come later.

So why in the hell are you still here?

She'd made it clear there was no more fun to be had, and what other reason could he have for sticking around? He scooped the documents she'd dropped up off the floor, the very real answer shaking him up inside: *you want to be with her.*

And that meant he should leave. Right now.

But he couldn't. Not until he knew things were okay. Isla certainly wasn't, from what Carrie had said. And considering the timing of her call, Carrie wouldn't be either. Her guilt, no matter how misguided, would be eating away at her if what she'd told him the other night was true.

He could *pretend* he was sticking it out because he cared about Isla, that he wanted to know what was going on with her, but in reality, he didn't want to leave Carrie. Not yet.

It was that realization that brought him to his senses and had him moving into action. He would seek out the foreman, catch up with him briefly, and get on the road. This was supposed to be about helping Isla's club, and the sooner he focused on that, the sooner he could get Carrie out of his head.

Help Carrie to help Isla. No more, no less.

Foreman. And then leave.

And he would have done just that, if he hadn't still been speaking to the guy when Carrie returned. Her eyes were puffy, and while her makeup was still perfect, her distress was too marked to hide. *What the fuck?*

He cut the conversation short and strode toward her, ignoring how his chest tightened the closer he got. "Carrie, what is it?"

He reached out, stroking her arm over the soft pink sweater that she wore. She looked up at him, eyes wide, so fragile and so un-Carrie-like that a chill washed over him.

"I've fucked up," she said softly.

"How?"

Behind her, Helen walked in with a tray of steaming mugs, and he stilled his caress. *Now's your chance. Let her mum deal with this.* His chest tightened further; he couldn't do it, he just couldn't. "Tell you what, let's grab one of your mum's teas and take it to the office. You can tell me everything."

Her eyes welled, her head shaking. "No, I…I'm not sure…I can't…"

A tear ran down one cheek and his throat constricted, his hand lifting to stroke his thumb over its trail and wishing it gone. "Come on, you don't want your mum seeing you like this. She'll only worry."

She shook her head and gave a small sniff. "You're right."

No, you're not. You should hand her over and let her mum deal with whatever this is, not you.

He walked around her, ignoring his raging brain, and gave Helen a smile. "You are a lifesaver." He took up two mugs and nodded to the stairs. "Carrie and I are going to take these up to the office and talk shop."

"Great idea." She looked past him to Carrie, a frown marring her brow. He waited for her to say something—there was no way she'd missed her daughter's distress—but instead she gave him a small smile of understanding and turned to walk away.

He watched her go, the realization dawning that she trusted him to fix it. Whatever it was, she trusted him to make her daughter feel better. A strange warmth spread through his gut. *You shouldn't be happy about it, for Christ's sake.*

But he was, and it had unease creeping up his spine, the past becoming a warning beacon in his brain. *You're getting too close.*

He heard Carrie approach, her heels clipping against the wooden floor, and he parked it all. He could suffer it later. Right now, he wanted the composed Carrie back. He'd never seen her this broken—this lost and distraught—and whatever was causing it, it had him worried. This was more than just guilt.

They headed to the office in silence. It wasn't until she dropped into the worn leather sofa, her slumped posture so unlike her usual grace, that he couldn't stay quiet any longer.

"What's going on?"

He offered her a mug and she took it, her fingers shaking as she wrapped both hands around it and brought it to her lips.

"I don't know where to start."

"The beginning is always good."

He perched on the solid wooden coffee table before her, his elbows resting on his knees. "Whatever it is, it can't be that terrible."

She looked at him and scoffed gently. "Can't it? This is me, remember."

Fair point. His own view of her, their shared past, what he'd thrown at her the other day about not caring…they all combined to rob him of a response. At least, one that wouldn't make it worse.

"See?" she said bitterly.

"Hey, I'm sorry, it's hard to forget the past."

"God, don't apologize." She rolled her eyes and gave a sniffle. "That only makes it worse."

"Okay." He smiled. "Apology retracted, so come on, talk. Maybe it'll help."

"Will you promise not to judge?"

"Tell you what, I'll go one better…" He knew what he had to say, knew it would change their relationship going forward and lift the guard of hate he'd built up, but he had to do it. She was trying to do right by Isla, and he admired her for it. He wanted to help her because she *was* different, and all the more appealing for it—it wasn't her fault he couldn't stop the way his feelings were evolving, and he couldn't blame her. "Let's wipe the slate clean. Start afresh."

She gave a small laugh. "Who are you, and what have you done with the Dan from three nights ago? The one that threatened to throw me out on the street?"

"He's still here…but let's just say he's seen the benefits of having you back in his life."

The innuendo was intended, her little laugh coaxing him into wanting more, and as her face lifted with humour, he soaked up its rays.

"You're insatiable," she teased. "You know that?"

"What can I say? A man has needs."

Her eyes heated, her teeth tugging on her lower lip. "As does a woman."

Her voice had turned thick, her mood shifting so swiftly he almost lost sight of the reason they were here. The reason her eyes although dilating on a hit of desire, were still spiked with her tears.

"As much as I'd love to explore those needs, I don't think it'll help get to the bottom of what's wrong, will it?"

The humour, the heat, the smile, it all drained from her face, and he almost cursed his Good Samaritan act. But it was the right thing to do. She needed help and comfort, not sex, no matter how worrying that was to his no-getting-in-deep stance.

"No." She took a deep breath and it shuddered out of her, the words coming with it. "You know how I told you I was spoken for?"

His gut lurched. It wasn't what he'd expected her to start with. In fact, her boyfriend stateside was the last thing he wanted to discuss, but he forced his expression and tone to remain neutral. "You did."

"Does the name Bradley King mean anything to you?'

Bradley King. Was she kidding? "Well, yeah, sure, who doesn't?...*why?*"

Even as he said it, he knew the answer. This *was* Carrie after all.

"We've been seeing each other for months..."

Months. His gut didn't just lurch, it twisted now, a continuing motion that had him struggling to keep his cool.

"...in secret..."

Secret? That's why he didn't know of it. Why no one knew of it. And he didn't want to know it now. It was too real, it had given the guy a face, someone to be jealous of. His twisted mind was already conjuring up the two of them entwined.

"...and a few weeks ago, he proposed."

"*He what?*" His fist flexed around his mug. *She couldn't be serious.*

"He asked me to marry him." She looked up, her eyes wide and far too perceptive as they locked with his own. He couldn't take it. He got to his feet and walked away, distancing himself physically and mentally.

"It sounds worse than it is." Her voice followed him, small and unsure.

Small and unsure? Christ, this is Carrie, there's nothing small and unsure about her. The woman had a man pining for her in the US who loved her enough to marry her, and she'd repaid the guy by hopping into bed with *him*—a nobody.

And what had *he* been? A quick fuck before she tied the knot? A moment of madness to get it out of her system? *Shit.*

He stared at the opposite wall, pulling at the back of his neck with his fingers as he worked to hold back the rising tide of emotion. She'd proved one thing: she really was no different. She was as selfish as she'd ever been.

And here he'd been suggesting they wipe the bloody slate clean and make amends.

She'd duped him. All over again.

You bastard fool.

"It *sounds* worse?" He spoke to the wall. "Really?"

"Please, Dan…*please*…"

Her desperate plea had him turning against his will. "What?"

His eyes locked with hers and she visibly recoiled, her lashes fluttering and her body straightening on the defense. "It's not like you think."

"Then what's it like, Carrie?" he bit out. "Because when you told me you were taken, I figured it was by some guy you were dating, not fucking marrying."

"I'm not marrying him."

"You just said—"

"I said he proposed, I didn't say I said yes."

She hadn't; that was true. He'd just assumed. Still, that didn't change the fact that the guy loved her enough to propose. *Christ, Bradley is as much a fool as you are.* "Right, so you turned him down?"

"Not exactly."

Now she blushed, the color invading her cheeks so similar to her post-orgasm glow that he hated his body for reacting to it. It made his tone all the more cold when he said, "What does that mean?"

"It means that his proposal is part of the reason I'm back here. It's a time-out for me, a chance to take stock of things and decide what I want for my future. Isla is in LA pretending to be me, keeping the press off my back and my location secret. Like I said to you before, I'm here on the quiet."

He remembered her saying as much but he couldn't get his head round it. "I don't understand. You dreamed of fame and now that you have it, what…you want to avoid it?"

"It's suffocating," she blurted, waving an agitated hand. "Having your every move under scrutiny, not being able to put a foot out of line, speak your mind, have a fucking life. It's why we kept our relationship a secret. We didn't want to be judged when it failed, or questioned to death when we just happened to step out with someone else." She was talking so fast now, her breath elevating; if he didn't know her better he'd think she was heading for a panic attack.

"But getting married would change that," she continued. "It would be headline news. A Hollywood Match. Can you imagine it? We'd never be able to escape it—not without some kind of public backlash."

He didn't want to agree with her. Didn't want to acknowledge she spoke sense.

"So this guy, Bradley," he said with forced calm. "Does *he* know you're here?"

"No."

He frowned. "How's that supposed to work? Surely you spend time together?"

"It was supposed to work just fine." She looked down into her mug, her voice quiet, and he had the sense that he was getting to the crux of the problem. "He was meant to be away filming for a couple of months. He was giving me the space I needed to think."

"When you say *meant*?"

"He's back," she whispered. "He came back a few days ago and scared the hell out of Isla."

Isla. Bradley King. *Oh, Jesus.* 'Wasn't he the guy she had plastered over her walls when we were teenagers?"

Carrie flushed further and gave a strangled, "Yes."

He narrowed his gaze, saw how white her knuckles were around her mug, and knew he wasn't going to like whatever was coming next. "I take it he knows now? About this little switch you guys have pulled?"

"No."

It was a squeak rather than a word.

"I don't know whether I want to hear the rest."

"They've slept together," she blurted over him.

"*What?*" He couldn't believe his ears. Didn't want to. "*Jesus, Carrie.* Do you know how *sick* that is? Sleeping with someone who thinks you're someone else! Where's the consent in that? There isn't any. It's fucked up, totally fucked up."

"I know, I know." She shook her head at him—in fact her whole body shook, remorse coming off her in waves. But he still couldn't calm down.

"How can Isla have let it happen?"

She stared up at him, wide-eyed. "I think that's the bit we *can* understand."

"Irresistible attraction?" he scoffed. "There's a difference: I know who you are."

He couldn't keep the bitter edge out of his voice and she crumpled before him, her body closing in over her mug and her eyes downcast. *Shit.* He didn't want to feel for her. She didn't deserve it. Not after this. And yet he couldn't help it, his words coming softer as he added, "Surely he must have worked it out by now? You two are nothing alike."

"We're identical twins, Dan, of course we're alike."

"I'm not talking about aesthetics…" And he hadn't been when he'd said it; the two couldn't be any more different. But… "Hang on, last I checked Isla was still a redhead."

"She bleached it."

"Right, how noble of her, of course she did." He was shaking his head over the madness of it all. The guy *must* be able see the difference. He *must*. "But she's still Isla—sweet, laidback, heart-on-her-sleeve Isla."

Carrie blanched as she stared up at him, eyes wide with obvious pain. "And what does that make me then, Dan? The hard, callous bitch?"

No. He swallowed; it didn't make her that.

But the words that came to mind scared the hell out of him. Strong, sexy, determined—*selfish, two-timing, single-minded*, his conscience was quick to append.

"Forget it, your face says enough." She looked back to her mug and took a deep swig, a hardness befalling her. "She knows me well enough to act the part, and besides, for all the time we spent together, Brad never got in too deep. We never had that sort of a relationship. It was companionship and fun in bed—that was all we needed."

"*All?* He asked you to marry him, for fuck's sake. It had to be more than that…to him, at least." He couldn't bring himself to say that Bradley must have loved her, and she must have given him some sign she felt the same. He felt sick. Sick and foolish.

"No," she said vehemently. "It really wasn't like that…you'll never understand…I didn't love him, and he didn't love me. The marriage was convenient—a front. It made sense on so many practical levels."

He could hear her words, could read the sincerity in them, but he couldn't stomach it. Couldn't believe someone would propose marriage and not be in it for love.

But at least it's the truth. At least she isn't in love with someone else…someone other than you.

"This is fucked up, Carrie," he spoke over the turn in his thoughts. He didn't like how the realization eased a part of him.

"Don't you think I know that?" she snapped. "And it's all my fault. I told her to keep up the pretense. I wasn't ready to call an end to our relationship; I wasn't ready to have that conversation with

Brad. It was all part of my career goal, part of what I've worked so hard for. I should have been racing down the aisle, I should have—"

"Fucking hell, Carrie, do you listen to yourself?" He couldn't take it anymore. Her rambling panic was bringing out too much of what he hated, too much of the girl who had left him to pursue stardom all those years ago. "It's still all about you, your career, the fame—"

"No Dan, *you're* not listening to *me*," she threw back at him. "It's the fact I didn't jump at the offer, the fact I realized it was wrong, that had me running back here. I needed space to think, to sort my head out."

He was listening just fine. "And so you've thrown your sister right into this mess?"

She nodded, swallowing hard. "It gets worse."

"How can it possibly get any worse?"

"She's falling for him."

He threw his hands up. This just got better. "Of course she fucking is."

"I'm serious."

"I am too, Carrie. I mean, Christ, she's gonna be jazzed up on endorphins and crazy loved up pheromones, or whatever they're called, being confronted with him. She isn't going to be thinking straight."

"The problem is she's convinced he's falling for her too. She has this crazy, deluded idea that if she confesses our swap, he will forgive us and they can live happily ever after. Like that's ever going to happen. It's an impossible fairy tale and it's all my fault."

"You got that right."

His voice was hard, and it hurt her. He could see it in the tears welling once more, but he wasn't taking it back. It *was* her mess. Unless of course… "But what if she's right—what if he is falling for her?"

She gave a bitter laugh, a tear rolling free. She brushed a shaky hand over it. "He's not capable of love, not in that way. It's why we worked so well."

Because Carrie doesn't do love... he quashed the voice and the pain that accompanied it.

"And what if you're wrong?" he pressed. "I know you say she can play the role of you well enough, but I'm not so sure."

"What? You think he's seen something in her that he didn't see in me? Something that has him confessing feelings he's shown no interest in before?"

She looked incredulous. But he knew from his own bitter experience just how different they were, and that it was easy to fall in love with one and not the other. "Yes. Don't you?"

"I am...I'm not..." She looked at him for a long moment, her expression unreadable, and then her eyes dropped back to her mug. "I don't know. I just know we didn't have it together."

"That's not to say she hasn't found it with him. What if he *has* fallen for her?"

"I don't know...life in Hollywood doesn't exactly cater to real life happily-ever-afters. Look at my mum; she never believed it was possible. She gave up on love to stay here."

"I'm sure there was more to it than that."

She shrugged. "Maybe. But Brad has his own baggage—I just can't see it in him."

"I think you're blinded by your own relationship with him."

"And so what if I am?" she burst out. "I've known him a lot longer than she has."

"Sounds to me like you're jealous." He hated admitting it, but it did.

"I'm not fucking jealous." Her eyes flashed to him. "Would I have slept with you if I was in love with Brad?"

"I didn't say you were in love with him. I just said you were jealous—that you don't like the idea that your sister may have earned what you didn't."

She frowned. "Is that how little you think of me?"

He hunched his shoulders, pushing against the knotted mass of muscle. "I don't know what to think."

"Look, she's all the way over there, her heart in pieces because I've put her straight and she has no one to talk to. No one to help."

"What about your father? Can't he go see her?"

She shook her head, the mention of her father triggering a fresh well of tears—*shit*.

"I asked her to go and see him even before all this happened. I'd hoped the trip would be a chance for them to make amends." She took a shaky breath. "They haven't spoken since we left for LA, but she's not interested. She blames him for breaking up the family; she blames him for Mum being miserable."

"Your mum's not miserable."

"No, but she's lonely, I can see that. She still misses him." She swept a hand over her mouth, keeping it there. "It's a mess, all of it, and it's all my fault."

She looked so desperate, so helpless, that the crazy heat of anger that had taken hold the second she confessed ebbed away. He wanted to hold onto it, to feed on it—anything to stop his concern, his worry for her, because its underlying force was too scary to acknowledge. He needed the anger—the reminder of how low she could sink, how shallow and hurtful she could be. He needed it to protect himself. But it wasn't working; not when she looked so broken, so remorseful.

"You could just tell her to speak to Bradley," he suggested, thrusting his hands into his pockets to stop himself from reaching for her again. "Let her tell him the truth. Let them work it out. If he cares for her as she suspects, he won't let this break them apart."

Her lashes wavered. "That's what she said."

"Then trust her. Give them the chance to work this through." The more he thought on it, the more convinced he was that it was the right move, even if Carrie wasn't. "What are you so scared of?"

She shook her head. "I honestly don't know, not anymore."

Her phone announced an incoming message, and she tensed before pulling it out of her pocket to check the screen.

"Who is it?"

"Isla."

"And?"

"She's going to lie low and call me tomorrow."

"Right, there we go," he said. "Let her sleep on it, then see what she has to say and make a decision. But my advice? One of you tells him."

She placed her phone down on the sofa, but her eyes stayed fixed on it. "I'll think about it."

"Okay, well, while you're thinking on it, one of us needs to be getting this building finished," he said, pulling her attention back to him. "Because if things go tits up stateside, she's going to be back here sooner than you thought."

"Oh, God." Carrie came alive, slapping her mug down on the table and launching to her feet. "Don't you think I know that? It's the other reason I had her keeping up the pretense—I didn't want to run the risk of her coming home early. This is a disaster, Dan. An absolute disaster." The helplessness was back, along with the desperation. "There's no way we're going to get enough done, and then all this will have been for nothing. She'll have nothing—no Brad, no club…I will have royally screwed up her life, and for what?"

"Hey, don't panic." He was reaching for her before he even acknowledged the move, and once his hands were on her arms he couldn't draw them back.

She looked up at him, her eyes wide and earnest. "I don't want this to fail, Dan. It can't."

He could feel himself drowning in her pleading gaze, and the last of his anger trickled away. "There are things we can do to keep it under wraps. We can keep her away from here if we have to."

She shook her head. "I don't know…"

"Carrie? Look at me?"

Slowly, she did as he asked.

"You trust me?" He was more than aware of the last time he'd asked that question, back at his club. And judging by the way her eyes sparked, she was too.

But this was important.

"Yes," she whispered, the simple word loaded with so much meaning and his lungs filled with air, the fact he'd been holding his breath totally lost on him until then. Until she'd told him what he *needed* to hear.

"We can do this," he assured her.

"Okay..." She started to nod, her focus coming back and her strength with it. "Okay...You're right. Of course you are. We can make up some sort of excuse." She stepped free of him, and instantly his body pined for her.

"Ideally we want to keep her away until most of the work is completed," she said, pacing now. "At least until the invites to the launch night are out, and then she can't back out."

He frowned. "The launch night?"

"Yes, it's the final move in my plan, I'll pull some strings and get some big names in—give the place the ultimate PR launch. It'll be perfect...we *can* do this." She looked to him, and he realized she was seeking affirmation. "Can't we?"

As if he would dare doubt her.

"I think you can do anything you put your mind to," he said truthfully.

She smiled then, her sadness from a moment ago fading into the background and replaced with a warmth that reached all the way to his toes. "Thank you, Dan."

She stepped forward, and before he could clock her intent she'd lifted onto tiptoes, her lips brushing against his cheek.

He should have let her drop back and left it there, but the second her scent invaded his senses and her lips touched upon his cheek, his arms were around her and his head was turning. He expected her to freeze or to pull back, but instead she met him mid-turn, her lips brushing against his own.

"Carrie?" He was asking for permission before his restraint entirely snapped. She'd told him they had to end things, but that was when she'd thought Isla to be in love with him. Now she clearly knew that wasn't true, so where did that leave them?

"Dan?"

She hooked his bottom lip with her mouth, her tongue tracing over the sensitized flesh. His body ignited, a growl erupting in his throat as he tightened his hold around her, and kissed her. It was as if their emotive discussion of seconds before had made everything more powerful, more desperate.

She moaned, the sound in tune with the explosive hit to his groin as she pressed herself against him. Her hands were clawing at his back, nails scratching against his skin as she dragged his T-shirt over his head. Throwing it away, her eyes lit on his exposed chest with such hunger that his cock pulsed in kind.

He moved to claim her mouth anew and she pressed her palms to his chest, stopping him, her eyes widening with what he could only describe as wonder.

"When did you get like this?" she whispered, her fingers tracing over his skin and making it prickle.

"You're only just noticing?"

"I've not had the time before to appreciate it. I think I was too distracted by your new addition, this tattoo...which I like by the way..." Her softly spoken compliment caught him off guard, warming him for reasons far greater than lust as she trailed her fingers lower. "You must train hard."

She looked up at him, the desire in her gaze stoking his own, and the answer came out honest and unthinking. "For ten years, ever since you left."

Her lashes fluttered, an emotion he couldn't quite place

thickening the air; was it guilt? *Christ*, he didn't need her guilt, he needed her riding the same wave as he was.

He cupped her chin and his thumb caught at her bottom lip, parting her mouth to him. He dipped his tongue in slowly, gently coaxing, sampling her unique taste, loving how she whimpered, her eyes closed, her head tilted back.

"I should be thanking you," he whispered against her lips, working hard to stay in control, to stave off the heat just a little longer so he could savour her like this—so wanton, so caught up in him. "The ladies loved the new me."

She stilled, her eyes snapping open, jealousy flaring in their depths and sending his lips twitching up. It had broken his spell, but for jealousy, he'd take it, the power it handed him, the control.

"Ladies?"

"Yes, the ladies." He stroked his fingers over her neck as he considered her. He had to make her see he wasn't weak. He had to make *himself* see it. That he didn't need her; that when she left again, he would be just fine. "You didn't think I'd been pining for you for ten years?"

"Well…no, I…" She was flustered, her uncertainty only making him desire her more.

Desire? It wasn't desire that had his chest warming over the real her, the person beneath the Hollywood mask.

But desire is what you can handle—just the sex, keep it at that. Enjoy this.

"And surely you can see how you benefit now too?"

He dropped his hands to the hem of her sweater, easing them beneath it. The moment his fingers touched her skin, she inhaled sharply.

Yes, this is what you can cope with—this doesn't have the power to hurt.

"How might I benefit?" She was all breathy, and all for him. *No one else.*

"You can't guess?"

He pulled the sweater over her head, his attention dropping to the white bra she wore. It was so innocent, so un-Carrie, that his smile resurfaced, an unwelcome whirl of emotion quick on its tail. *Just ignore it.*

"What?" she asked, her chin lifting in a gesture that smacked of uncertainty and confidence all at once.

"You." He unfastened her bra clasp, her skin hot beneath his fingers. "In white."

She eyed him beneath her lashes. "I'm wearing white jeans, Dan."

"You sure are...but white underwear, Princess?" He shook his head, his fingers hooking beneath the straps at her shoulders and pulling them down her arms. It fell to the floor and she shivered, her breasts quivering with the move, nipples hard and pleading.

"You saying I'm not innocent enough?"

He bowed his head. "With the things that I want to do to you," he whispered against her earlobe, teeth taking hold of it to deliver a sharp nip. "Far from it."

"*Fuck, Dan.*" The words shuddered out of her, her hands lifting to grip at his shoulders and he wrapped an arm around her waist, letting her curve back over his support.

He looked down at where the fingers of his free hand trailed over her skin, watching as color flooded her cheeks, her neck, her chest. Her nipples were swelling hard for attention, and when he circled one, she whimpered, her head falling back further, her teeth clamping into her bottom lip.

She was so much more than the girl of ten years ago now, her curves so delicate and full. Gently, he palmed one breast, his thumb rolling over its hardened center. "You're beautiful."

The words held so much meaning, the husky tone in which he said them shaking him inside out. But he couldn't help it—with her, he couldn't help anything. Alarm bells sounded in the recesses of his mind, but he wasn't listening; not anymore.

He dropped his head, his tongue mirroring the roll of his thumb. As he explored every dimple, every crease to the sensitized bud, it puckered tighter—coaxed to attention by his teasing caress—and still he kept going. He was high on her harried breath, her desperate little moans, the feel of her nails biting into his skin.

And then he dropped lower, desperate to enjoy every inch of her soft, golden skin. She sucked in a breath as he reached her navel, his tongue dipping inside and then tracing around it as his fingers undid the button of her jeans.

"Let me," she breathed. Her hands shifted to take over, but he grasped her wrists, his eyes meeting hers.

"Stay still."

He wanted to devour her, he wanted her to come apart, all by his hand.

He hooked his fingers inside her waistband and eased the tight denim down her thighs enough so that he could get what he wanted—what she needed.

He rocked back on his heels, his eyes taking in the dampness of her delicate white thong and heat assaulted his groin, his cock pulsing against the confines of his clothing.

Raising his eyes to hers, he lifted his hand to trace the wet fabric with his fingers, losing himself in every fleeting reaction she gave; the flare to her nose, the lustful heat to her gaze, the sounds down deep in her throat. He rocked his hand back and forth, varying the pressure, coaxing her body into the motion. He'd never seen anything so goddamn hypnotic, so fucking erotic. Would she taste as good?

He *needed* to know.

Leaning forward, he cupped her thighs from behind, forcing them to part wider, to grant him the access he craved.

He nudged her slickened folds with his nose, grinning as she bucked on a small cry. He looked up to see her head fall forward, her eyes colliding with his, her mouth beautifully parted. She raked her hand through his hair, her eyes marvelling at him, and then he tongued her firm enough to part her beneath the fabric and she clamped down on her bottom lip, her body bucking.

God, she tasted sweet, her scent laced with sex and need. He was intoxicated, his entire body fuelled on her desire, his cock seeping as even the loose-fitting pants became too restrictive.

He repeated the move, only this time he didn't draw back; he surrounded her, sucking back hard and taking in the juices that coated the fabric.

"Fuck, Dan...*more. Fucking more.*"

She was losing it, her voice unrecognizable in its lustful quality. He could leave her right now, and he'd swear she'd cry. *Leave her? You could never leave...*

"*Dan.*" Her moan obliterated the crazed thought, her hands sliding inside the waistband of her thong and forcing it down her thighs.

"I told you to stay still."

"So? Bite me."

He grinned and nipped the inside of her thigh hard, making her gasp. "Don't tempt me."

She returned his smile, but it was weak, pleading. "Please Dan, *please.*"

She stroked her hand over his head, encouraging him in.

"No, you don't." He took hold of both her wrists, pulling them around her back and fixing them there with one hand. "Now stay."

He dipped forward, his free hand parting her, and flattened his tongue against her wetness. Swiping it upwards. He cleaned her off, readying her for more, and then he went straight for her hardened bud and felt her freeze in anticipation. His lips quirked as he rotated around it, circling and circling until she was forced to move and then he flicked over it, making her cry.

She writhed into him. Her wrists pulled in his hold. He did it again, circling her, flicking over her, driving her wild. He wanted to be a fly on the wall, wanted to watch her as he drove her over the edge. He kept on until she was dripping, so wet and needy for him, and then he sucked over her, making her cry out.

"You taste so fucking good."

He pressed a finger inside her, and then another, and finally a third; all the while, his tongue was unrelenting. Coating his entire hand in her wetness, he buried his thumb inside her as his fingers slipped back between the crease of her arse, seeking her puckered opening and pressing over it. *Has she ever played here? Will she now?*

Carrie moaned with abandon. She was close, he could hear it; could see it in the flush to her skin, in her jagged movements. He picked up the pace over her clit, the pressure of his thumb and the invasion of his fingers pushing her to the edge until she screamed his name as she came. Her orgasm riding out long and hard above him.

"Thank you," she whispered as her legs buckled and he swept her up, his smile soft over her gratitude, her heavenly scent washing over him.

God, you can never give this up. You can never give her up.

He walked to the couch, ignoring the wild notion, and laid her down before stretching out alongside her.

She turned to look up at him, her face so heavenly, so blissful that his heart swelled inside his chest, a sensation he hadn't felt in years—ten years to be exact—and his cock came to the rescue, surging against his jeans.

This is sex—just sex.

Don't confuse it. Don't let it be more.

Chapter Nine

CARRIE FELT WINDED. IT WAS THE ONLY WAY to describe how she could hardly draw breath. Even now, curled up half-naked against Dan, her heart raced out of control; her skin burned with the heat of his against her; her head swam with a multitude of wants and desires.

He nuzzled beneath her ear, his arm tight across her middle and his hardness pressed distractingly against her thigh. "You okay?"

"More than okay," she murmured. "That was incredible."

"See, I told you those ladies paid off."

She tensed. She didn't want to hear about other women; didn't want to think of him with anyone but her.

Jealousy wasn't an emotion she was accustomed to, but she *was* jealous. She knew it as readily as she knew that she wasn't ready to turn her back on this heat between them.

And that's all it is—heat?

She wriggled against him—against the fear that came with the probing question. What if Isla did have a future with Brad? If Dan was right to think it possible, then where did that leave her? Where did that leave the feelings she'd once turned her back on to protect her sister?

Without that barrier, was she free to hope? To give in? *To love?*

She stroked over his arm, his hairs prickling beneath her touch.

She felt him straining against her thigh, calling her to him, and yet he made no attempt to ravish her. Was he waiting for her to recover? The sweetness of that reminded her of the old Dan. Was he still in there, deep down? The man that had once loved her?

Her heart squeezed, and she closed her eyes against the weird pang that struck her. Remorse, guilt, uncertainty, more fear…

"I could get used to the jealous version of you."

His gibe pulled her back—*just enjoy this, whatever this is. Live for the moment and stop over-thinking.*

"Jealous? *As if.*" She pushed him onto his back, his eyes smiling up at her and causing her heart to squeeze ever tighter.

"Oh yes," he nodded, his hand lifting to twist through her ponytail. "Definitely jealous."

"Careful, Dan, or this…" Brazenly, she tracked a path down his chest to his cock and squeezed—hard. The air hissed through his teeth, the muscles of his chest pulling taut, and she smiled teasingly. "This will be left for you to sort."

"You wouldn't be so cruel."

She raised her brow, releasing him to trace his hard ridge with her nail. "Wouldn't I?"

"I—"

"Carrie!"

Christ, it's Mum!

They both started scrabbling for their clothes; they could hear footsteps on the stairs outside, Dan tossed Carrie her sweater. She threw it on, and just as he did the same with his T-shirt the door opened, her mother walking straight in.

"Mum," Carrie blurted.

"So sorry, dear, but the guy downstairs—the one in charge—he says there's something about…"

Her mum's voice trailed off, her eyes lighting on Carrie's bra where it lay strewn across the floor—*ah, hell*. Dan side-stepped in front of it, but it was too late; the color creeping into her mother's cheeks said the damage was done.

The woman cleared her throat and pulled her eyes back to Carrie's. "Erm, yes, the guy says there's something going on with a light fitting that needs your direction."

"My direction?" *Christ, she'd been on helium again.* "Sure, of course. I'll be right down."

She sent Dan a sheepish look. "I'll just finish up here."

Oh God, why did that have to sound so bad?

And Dan—big, strong, fierce Dan—flushed red. And she couldn't look away. His hangdog look threw her back ten years and made her heart pound in her chest. A myriad of feelings had butterflies spinning up inside, and she gripped the edge of the couch, scared her legs would give way.

"Okay, I'll just go and let him know." Her mother looked from her to Dan, his crazed mop of hair added confirmation of what had been underway seconds before, and returned to her, eyes even wider. Carrie could practically see the cogs turning in their depths, could feel the grilling that was coming the next time mum had her alone.

"Bye, Mum."

"Mrs. Evans," Dan said, with a swift nod, and this time her mother didn't even comment on his formality—she simply glowed red and smiled brightly, floating out of the room on a palpable wave of happiness.

"I guess we should get to it," he said to Carrie, his disappointment so obvious, even with his recent attack of the blushes, which she fucking adored if she was honest with herself. And hell, *she* was disappointed.

He started to move past her and she reached for him, her hand closing over his upper arm. "If you wanted…" she broke off, nerves making her suddenly wary of offering what she was about to. What if he rejected her? She still didn't know where she stood with him, despite all they'd shared.

"Wanted?" He searched her gaze, his lips so close she could taste them if she chose. She lowered her eyes to their fullness, the evidence of their lovemaking in their swollen state.

Heat swirled through her middle and she tugged on her lower lip with her teeth, desire ramping up her heart rate and forcing out her next words. "…I could come to your place tonight."

Her voice was so husky it was barely there, but he'd clocked it. His lips quirked as he hooked a hand around her neck and lowered his head to taste her. Once, twice…she sighed into him, her body like liquid in an instant.

"Eight o'clock?"

She nodded in his hold, and then he released her and headed for the door. "Come on, let's get this show on the road."

She watched him go, her feet rooted. Something had changed—a weight had been lifted. Yes, she was worried for Isla, but Dan had given her hope that maybe things could be fixed. Her sister had a chance at happiness, and not only that, but maybe she did too. Maybe waiting a decade had given them all a chance to have what they'd once dreamed of; maybe it wasn't too late for them after all.

Dan checked his watch. Just gone six.

For the past half hour he'd been sat in his office, trying to catch up on work. He'd spent far too long at Isla's club, overseeing the work with Carrie and talking through plans that were already fleshed out enough; he'd run out of excuses to stay and had finally made himself see sense enough to leave.

But here he was, getting nowhere, as he stared blankly at his inbox and the influx of emails that had arrived that day. Mindlessly he clicked on one. Text appeared; a load of words, not a single one registering.

This was useless—he needed to burn off some steam. His body positively thrummed with nervous energy and it wasn't just anticipation for her arrival that evening; it was the deeper hit of emotion her reappearance in his life had evoked, and he needed to get it in hand.

The only thing capable of taking the edge off was a round with her, and since that was hours away, his gym and personal trainer would have to do. Axel could take his angst and wouldn't ask questions. Hopefully, by the time Carrie arrived, he'd have regained some of his senses.

An hour later, gloved up and several mistimed punches later, even Axel was looking like he might cross over into the role of therapist.

Shaking off Dan's last punch, Axel gave him a nod. "You gonna pay me danger money to stay?"

Dan hopped from one foot to the other, his fists lined up for attack. "You gonna quit being a wuss?"

"I just don't fancy a black eye for my date tonight."

Dan laughed, swiping sweat-slickened strands from his brow with the back of his gloved hand. "A date, hey? Why didn't you say? You should take off. I'll take it out on the punchbag before I hit the shower."

Axel looked past him, his brow raised in surprise. "Looks like I'm not the only one."

"You what?" He frowned and followed Axel's gaze before he froze, his lungs trapped mid-intake of breath—*Carrie.*

She was leaning against one of the brick pillars supporting the basement gym, her hair falling loose about her shoulders. A slinky leopard-print dress dipped low at her front and skimmed over her curves before halting mid-thigh, her exposed legs bare right down to her heeled black boots.

Blood surged south, his erection instant and painful.

"Don't let me stop you," she purred, her arms crossing over her middle as she settled in against the pillar. "I'm glad I'm early—I was quite enjoying the view."

He swallowed as he came alive. "How did you get in?"

"The doormen are getting used to me now, it seems. They sent me down."

He nodded, more words slow to come.

"I can leave if you want me to?"

"No," he said, too quickly, and her brow twitched. *Way to go on keeping your cool.* "Why don't you join me?"

She snorted out a laugh. "Me? Box?"

"Yeah." He gave her a lopsided grin, the idea of her working up a sweat with him suddenly appealing greatly.

"I don't do contact sport."

"No? Not even in Hollywood? I would have figured it a great way to let you celebrity *biatches* go at one another…" He made claws with his gloved hands. "Let those talons out in a safe environment so to speak."

She erupted on a giggle. "You make a good point, but not *this*—" she gestured to herself, eyebrows raised, "—celebrity *biatch*."

He laughed as she mimicked his pronunciation.

"I *always* make a good point…so, come on, what sport do you do to keep yourself looking this…" He ran his eyes over her again, loving how she straightened just a little, her breath bated. But what word could possibly do her justice? He had to settle in the end because truth was, there wasn't one. "Breathtaking?"

And you had to go with the most mushy—Jesus!

Her lashes fluttered, her lips softening and curving into a smile. "Breathtaking?" She cocked a brow.

"Yeah, yeah, don't get a big head, just spill."

She grinned and waved one hand. "Yoga, pilates, swimming. Anything that doesn't involve an unsightly amount of sweat."

"You saying you find sweat unpleasant?"

He gave himself a blatant once over, his naked chest slick, and she followed suit, scanning him slowly. The flush to her skin telling him exactly what she thought.

"On you, not so much…but on me, definitely."

"I disagree."

Her eyes flashed to his, heat firing the air between them.

"Right," Axel piped up, "definitely my cue to leave."

"Actually, could you stay? If you have time before your date, that is?" he said, the idea of having Carrie train with him taking hold. "I think my lady friend here could do with loosening up, and you're the perfect teacher."

He watched Axel look from him to Carrie and back again. It then struck him that his PT wasn't just surprised; he was downright starstruck. And he had every right to be—it was the actress he bloody well saw, not the girl. "Carrie's here on the quiet from the states. We're friends from way back."

"Oh right." He nodded and gave Carrie an almost impish look—one at total odds with his giant, imposing frame. "It's a pleasure to meet you."

She smiled and straightened, crossing the floor towards him and holding out her hand. "You too…?"

He handled her like china as he shook her hand and gave a gruff, "Axel."

"Ah, Axel," she cooed, her hand falling back to her side as she considered him. "A good name for such a strong-looking guy."

His PT practically melted into the floor, and Dan had the urge to roll his eyes.

"I'd be happy to throw in some time for you both. I have forty minutes before I need to be getting off."

"No, no, it's fine," she assured him. "Boxing just isn't my scene."

"You're going to upset Axel if you keep that up—he's an ex-champion."

"Enough with the 'ex'," Axel was quick to throw at him.

Dan grinned and raised his hand in apology.

"Well, no insult intended," Carrie chipped in, her smile worthy of captivating the world and making him think of her on screen persona.

He wanted it gone; he wanted the real her—the Carrie beneath the façade—back.

"You're just chicken."

Her eyes snapped to his, instantly bristling, and his gut rolled with laughter, not that he dared let it out. "I'm *not* chicken."

"*No?* Prove it."

She rolled her shoulders and narrowed her sights on him. "You have an old tee I can borrow? Some *tight* boxer shorts perhaps? I'm not ruining this number."

Carrie, in his clothing? The vision was payback, his gut contracting over the rush of heat to his groin; like he needed the added fuel. He turned to Axel, praying his erection was contained by the compression layer of his shorts, and pulled off his gloves. "Make sure she doesn't chicken out and run off before I return?"

Axel nodded with a laugh, though Dan was only half-joking.

He shrugged on a zip-up hoodie and legged it to his top floor pad, rooting out some clothing and returning in record time.

"There you go." Dan tossed Carrie the clothes and crossed his arms over his chest. He was amazed that she caught them; her eyes seemed far too busy trailing over him, her gaze nearly as tangible as her touch.

He nodded to a door across the room. "There's a toilet through there you can change in."

She started, her gaze sweeping from him to Axel, and then to the door. "Be right back."

She crossed the room, her heels clipping the concrete floor and lending a provocative sway to her hips. He soon realized he wasn't the only one staring.

"Thought you said you had a date to look forward to?" he muttered under his breath.

Axel coughed and looked at Dan.

"Too right I have," came Axel's response. "But she's something, ain't she? I mean she's hot on screen, but in the flesh…"

His PT was rooting through his gear and wouldn't have seen Dan's nod—the sheer sincerity of it—but Dan felt it under his skin, in his chest, in the swell of his heart. *Christ. Too close.*

"Ah, sound, these will do for her; they're my son's." Axel pulled out some bag gloves. "You take the pads. I think she'll enjoy trying to punch the crap out of you."

Dan grinned and shook his head. "You can tell that already?"

Axel shot him a look. "You're kidding, right?"

"Okay, how'd I look?" The toilet door shifted open with her question and they both froze, their teasing smiles locked in place.

Axel gave a low whistle. "You wanna go first, boss?"

Did he want to go first? Christ, he wished the guy gone. He'd seen Carrie in varying states of dress but never in his clothing, his underwear, and hell, it shouldn't be this sexy.

She'd tied his old Guns N' Roses tee in a high knot, pulling it taut over her curves and leaving her midriff bare. His boxer shorts hung low on her hips, too big but secure enough…that is, unless he chose to slip them off.

And he would.

Later.

His eyes came back to hers, his desire blatant he was sure, and he heard Axel cough. "Right, let's get you warmed up. There's a rope over there, a couple of minutes skipping to start—"

She laughed. "You want me to skip?"

"Sure do."

She eyed the rope sceptically. "I haven't skipped since I was a girl."

"It's like riding a bike. Show her, Dan." Axel tossed him a rope and he caught it on reflex, his brain having no part in it. It was still fixated on Carrie, or more specifically, on just how much he wanted to carry her upstairs and reacquaint himself with her entirety.

"Now this, I have to see." Carrie crossed her arms over her chest, laughter clear in her eyes, and his pride bit back. He'd show her, alright.

He moved into a clear space on the mat and took to it, fast and easy. He was showing off, but watching her appreciation only kept him going. And then she was trying to match him, her moves awkward at first but her concentration palpable, and something softened deep inside him; something he didn't want to pay attention to. It broke his rhythm and had the rope catching on his heel, halting his movement. He eased off, but she was well away now, her determination as sexy as her getup.

"You giving up?" she called.

"It spoils the view." He said it teasingly, but he meant every word. "Besides, I'm warmed up already."

Her eyes grazed over his skin as her pace slowed. "You are that."

"Hey, enough. Back on task," Axel ordered. She gave him a smile, happily doing exactly that. Her body was hypnotic as she effortlessly re-found her rhythm, and it set Dan's pulse racing off to match.

Carrie was panting by the time Axel told her to stop; there was sweat breaking across her brow, and she tried to sweep it away with her forearm before they could spy it. He had, though. And it made him wonder…had she really meant it when she said she didn't let herself break a sweat?

Of course she meant it, she's the ever-composed Carrie Evans, for fuck's sake.

Only he wasn't seeing as much of that in her anymore. The more time they spent together, the more real she appeared; she'd started to let go and seem more at ease, and he was loving it far too much.

Axel continued to fire off instructions for the next five minutes, making sure she was properly limbered up. Then he tossed Dan the pads, and Carrie the gloves. "Get these on."

She looked to the gloves as she caught them against her chest and frowned. "Really?"

"Yes, really," Axel said, taking hold of one glove and starting to help her put it on. "We don't want you hurting those pretty little fingers of yours."

"But they look ridiculous."

"I won't tell my son you said that."

"Your son?"

"Aye, they're his gloves."

She smiled. "In that case, please thank him for the loan."

"I will." Axel grinned down at her as he slotted the second glove into place. "There you go. How'd they feel?"

She knocked them together, the move studious and strangely endearing. "Big."

"Good." Axel nodded his approval. "They'll give you plenty of weight when you take him out."

Dan laughed, but it sounded awkward even to him; he was enjoying this far more than he should. "Whatever! Let's get to it."

He slotted on the focus mitts, trying to ignore the unease building at his and Carrie's interplay. It was too comfortable, too at home. He could imagine doing this regularly, the two of them working out together, working off the day's stress and then taking it upstairs afterwards. Like it was the most natural thing in the world having his film star girlfriend in his basement gym.

Girlfriend. His skin prickled, a chill sweeping over his spine.

She's not even close. Never would be.

"Dan?" It was Axel, his prompt pulling him up. "You ready?"

He nodded, looking to Carrie. A frown creased her brow, her eyes almost concerned. Had she read him? She couldn't possibly have. He hoped not—he didn't want the mood ruined by his runaway imaginings. He wanted this moment, wanted to enjoy it. "You ready to sweat?"

Her brow eased, and she gave an exaggerated shudder. "Enough of the sweat talk."

She raised her fists and bounced up and down, presenting the perfect warmed-up apprentice, ready to learn, and he shook his head. This was too much fun.

"If you stand here, Dan," Axel said and pointed to a spot on the mat, "I'll help Carrie."

Dan stood as Axel directed and watched as he coached her stance and strike. Her look of concentration was addictive to watch.

"So like this?" she said, giving a sweet little wriggle that made his cock twitch.

"You got it," Axel said approvingly. "Now aim for the mitts and give him hell."

She grinned, her eyes locking with Dan's, and he prepared himself for her onslaught.

"You best watch my tootsies," she said. "That pedicure is fresh and I really will whoop your ass if you ruin it."

He looked down at her dainty pink toes, and off went that strange spread of warmth again; not that he could dwell on it as he took a direct hit to one unresisting mitt. She'd tried to disarm him—the realization had him laughing, and she furrowed her brow, her sights locked on his mitts.

"What's so funny?"

"You hit like a girl."

She blew a lock of fringe off her forehead. "Funny that."

God, how he loved winding her up. "Sure is."

She sent him a fierce look, her speed picking up, her power not so much. But her determination was there, so much so that she stopped swiping at the sweat as it started to form over her brow, her focus entirely on her next punch.

"Place your feet a little wider," came Axel's command. "Get the heel on your back foot up. Extend your knees as you land your punch."

Dan could see her listening intently to each instruction, doing exactly as Axel asked, the power building in her punches. It was fascinating to watch, and his guard started to lower, the focus mitts with it.

"Careful, Dan, she'll have your face you do that again."

She smirked then. "Would hate to mar that pretty face."

He arched his brow. "Pretty?"

She delivered a hard right-left-right. "Yeah, especially those eyes."

"My eyes?"

"Yeah…they take me back."

He wanted to ask her what that meant, could feel the sincerity in her words but then Axel moved in, his hands holding her by the sides. "Watch your hips and torso…you need to swing back like this, load the punch up and then reverse it…swing your torso at your target."

She swung at him hard, his hand shifting under the sheer force and making him curse.

"Yes!" Axel declared, his fist pumping the air. "You got it!"

"I got it?" She jumped up and down on the spot. "I did, didn't I? That felt amazing."

"Never mind celebrating," Dan said, his voice tight. Truth was her, jubilation was driving him crazy. She looked like a kid that had just won the biggest bag of candy, her carefree turnaround both surprising him and pushing the uneasy shift underway inside. "You only got one."

"I've got a lot more in me."

"Prove it."

She laughed. "Oh, I will."

She got straight back down to it, her punches landing harder and faster. He lapped it up. Axel would shout the odd instruction, a reminder that he was still in the room, but Dan was so hooked on watching her he barely noticed.

He started to move—to make her work for the shot—and she matched him every step. Time disappeared. They were so in tune with one another, they barely noticed when Axel announced he needed to go.

He had to brave an intervention, his arm sweeping between them. "I'm gonna need to take those gloves with me, love, or my boy isn't going to be best impressed."

"Oh right, sure. Of course." Carrie's disappointment filled the air as she backed up, and Dan could see Axel waver.

"It's okay, Axel, I think Carrie's sweated enough for her liking."

Her eyes widened, her hand sweeping across her brow and sliding away. She grimaced. "Oh God, I must look frightful."

Yeah, totally frightful.

She turned to offer out her gloved hands to Axel with an apologetic smile. "Sorry, they probably need a good clean."

"Nothing they've not seen before."

Dan laughed, the idea of Carrie wearing someone else's sweat-ridden gloves tickling him just as much as it probably freaked her out. Even if outwardly, she didn't show it.

She let Axel strip them off and then flexed her hands in wonder. "That was so much fun."

"Worth getting sweaty for?" Dan asked while Axel packed up his stuff.

She grinned, her eyes locked in his, still filled with wonder and something else that he couldn't quite fathom. "Surprisingly so."

It pleased him more than he wanted to admit; everything about her in this moment bloody well pleased him.

He tossed Axel the training mitts and headed to a rack on the wall containing towels, grabbing two and returning just as Axel swung his bag over his shoulder.

"Right then, I'll leave you both to it."

"Aye, see you later." He gave Axel a fist bump and then tossed Carrie a towel. "For your sweat."

She caught it mid-air, her smile breathtaking with the exuberant color in her cheeks, the fire in her eyes. "Bye, Axel, and thanks."

"My pleasure."

With every step the PT took towards the exit, the tension in the air ramped up. He wouldn't be surprised if Axel could feel the heat radiating down his back—it felt like the air positively crackled with it.

He towelled his hair, then his face, his neck, his eyes fixed on her doing the same—on the flex of her torso as the sweat glistened over her exposed skin, the cling of his damp shirt over her curves that undulated with her breath. Every muscle in his body felt primed, his cock hard and painful in his shorts.

Axel pulled open the door and Dan threw his towel to the ground, striding straight for her—he wasn't waiting another second.

Chapter Ten

CARRIE'S HAND FELL AWAY FROM HER FACE, the towel slipping from her grip. Dan was coming for her, everything in his predatory stride telling her what for. And she wanted it. Bad.

He didn't break step as he reached for her. One hand snaked through her ponytail; the other reached around her to lift her against him. The heat of his chest, his arm against the exposed skin of her lower back, his scent—they all stoked the fire in her veins.

And then his lips crushed hers, her eyes closing as fireworks exploded behind her lids, the passion so fierce, so all-consuming that she wasn't aware of their movement until her back hit the wall. Its rough surface grazed against her skin, his arm shielding her from the worst and protecting her even in his heightened state.

"You drive me crazy…" He bit into her lip, tugging at it. "You know that?"

Her response was a whimper. *Crazy—What does he think he's doing to you?*

She yanked at the zip of his hoodie, shoving it from his shoulders as her mouth returned his assault, making sure he didn't doubt for a second that she reciprocated his feelings.

He fumbled over the knot she'd tied in his top. "*Blasted thing.*"

He gave up on the tie to grope her breasts through the fabric and she arched into him, her body singing at his crazed attention. He rolled his thumb over her hardened peaks and squeezed his fingers into her flesh, but it wasn't enough, for her, for him.

"It's gotta go." He took hold of the shirt collar with both hands and pulled.

The fabric bit into the back of her neck as it tore open, and he swallowed her gasp with his mouth. He continued to jerk it apart, the sound, the force, the growl he made, upping the wildness within her. He shoved it from her shoulders, her bra straps along with it, imprisoning her upper arms in place as his head dropped, his hands sliding inside her cups. The heat of his palms encased her, followed swiftly by the hot cavern of his mouth, his tongue, his teeth as he swung from one breast to the other, seemingly unable to get enough.

She started to undulate against the pillar, the brick grazing her skin and the burn only adding to the crazy well of heat within. She was a hot, moaning mess, and she couldn't take much more of this. She was going to come with his head at her breast. But it wasn't how she wanted to go. She wanted him inside her when she shattered; she wanted him going over the edge with her.

She clawed at his shoulders. "I need you," she pleaded. "Now."

He dropped to his knees, his head at her navel. He shook his head, his nose brushing teasingly over her mound. "I don't have any condoms down here."

Fuck. She looked down at him, meeting his desire-filled gaze. "I'm clean."

His eyes widened, his head shaking again. "But..."

"I'm on the pill."

He lowered his gaze, his forehead pressing into her belly; she could tell he was fighting with himself, his body strained with tension, his breath rasping hard and uneven.

She stroked his head and coaxed his eyes back to hers. "Are you?"

"Clean?"

"Yes." It was a whisper as he nodded, his eyes softening. The fire still blazed but there was something else—something deeper in their depths—that gave her hope.

"*Please.*"

He rose, his hardness coming to rest against her bare midriff, and his hands reached to cup her face. "You sure?"

"I've never been more sure." *Of anything. Of you, of me…of what I want.*

He searched her gaze, his eyes flickering—could he read her silent declaration too? And then he lowered his mouth to hers, but they weren't manic or hard; they were soft, gentle. He sipped at her mouth, his hand trailing down her front to slip inside the boxers and thong that she still wore. They probed just as gently, just as teasingly. Stroking her clustered nerve-endings with a feather-light touch that had ripples firing through her limbs and her knees threatening to buckle. Her hands flew to his shoulders for support before he sunk low, his fingers slipping through her wetness, and she knew she'd have to beg.

"Now, Dan—*now.*"

He broke away, his eyes remaining fixed with hers. "You trust me?"

And there's that phrase again…

Through her lust-filled fog, she whispered, "Of course."

"Turn around."

She did as he asked, looking over her shoulder at him, waiting for what came next.

He cocked his brow. "I think you can lose my briefs now, don't you?"

She gave a soft laugh, milking it as she drew the movement out, his appreciate gaze feasting on her behind as she bent forward and slid both his boxers and her thong off in one motion.

She moved to straighten and he stepped forward, his palm smoothing over one buttock to stop her. "Stay like that."

She swallowed. Desire was so tight in her throat she could scarcely breathe, all senses honed on his touch.

"So soft," he murmured as he caressed her. "So smooth."

He stroked down to cup her between her legs, his fingers dragging back and gathering up her wetness before they slid inside. She undulated with his invasion and her hands reached to grip the pillar before her as she moaned.

He went deep, his free hand palming her other cheek and the tip of his cock nudging at her flesh.

"Have you ever played here?" he asked.

She was about to ask what he meant, but his fingers slid out from inside her, travelling to her arse, and instead of skimming over it, his slickened fingers dipped inside, teasing at the puckered opening.

"*No.*" The word came out on a pant, voice and body tight with anticipation. She remembered the raven-haired woman—remembered how she'd moved, how she'd moaned, how her skin had flushed in pleasure. "Do you want to?"

She sensed him smile. "I should be asking you that."

He probed at her with one finger, and she pressed into him. "Oh, *yes.*"

His breath hissed through his teeth, his tension vibrating through his palm as he steadied her. His fingers continued to coax—to invade further—her wetness giving them the lubrication her body needed, until she was brazenly riding his fingers. She was unable to get enough, the sensation so unfamiliar and like nothing she'd ever known.

He shifted, his free hand cupping her front and giving her friction against her throbbing clit as he took himself in hand, rubbing between her legs and coating himself in her need.

"You ready?"

His voice was tense, her nod just as stiff. He positioned himself between her arse cheeks, the tip of his cock nudging at her, and instinctively she pulled herself taut.

"Relax," he rasped.

And she did—at least she tried to—but her whole body was alive; desperate.

Slowly, he pressed into her, stretching her, and she moaned with the wave of heat, her tummy contracting over it. It hurt, but it didn't. The sensation was confusing, powerful, compounded by his palm still pressed against her beating clit.

He eased in and out, each time going that bit further—making it that bit more painful, that bit more thrilling. She could hear him struggling for air, feel his thighs trembling against her own. He was close, and he wasn't even fully in. Would he even be able to fit?

She looked to him over her shoulder, the veins corded in his neck. His eyes blazed, locked on where their bodies met, and she bit into her lip so hard she tasted blood.

"Your arse is so perfect," he seethed through his teeth. "So tight, I can't…"

His voice trailed off, both hands shifting to cup her hips and better control his movement. He was scared of hurting her—she could see it, and it turned her on all the more—but she wanted him losing it; she wanted him out of control, fucking her hard.

She pushed back over him, squeezing him tight. "Let go."

A second's hesitation flared in his eyes and then he let go, his cry guttural, trembling through her as he started to pump, his moves jagged and fierce. She gripped the wall with one hand as the other dropped to her clit, feeding its demand for more. The movement pulled the torn T-shirt taut against the underside of her breasts, biting into her skin, her nipples puckering in the cool air of the gym, so many sensations all at once and the telltale heat started to spread.

She tightened up her stance, her fingers claw-like against the brick, her breath catching in her lungs.

"Fuck," she cried out as the first wave hit. "Yes…*yes*."

She exploded, her body jerking forward, and she felt him follow suit, his cock pulsing within her, his hot fluid filling her. The sensation was raw, exhilarating, new. He rocked back and forth, his breathing ragged as he smoothed his hands up her body to pull her against him. He wrapped his arms around her tight and dropped his head to the curve of her neck, his breath hot and blustery against her skin.

"I hope I didn't hurt you."

His cock was still planted deep inside, still pulsing within her, and yet he was making sure she was okay.

She turned to nuzzle his ear, a jagged breath leaving her lips as her heart swelled. "Are you crazy? I loved it."

He lifted his head to meet her gaze, and her breath caught at the emotion flaring behind his eyes. Something had changed—something between them had shifted. She was sure of it. The question was, did he feel it too? Was he about to confess as much? He was looking at her so intently, so passionately—

"You want to take a shower with me?"

She stilled, disappointment landing heavy in her gut. *What did you expect?*

"Hey?" He frowned at her, seeing too much, and his arms squeezed around her middle.

"Sure, yeah, that'll be nice."

She lowered her lashes, but could sense his frown still upon her as she encouraged him to release her. A shower was better than a "you can leave now".

She'd just wanted so much more in that moment.

And that told her everything she needed to know. That she loved him; that more than anything, she wanted him to love her back.

No more hate, no more resentment, just love.

And a future she'd refused to believe possible ten years ago…

He turned the shower on, watching the water fall from the oversized showerhead before turning to see her enter the gym's wet room. She pulled his ruined tee over her head while he hung back, unable to look away—almost unable to believe. Only he *had* to believe, after all they'd shared. She was really here; they were really doing this.

Her eyes came back to him as she unclasped her bra and the fabric fell to her feet; her rose-tipped buds were pert and alert, calling to him from across the room. Red streaks ran over her skin from where his T-shirt had been stretched tight and where his mouth had sucked and teeth had nipped. Possessive heat rushed his system. He'd done that. Marked her. Staked his claim. His throat thickened, his hand tightening over the shower dial—*how can you want her again so soon?*

Because it will always be like this with her.

It was then, it is now.

Only it's more intense, unstoppable.

She sauntered towards him, her hands lifting to her hair and freeing it from its tie. Honey-blonde waves fell to frame her face, trailing over her shoulders, her breasts…she really was breathtaking, and right now, she was his.

"You going to shower in your clothes?"

She gestured to the shorts he'd slipped back on, and he smiled. "I was hoping you might take them off."

"Aaah."

She reached out to trail her fingers over his skin, goosebumps pricking in their wake and a thrilling shiver ran through him. She stepped around him, peppering kisses across his collarbone and then his shoulder blades as she hooked her fingers into the waistband of his shorts.

Slowly, she crouched, taking them down, her kisses travelling down his back with her descent. She nipped the base of his spine and trailed her tongue lower, lightly over one arse cheek before delivering a sharp nip to the other.

He bucked forward. "*Fuck.*"

"Easy, tiger," she murmured against his skin. Even the brush of her lips had his cock twitching, his breath hitching.

Stripping him of his shorts, her fingers returned, roaming freely over his legs, teasing at his inner thighs, the backs of his knees, his calves, his ankles. "Turn around."

He did as she commanded; was willing to do *anything* she commanded.

She rose up, her nipples brushing provocatively against his chest as she arched into him, his cock coming to rest against her stomach, gently nudging. "That's better."

She slid her fingers into his, the move as intimate as her caress, and then she stepped back, pulling him under the water with her.

"This is nice," she said softly. *Nice?* He could think of a thousand other words, but nice…

He looked down into her gaze, so intent, so devoted even, and realized the word did have its place, she was right. He cupped her sides, his palms gliding with the water as he stroked over her skin and she smiled, the gesture adding to her gaze tenfold and a warmth that had nothing to with desire flooded his veins. He was happy; content—too much so.

He closed his eyes against the old fear—*not now*—and felt her turn in his hold, her pert behind caressing his hardness and emptying his brain of all but the sensation.

He let the water run over the lower half of his face and opened his eyes to watch her raise her face to the stream, her hair falling to cling against his chest and creating a waterfall down his front teasing at his groin. He reached for the soap, his intent to clean her, to enjoy her body beneath his palms, but she turned into him once more, her hand stopping him.

"Let me." She took up the bottle and squeezed the blue liquid into her palm before returning it back to the rack. She rubbed her hands together, the air filling with its masculine-soapy scent, and then she looked to him beneath her lashes, her smile deliciously provocative as she reached out to palm his pecs. She circled her hands over him, her caress firm and encouraging him to sway into the move.

He smiled with teasing. "You saying I'm incapable of washing myself?"

"No," she whispered. "I'm saying, I owe you."

"Owe me?"

"After today, I owe you."

It baffled him, but any need to question it died as her hands travelled lower, turning them both and urging him back under the water. He raised his head to the jets, every sense focussed on the downward progression of her hands as her thorough exploration coaxed him harder and tighter. She slid a hand between his legs, her fingers gently cupping, massaging; then her other hand took hold of his length, pumping him back and exposing his head to the spray.

She stroked over his slit and he gritted his teeth, pre-cum swelling at his tip and beaten away by the stream of water as a multitude of sensation ripped through him at once.

He dropped his head forward, his eyes locking onto the now primal heat of hers.

"Make love to me, Dan."

Make love to me...Christ, just hearing her ask had his heart rate soaring, his chest expanding.

"I don't have a condom here."

"We've been through this…"

He squeezed his eyes tight. We had. And then he'd taken her from behind, bareback instead, and she'd felt so perfect. But it would have nothing on this. To feel himself deep inside her warm, slick heat. To share that bond.

Fuck, how he wanted it.

But not here, against his cold shower wall.

He wanted her in his bed.

He wanted to make love to her like this was something more,

something real, something long-term, and the realization should've had him running.

"*Please*, Dan, *I need you.*"

Screw running. He was already slamming off the shower.

"Dan?"

He pulled two fresh towels off the rack and turned to her. "This time we're going to make it to a bed."

"A bed?" She gave a soft laugh as he threw her a towel. "It's a bit late for such standards, don't you think?"

He studied her—her flushed skin, her hair trailing water over her curves—and leant forward to twist a blonde strand around one finger. "If I'm going to make love to you, I'm doing it properly."

She gave a little intake of breath, her lips parting, and he allowed himself a sweeping taste. "Now move it, before I change my mind."

He tapped her arse and she giggled, the sound flooding him with yet more warmth. This was madness. He was losing it. But in that moment, he didn't care.

Chapter Eleven

Dan slung his towel around his hips, then held a hand out to Carrie.

She looked at him with a peculiar, almost bashful expression as she wrapped her towel around herself before lacing her fingers through his. Had his words left their mark? Something akin to what he was feeling far too close to his heart?

She offered him a small smile when he failed to move and he mentally shook himself out of it, pulling her along to his private staircase, not daring to pause and risk his restraint snapping. Because all he wanted right now was to drown out his emotions in the passion she instilled. To forget all else. And yes, the stairwell would be deserted, but getting carried away beneath his CCTV wasn't happening. He wasn't sharing this moment with a lens.

She was for his eyes to capture as he took her, and his eyes only.

He pushed away all thought as they walked, not stopping on the threshold, or in the hallway, or at the bedroom door. When he got to the foot of the bed, he turned to sweep her up, the force of the move sending her towel to the floor.

She gave a little squeal of delight as he threw her onto the bed, her naked form sprawled and open to him. He whipped off his own towel and she gave another delighted sound low in her throat, driving him to grin. "You ready for this?"

She nodded, her teeth pulling back over her bottom lip, her eyes alive with anticipation as he lowered himself to all fours on the bed before crawling towards her.

"How can you be so hungry for me already?"

"You complaining?" he said gruffly.

"No." Brazenly she eyed his length, hard and probing between them. "I'm just as wet, see for yourself."

She trailed her fingers down her stomach, between her legs, pulling them back in a V to part herself to his gaze. He swallowed, his tongue sweeping over his lower lip and then he dipped to lick over her, taking advantage of her parted state.

Her breath rasped as her body bucked, the hard nub of her clit protruding and calling him back. He tongued it, lapping up every little jerk she made, every little whimper, and she gripped him to her, her hands forked in his hair. He raised his gaze to see her staring straight back at him, taking it all in, and his cock throbbed in response, begging for completion, to be inside her.

But he pushed on. He wanted her close; wanted her on the cusp just as he was. He continued to feast on her, his fingers joining in on the attention—one finger dipping inside her, then two, then three. She stretched for him, her readiness making it easy to move within her. She was ready. So ready. And he couldn't wait any longer.

He rose up on his knees and looked down at her, wanton, desperate, her hands reaching for him. "You are so beautiful."

That hint of bashfulness was back, mixing with the glaze of desire and he moved over her, loving how she stroked her hands down his back, how her eyes stayed fixed with his. He rested his weight into one elbow beside her, nestled his cock between her legs, wanting to savor this moment, to savor *her*. He brushed her damp hair from her face, felt the heat of her cheeks burn through his palm and lost himself in her eyes that glittered with so much emotion and yet he daren't read a single one, save for desire. The one he understood, the one he could cope with.

He lowered his hand, his fingers trailing over her front and her tummy contracted, her teeth dragging on her lower lip as she arched into his caress.

"You want me?" He wanted to stress the *me*; wanted her to make him worthy. Make him believe the great Carrie Evans would be happy with him and only him. Even for just this moment.

She nodded, her legs wrapping around him, her eyes serious and blazing and telling him all he needed to know. His cock nudged at her entrance and she angled herself towards him, her hands soft upon his shoulders as her teeth once more found her bottom lip. She nodded again. "I want *you*."

Her words, her gaze, her liquid heat surrounding his tip, *this*...it was perfect. He drove forward, sinking himself within, surrounding himself with her. His ears rang with her moan, his eyes lost in the sight of her pressing back into the pillow, the flush to her skin, the ecstasy etched in her face. *Christ*.

He eased out slowly, her need coating his length, hot and wet, and fuck, he was going to come. He stilled, too scared to even breath.

She shifted beneath him, her hands dropping to claw his arse, her fingers and heels biting into his flesh as she looked to him, desperate, pleading. "Don't tease."

Tease? Jesus.

He couldn't if he tried.

But they had all night for longer performances...

"Hold on, Princess."

He thrust in deep, sending her up the bed with a moan of pure bliss. *Fuck*, he could get hooked on hearing those sounds from her. He pumped harder, faster, wanting more noise, more of the wanton, the real her; and she obliged. He lost himself in her every reaction; in the moans that filled his ears and the wet heat that surrounded him, squeezing him tight, holding him deep. No barrier between them, no protection, no nothing, and he'd never felt closer to anyone; never felt more at home.

"Dan, *Dan*..." Carrie clung to him, her impending climax evident in the strain of every muscle, and he was so absorbed in her that his own erupted with the first ripples of her orgasm around his length.

Ecstasy flooded his veins, his muscles, his brain...*his heart*. And he couldn't take his eyes off her. She was stunning. Hell, she was always stunning, but when she came...

She wriggled and sighed beneath him, tension seeping from her body her fingers trailing along his skin and making him shudder.

She smiled, her head cocked to one side. "Still ticklish in the aftermath?"

She remembered. A mixture of pain and love winded him, and he dropped his eyes, rolling to the side and pulling her into him.

"You could say that." He traced a path along her side, past the dip of her waist, over the curve to her hip, pushing away the past. He wouldn't ruin this moment. In fact, he didn't want it to end... "Stay the night."

She placed her palm on his torso, her fingers stroking his skin. "I'd like to."

But. He could hear it coming, and he didn't want it to. He could take 'but' later; just not right now...

She gave a soft sigh, her lips pressing into his chest. "I don't have anything with me to stay."

She couldn't be serious. "What do you *actually* need?"

"Typical man!" She looked up at him with a laugh. "I need clothes for starters; a toothbrush, a comb, makeup..."

Relief, happiness, it all flooded him and had him teasing her with a squeeze to her hip. "You don't *need* those things, you simply desire them."

"Well desire or not, I'm not wearing my underwear two days running. Especially after our escapades."

He laughed at that, a genuine, hearty laugh that beat back the unease. "In that case, send your mum a message. Ask if she'll pack you a bag, and I'll get one of my men to go and collect it."

She raised her brow, her head pressing into his shoulder. "Seriously?"

"Yes, seriously."

She smiled, light lifting in her eyes. "Okay. I will."

Even as he shared in her joy, his relief swelling, there was that tiny part of him that couldn't keep quiet. *You're in too deep. You're letting the past repeat itself.*

But could he stop it?

Did he *want* to stop it?

She rolled from the bed.

"Where are you going?"

She looked back at him, her feet hitting the floor. "Well, if I'm to message my mum then I need my phone, and that's still in my bag downstairs."

He reached out and grabbed her wrist, tugging her back so that she landed on top of him. "That can wait a minute. I haven't finished here yet."

She laughed and pressed against his chest to meet his eye. "There's no way you want to go again."

"No way?"

She shook her head with another laugh.

"Let me be the judge of that." He pulled her down to the mattress and rolled on top of her. Her continued laughter washed over him, full of sheer pleasure, injecting him with the same. *If only we could stay like this.*

He lowered his head, ready to devour her all over again.

"Dan?"

His name pulled him back up. "Yes?"

"This feels right, doesn't it?"

Right? It felt *right* in more ways than he wanted to contemplate, but… "You mean, now that Isla has convinced you she no longer has feelings for me?"

Her lashes fluttered. "Well yes, there's that…" She broke off, her head shaking as she dropped her sights to his mouth. "Ignore me, I'm having a moment."

"A moment?"

"Yeah, it's all good, come back." She pulled his head down, her kiss fierce in spite of her recent release, as if at any moment it would all be taken away. As if they were living on borrowed time.

But you are. This isn't forever. It's for now.

Carrie Evans didn't belong in his world, and he certainly didn't belong in hers.

He knew it.

She knew it.

But what if they could change that? Find a way?

Chapter Twelve

CARRIE STRETCHED OUT, HER LIMBS protesting at the move, and she smiled. The pleasing ache reminded her of the cause, of the man pressed tight against her back with his arm draped over her waist, surrounding her in warmth.

Slowly she turned, careful not to wake him. The strips of light breaking through the blinds told her it was late morning, and yet Dan slept soundly, his deep and even breath brushing over her. She angled her head, enjoying the opportunity to study him unobserved.

His features were softer in sleep; even the dark shadow of his stubble seemed less severe—*he* was far less severe, at least compared to that night she'd appeared in his office.

Or maybe it had nothing to do with sleep, and everything to do with the fact that he'd given her so much pleasure—so much of himself—since then. The hatred he'd made clear upon their reunion was now a distant memory, replaced with feelings a decade old.

And now that she was here, in his bed, it all seemed so obvious to her. The reason she had been so dissatisfied, so keen to land the next big role, the next big award, the next whatever.

She wasn't fulfilled. She wasn't anything without him. She was lonely. And no acting career could change that.

How could she have been so blind to it?

Being with Brad played a part in it for sure; ticking a box that had never really been ticked at all. He was still perfect on paper, and she cared for him, but not like this; not with this all-consuming passion that she was helpless to control.

The very idea of going back to her life in LA and leaving this behind terrified her, particularly now that she knew how life could really be with Dan back in it. She couldn't walk away from him again.

But what about Isla…and what of Brad? Had they found this, too? Were they wrapped up in their own love affair right now? With Isla's falsehood forgiven and their relationship on an honest footing, being given a real chance?

Carrie wanted to believe it, but this was no romantic fairy tale with a guaranteed happy ending. Before she pursued a life with Dan, she had to know Isla was okay and that Brad understood and hopefully forgave.

It seemed too much to hope for, no matter what Dan had said to the contrary.

And with thousands of miles between them, it wasn't like she could help her sister. She couldn't protect her, or even just be there for her.

No, first and foremost, she had to get Isla back here, and then she could worry about the rest—not least of all her mission to save Isla's business, because with Dan's help, she knew they could do it.

Perhaps she should just go ahead and book her sister's return flights. That way it would be out of Isla's hands and she'd have to fly home. She'd be surrounded by those that loved her and would look after her.

Or—Carrie's pulse tripped—maybe her sister already had the tickets in hand? Maybe it had all gone south and she was winging her way back right now? *Shit.*

Carrie needed to check her phone; she needed to see if Isla had been in touch.

"Hey, why so tense?"

Dan's sleep-ladened voice rumbled through her worrying thoughts, and she refocused her gaze to give him a small smile, lifting her fingers to brush over his cheek in an impulsive caress. "I can't help worrying about Isla."

He tightened his arm around her and pressed a kiss to her temple. She hummed her appreciation, her stress easing just a little— *see, there he goes again, his simple gestures making everything feel better.*

"She's a grown woman," he murmured against her hair. "She can take care of herself."

"But this is my mess." She shook her head softly. "I should face his wrath when this all comes out, not her."

"Perhaps." He bowed to nuzzle at her earlobe, his arm lifting to stroke his fingers along her side and lighting up her skin, her body stirring so readily.

"Maybe I should just get her flights sorted," she continued, trying to douse the heat, to stay on track. "Insist she come back so we can deal with it together."

His groan danced provocatively along her spine. "That's hardly giving her the chance to fix things, is it?"

"I know, but…"

"And she told you she would be in touch today," he pressed, his fingers continuing their exploration. He coaxed the quilt down her body, her skin prickling as he exposed her to the cool air of the room. "So I say, wait for her to call." He traced a circle behind her ear with his tongue and she shivered. "Then we'll take it from there."

Focus, her brain demanded, the breathless argument fluttering out. "I'd just feel happier knowing she was on her way home."

"It's far easier to keep her away from the club when she's on another continent."

His hand dipped low over her belly, and she sucked in a breath, her hand dropping to cover his. She'd intended to stop him, but instead she moved with him, her body fighting her good intentions.

"And as you assured me," she said, determined to talk this out, "there are ways to keep her away, and I'd feel better knowing she was here, where I can look after her."

Their fingers brushed over her curls, so close that she caught her breath, ready for it.

"What's got into you?" he rasped out, his choice of words surprising her as her fingers stilled, his own too. "When did you get so protective? Or selfless?"

Her gut twisted, the heat of desire snuffed out in an instant, his hidden accusation crushed her—*you were selfish before; you didn't care before.*

And he'd uttered it so easily.

"I've *always* been protective of her."

Pulling his hand away, he raised himself up on one elbow to look down into her face. "Sorry." He frowned, tucking the hair that had fallen across his eyes, back behind his ear. "I didn't mean to upset you."

She wanted to tell him he hadn't, but that would be a lie, and she was done with lying.

She was done with the entire Carrie Evans persona that had her pinned as selfish, impenetrable, unfeeling. The evil yin to Isla's yang. She wasn't any of that. Christ, she'd left because she *wasn't* selfish. She'd left *for* Isla. She'd set aside her own happiness, for hers.

"Carrie?" He lowered his hand to hers now clutched tight over her belly, his stare intense, concerned, and she stared back at him. Hard.

"How else should I take it?"

He looked away and waved his hand in frustration. "I don't know, it's just…this whole drive to save her business, the barrier you put up between you and I when you thought she had feelings for me, versus how you were all those years ago…" His voice trailed off and he dropped onto his back, his eyes on the ceiling and eventually he said, "You've changed."

Her head spun with the confirmation of what she'd known to be true, of how much he'd disliked—no not disliked, *hated* her. And still her body pined for the loss of his.

She wasn't ready for this conversation, but there was no shying away from it. It was time he knew the truth, to face the past head on and deal with it once and for all.

She curved into him, her head coming to rest on his chest. "I've not changed that much."

"No?"

She swallowed back the lump forming at his disbelief. "No."

But it was no use, her eyes spiked with tears, as the memories flooded in. Memories of their argument ten years ago, the last time they'd seen each other—the night she'd told him her career was everything, that she deserved better, that they were destined for different lives; lives that didn't mix, just like her parents had proven, just like…like…

She closed her eyes, her breath shaking from her lungs.

"Look, it doesn't matter." He wrapped his arm around her, his fingers gently squeezing her shoulder. "I really didn't mean to upset you."

"I know you didn't."

"Then forget it. I shouldn't have said it." He hooked his fingers under her chin, coaxing her to look up at him. "It's all in the past."

"That's just it, we have two different versions of the past."

His brow drew together, his eyes deep and confused. "I don't know how you can say that. We were both there."

"But you don't know the truth of it," she started, and then stopped, not knowing where to begin. No, that *was* a lie, she knew, but it was just so hard to put it into words, to let it out. "The night I left…"

She felt his body stiffen; his eyes flickering with a barrage of emotion. Was he reliving it, just as she was?

"What about it?"

"I lied to you."

His throat bobbed, his lashes fluttering as his fingers flexed against her chin. "Which bit?"

God, how could she tell him now, after all this time—*But how can you not? How can you let him go on believing you put your career before him? You owe it to him. Christ, you owe it to yourself.*

"All of it." Pain swelled, and she lowered her gaze, she couldn't say it with him looking right inside her this way. "When I told you I had no place for you in my life, that my career had to come first, that I...that I deserved..."

The words died, the memory alone too much to bear, the decade-old lies weighing heavy on her heart.

His chest was completely still beneath her, the pounding of his heart against her ear the only sound in the room as she took another breath and tried again, but he spoke up first. "Why would you bring that up now?"

"Because it was all a lie."

"A *lie*?"

"Yes," she said softly, the pain in his words crushing her. She lifted her eyes to his, praying he would see how sorry she was. "I told you that because I knew it would stop you coming after me—that it would make you hate me enough to stay away."

His eyes flared, his head dropping back as his fingers left her chin to fork through his hair and stay there. He stared at the ceiling and she waited. Giving him time to let her words sink in. "What are you saying, Carrie?"

She pressed herself against him tighter. She needed to stay near him; needed that reassuring bond as she confessed, "That I broke it off because I couldn't break Isla's heart any more than I already had."

He trembled beneath her. "So you chose to break mine instead?"

She squeezed her eyes tight, the pang inside like a blow to the stomach, brutal and winding—*I broke mine, too.*

But this isn't about self-pity.

It's about telling him the truth.

"If I'd told you my true feelings, you wouldn't have let it go…I'd already done enough damage."

"How can you say that?"

"Because it wasn't you that caught Isla crying into her pillow. It wasn't you that had to cope with the look in her eyes every time she saw us together. We pushed her out—"

"Like hell we did."

"Not on purpose; she just couldn't handle it. When I asked her why she no longer walked to school with us, why she couldn't come to the park, the cinema, whatever…it was that same look. And no matter how hard she tried to hide it from me, it was so obvious. I just couldn't do it anymore."

"But you could crush *me*? You could leave me?"

His words wrapped around her heart, her chest squeezing too tight to breathe.

"I didn't want to," she said eventually. "When Mum and Dad announced they were splitting up, that he was leaving the country…" She broke off, the wedge in her throat getting too big—she needed to swallow to speak past it. "It was just too much. I saw a way out—a way to help Dad cope with the split, to do right by my sister, to help her—"

"Help yourself you mean?" He scoffed. "To get the career you always dreamed of?"

"Yes, I got my career…" She deserved his bitter recall. "…but it came at a price."

"And was it worth it?"

"In some ways." She was being honest. It had been. She wouldn't have the relationship she had with her dad if she hadn't gone, and no, she wouldn't have her career. But she had missed out on so much. Missed out on them…*on Dan*.

Suddenly he rolled away, and she fell to the bed, alone and cold. Her eyes welled as she watched him rise to sit at the edge of the bed, his head in his hands. He was shaking, the sight so vulnerable it killed her.

"Dan?" She reached out, her fingers soft upon his shoulder and he flinched, shrugging her away. "*Please.*"

He pushed up off the bed. "I need a minute."

She watched him walk away, his pain weighing heavy in the air and leaving her fixed in place with her hand still raised. A solitary tear traced down her cheek.

It will be okay. It will be okay. It will be okay.

"I never said I didn't love you," she whispered.

He faltered, his head twisting just a little—*come back to me,* she silently pleaded. And then his focus returned to the bathroom door and he strode for it, this time quicker and more determined.

She swallowed, forcing herself to sit and pull her knees to her chest, fighting off the flutter of panic taking hold in her gut.

It was out there now. It was for the best. They could move on properly; no secrets.

She dropped her head to her knees. It had to have been the right thing to do.

It *was* the right thing.

She only hoped it hadn't ruined everything.

Dan could feel Carrie's eyes burning into his back, but he forced himself on, her words echoing through his skull and slamming in his chest: *I never said I didn't love you.*

What the fuck was that supposed to mean?

He swung open the bathroom door, striding inside and closing it again with considerable calm—he was scared that if he slammed it with the force he wanted to, then everything would break free. The pain, the anger, the confusion…

Had she loved him?

Actually loved him, and still left?

Hell, she hadn't just left, she'd had him hating her. *Real, visceral hate.*

His insides twisted. He wanted to vomit—wanted to get rid of it all.

He lay back against the door, dragging air into his lungs and fighting for calm. He wished she'd never told him any of it. They'd been getting by just fine, enjoying the present and leaving the past where it belonged.

But now it was all a lie. Another of her goddamn lies. Only this one crucified him.

It turned the last ten years on their head, messed with everything he'd once taken as fact.

Ten years of hating her for what she'd done, hating himself for falling for a woman that couldn't love him back. Ten years of refusing to fall into that same trap again; of keeping women at arm's length, giving them a place in his bed but never in his heart. And now the one that he'd wanted all along was back, and she was telling him shit like this.

Shit that changed everything.

Or did it?

They were worlds apart now—Did it really matter that she'd loved him then?

She would up and leave again soon. Go back to her glitzy career, back to the people that belonged in her world.

And when she was gone, life would return to normal. Only now, he knew the truth…now he knew she'd been protecting Isla, putting her sister first, and that *did* change things.

He clenched his fists, his mind dizzy with the revelation.

It was messed up. It messed *him* up.

And yet, everything made so much sense now. Carrie's passion to help Isla, the guilt he'd glimpsed, the way she worried about her sister. And above all, the crazy, uncontrollable heat that persisted between them.

No, not heat. *Love.* Real, unadulterated love. Was that what this was? On both sides?

There was a gentle rap on the door. "Dan? I'm sorry. Please don't hate me, not all over again. I can't bear it."

His heart convulsed over the ring of hurt in her hushed tone—*hate her?* It wasn't hate that had him this crazed. His hand reached for the door handle.

She had suffered just as much as him. He understood her motive, could respect her for it, love her for it even, and that terrified him. Because one thing hadn't changed: they had no future together.

But you still have the present.

And though he got her reasoning, part of him wanted to punish her, wanted to hurt her like she'd hurt him. The anger warred with his sympathy and his body surged with adrenalin, fuelling a far greater need, to have her.

He swung open the door and she stepped back startled, her lips parted, her bare skin flushed and marred from their night together. From him.

He stalked towards her, grabbing hold of her wrist and tugging her against him.

She gasped, her head leaning back to look at him in question, but he was already crushing her lips with his own. He squeezed his eyes shut, his kiss brutal, sparring with her tongue until she could do nothing but fight back.

She clawed at his shoulders, his neck, his hair. Their teeth clashed, their tongues duelled, breath rasping through their nostrils as they pressed so close together. His hands were just as crazed, fierce on her thighs as he forced them apart, raising them around his hips as he spun her hard against the wall. She hit it with a soft grunt, her head pressing back against it as he dropped his head to her neck, wrapping himself in her scent: sex and honey. *Carrie.* Perfectly Carrie.

She panted heavily, her hands hooked around the back of his neck and nails biting into his flesh. His cock thrust between them, seeking her out, and he bent his knees, steadying himself before thrusting forward, entering her in one.

She cried out, and for a solitary second, he panicked that he'd hurt her. He knew she'd be raw after the night they'd shared. But then her hands were clawing deeper, her whimpers pleading. It was reassurance enough. He gripped her arse and let go, slamming her hard against the wall with every thrust, every grunt. And she moaned with him, screamed even, her pleasure ringing out in the quiet of the room.

It was desperate, it was carnal, and it was everything he needed. He came with a roar, his body bucking forcibly within her at the same time she spasmed against him; her thighs locking tight and squeezing as she pulsed around him.

He buried his head beneath her chin, his forehead pressed against her clavicle as he let his breath and sight sweep down the valley of her breasts to where their bodies joined. He didn't want normality to return; he didn't want their conversation of a moment before to rear up, dragging the distant past with it.

She stroked her fingers up his back, her breath soft upon his head. "I *am* sorry."

She said it so quietly that he could have pretended not to hear, but fear that she would push him to talk more had him raising his head and silencing her with a kiss.

He coaxed a whimper out of her, felt her body soften around him, and then he raised his head to look down into her eyes. "Let's just enjoy this while we can, yeah?"

Her eyes wavered, blazing with emotion, and then she smiled. "Okay." She wriggled out of his hold, her hands stroking down his chest. "In that case, how are your cooking skills?"

He gave her a bemused smile, ignoring the protestations of his cock as it slipped free. "My cooking skills?"

"Well, I'm voting for a shower and then breakfast in bed. If we're on borrowed time I say we make the most of it."

She didn't wait for him to respond; she was already heading into the bathroom, her appealing behind beckoning him to follow.

He was still a mess, a torrent of emotion pulling him apart inside, and he couldn't make sense of a single one. Or maybe he didn't want to make sense of it, because then he'd be forced to accept the truth?

He cursed and made after her. Because one thing was certain, he was going to do exactly as she suggested and make the most of every last second they had together.

The future could go screw itself for now…

Chapter Thirteen

ISLA WAS SOBBING—GREAT, WRACKING SOBS—but Carrie couldn't reach her. She could only watch through the glass as her sister curled tight into a ball on the concrete floor, cold and alone. Broken.

Some part of Carrie knew it was a dream—the surreal surroundings, the alien atmosphere all told her as much—but she couldn't shake it off, couldn't wake up. She tried to call out, to yell Isla's name, to break the glass, but her fists only clenched tighter, her mouth clamping shut and trapping her cries.

"Hey, easy." She could hear Dan. His voice was close and coaxing, calling her to him out of the darkness. His hand was in her hair, gently stroking. "It's a dream, Princess. Just a dream."

Her lids fluttered, her eyes slow to adjust. He leant in, warm and inviting, his lips gentle on her brow as he pulled her closer against him. "You're okay."

She nudged him with her head and cozied in beneath his chin, relief making her breath ease and her brain kick in. "What time is it?"

"Half-six."

Half-six in the morning, which made it the dead of night back in LA. Isla should have called by now; she'd promised she would. And the phone was on the bedside table, set to vibrate, so it would have woken Carrie had Isla called.

Or would it?

Cold sweat broke out across Carrie's skin, her panic quick to resurface thanks to her dream, and she shimmied out of Dan's hold just enough to feel around the bedside table in the dark for her phone. Eventually she found it, and grasping it up, she snuggled back down and lit the screen.

"Anything?" Dan rumbled against her ear, knowing exactly what she was doing.

She looked at it. Two texts from mum. Nothing from Isla. "No."

"She'll be okay," he reassured her, his arms gently squeezing.

"I hope so." The dream had left its mark, as had the last two days of worry. She unlocked the phone and fired her sister a text asking her to call when she woke up, then opened her mum's messages and groaned.

Dan raised his head off the pillow, his brow wrinkled as his sleep-filled gaze adjusted to the glow from the phone, and he mimicked her groan as a question.

"Nothing. Just Mum." *Mum and her over-excited chatter about Carrie's relationship status with Dan.*

His lips quirked and he dropped back down to the pillow with a soft snort. "Dare I ask?"

"She wants to know if you'd like to come for Sunday dinner today."

"She's asking that at this time in the morning?"

"No," she wriggled against him playfully. "She sent it last night, while we were otherwise engaged."

He grunted, his arm maneuvering her into rolling on top of him, and his hardness greeted her lower belly. Heat, instant and fierce, licked at her loins, her tummy contracting over it just as he grumbled, "I'd like to be otherwise engaged right about now."

"You're insatiable," she breathed.

"And you are a bonafide tease."

"Tease?" She gave a small laugh, her belly rippling over him. He gripped her tighter. "A tease wouldn't have let you have your wicked way with her for virtually an entire weekend."

He considered her, cocking his head to one side with a deliciously boyish expression. "True."

"But I am going to resist you now and make coffee," she said, pushing up on his chest. As much as she hated to admit it, she was worn out, both in body and mind, and physically sore. That was a new one for her: too much sex. Who'd have thought it?

He squeezed the cheeks of her arse and gave her a pout that set off her giggles again. "So long as I get you post-caffeine fix."

She rolled away from him, shaking her head. The sudden lightness after the weight of her nightmare had made her feel disorientated. But with Dan around, it was easy to feel like nothing could cut too deep, he had that magic power…her heart fluttered as she rose off the bed and picked up his T-shirt from the floor. She slipped it over her head. It was the same tee she had taken to wearing since hitting his bed Friday night, but it still smelled appealingly of him—a deep, oceanic scent that flooded her nostrils and soothed her further as she headed to the kitchen. It was no surprise her own smell hadn't smothered it; not when she'd barely been clothed since that night.

A small smile played about her lips as she entered the open plan living space that was so him. The clean, masculine lines; the soft tones to the furnishings; the predominantly glass walls that let in the early morning sun and the view that carried for miles—it was his own rooftop paradise. No wonder he chose to live here, above his place of work, when he woke to this every morning.

She loaded the coffee maker and set it going. Her eyes returned to the sun peeking on the horizon and she headed to the balcony doors, testing the handle and finding it unlocked. She pulled it open and cool air swept over her, its crisp, clean scent encouraging her to take a deep, slow breath.

She loved this time of the day. The calm before the storm, before the world started to move in earnest. And with it being a Sunday, everything was still so quiet, so at peace.

"When you said you were making coffee, I hadn't expected you to babysit the machine," he drawled, his presence surprising her.

"Not jealous of a coffee maker, are you?" She turned to give him a smile over her shoulder and froze midway, her mouth drying up in an instant. He'd thrown on a pair of low-slung lounge pants, his broad chest, his glorious tattoo all deliciously bare. His hair was mussed-up, post-fuck style. But it was his eyes that truly got to her, the emotion sitting just beneath the surface. She swallowed. *What was it you'd said about being too sore?*

"I could be." He stalked towards her and she felt her heart skip, love running so thick and fast in her veins she was scared she'd never be the same. She'd loved him before, but she'd been strong enough to leave; this time, she knew she'd do anything to stay.

Or maybe you've grown as selfish as everyone assumes? You don't even know if Isla is okay, and yet here you are, living out your fairy tale…

She swallowed down the thought, turning to look back at the view and hide her sudden guilt from his astute gaze. "Well that's a ridiculous thing to be jealous of."

"Is it?" he murmured, his arms slipping around her middle. "In that case, I am one hundred percent ridiculous."

She rested back into him unable to help her amused giggle, her tension easing as quickly as it had surfaced. "You have a beautiful view."

"I do. It's part of the reason I live here…that and the convenient commute to work."

She smoothed her palms over his forearms and hugged him to her, loving how the rising sun's rays washed over her front as his heat radiated against her back.

He dropped his head to her neck. "This is where I enjoy my coffee most mornings."

"Really?" She smiled, imagining the domestic scene and painting her own presence in it. She wished that could be their new norm—every morning, here, together. "I got the impression the bedroom was more your home."

He laughed against her. "Only with you around."

"Well, this time, I want to do what you do. Like a normal morning."

"A normal morning?"

"Yes. What does the wonderful Dan Stevenson do on a typical Sunday morning?"

She felt him stiffen, his head lifting a little, and she wondered if she'd overstepped some hidden boundary that had put him on edge. But then he moved away, his stride light as he headed into the kitchen. "In that case, it's coffee with salmon and eggs on the balcony, followed by gym and work. You sure you want to do all that?"

She smiled and hugged herself, instantly missing his hold. "Okay, I'll take the coffee and the food, but the rest you can keep."

"I hoped you'd say that. I have something else in mind for later."

"You do?" A little bubble of excitement erupted in her belly.

"I do."

"And am I going to like that something?" she drawled out.

He gave her a look, his eyes sharp and unreadable. "I think so."

"Can you at least tell me what it is?"

"Nope, it's a surprise."

"A surprise?" She frowned at him. "I don't do surprises."

"Trust me, you'll do this one."

"A clue, then?" She batted her lashes for effect and he rewarded her with a laugh, it's husky lilt thrilling her to the core. "Pretty please?"

"Okay, okay. I'm taking you out for lunch."

"Ah." Her heart sank. "I can't do that, Dan. Not without panicking someone's going to recognize me."

He grinned at her. "You don't need to worry about that—not where we're going."

She watched him navigate the kitchen, taking out the eggs and salmon from the fridge and digging out the pans. He was completely at ease, while she…

It's okay, she told herself. At least lunch meant he wasn't suggesting they part just yet. *And if he says it's okay, it will be.*

"You fancy helping?"

His question pulled her back and she shook her head with a grimace. "I'm rubbish in the kitchen."

"In that case, I'll teach you."

He held out his hand to her and she walked towards him, every step taking her closer to calm, to the sense of belonging and being exactly where she wanted to be. Always.

***

"Oh my God, Dan. You remembered?"

He looked across at Carrie in the passenger seat of his car, her face alive with wonder, and felt his insides soar. He was in so deep now that he couldn't imagine climbing out. And now maybe he wouldn't have to.

So much had changed in the last twenty-four hours alone. Having her to himself, enjoying one another and talking openly about the past—both before and after she'd left—had made things between them feel different. *He* felt different.

"Of course I remembered." He bent forward to look through the windscreen and up at the mountain trail laid out before them. "It's not every day a guy gets to kiss the girl he's been infatuated with since forever."

He heard her little intake of breath, caught the little flicker of her tongue over her lips and his body warmed.

"It was pretty special," she said softly.

Special. Memorable. The works. And here he was wanting to relive it. Only this time he was aware of the risk he was taking and doing it anyway.

He reached into the back for the thermal sweater he'd thrown there earlier and a woolly hat. "Here, it's going to be windy up there, pop these on."

She looked at the clothes and then back at him, her expression priceless. "You want me to wear these?"

"It's either that, or freeze."

He reached back for his own sweater and shrugged it on. "Think of it as a disguise. No one will recognize you in those."

"I'm beginning to think you'll do anything just to get me in your clothing," she grumbled, the sound muffled as she pulled the top on over her own sweater. Her head emerged, her hair over her face, and she blew it away with an upward huff that had him keen to comb his hands through it before sealing off her lips with his own.

"Maybe I will." He couldn't deny it; he loved the sight of her in his clothing, almost as much as he loved her—*shit, there really isn't any going back now.*

He had to take the leap and hope she was ready to come with.

He took a breath to take the edge off, and reached across her to open his glovebox and retrieve his own hat. Somehow, he forced his hands to stay on task and not curve over her thighs. They'd had enough sex—they were practically raw from it—and yet his body refused to quiet, as did his heart.

He straightened and pulled on the hat, yanking open his car door before he did something that could get them arrested for indecent exposure.

He climbed out, slamming the door shut and heading straight for Carrie's side. She had it open before he got there and stepped out, running her fingers under the brim of her hat as she scowled at him.

"I must look hideous."

"Yup, totally hideous." He grinned, reaching around her to close the door and then taking her hand. "Better than being spotted though, hey?"

She gave an unladylike snort and his restraint snapped. *Fuck onlookers.* Pulling her to him, he crushed his lips to hers with punishing intent. He'd only meant to make it a short demonstration, a swift release from the pressure building inside them both, but instead her little whimper and instant putty-like state had him going for broke. His body was high on hers by the time he finally broke it off.

She blinked at him, adorably dazed. "What was that for?"

He stepped away before he could throw her into the backseat of the car and do what his every nerve ending was screaming at him to.

"To prove to you that you look far from hideous," he said, heading to the boot of his car and triggering it to open. He leaned past it to give her a pointed look and stilled, his heart taking another hit of her flustered glory. "Did it work?"

She blushed deeper. "Perhaps," she said, smoothing down the dark gray thermal he'd lent her and patting at his similar colored beanie. All the while, her blue eyes evaded him. Their color had never been more striking than it was against the green of the hills and his muted clothing. He chuckled over the pull in his gut and pulled out the backpack he'd asked Max to load up that morning. The guy had practically gaped at him when he'd made the request, then gaped further when he'd asked him to continue fielding his calls for the rest of the day.

"You're taking *another* day off?" he'd asked. Dan had simply smiled and told him he'd be in touch. It wasn't like he hadn't earned it, but then he knew that wasn't what had Max so on edge; Dan didn't forego work for anyone, least of all a woman.

But Carrie wasn't just anyone. She was the one that got away—the one that he now wanted to tie down and keep to himself. If only she could hide away forever, with him. Leave Hollywood behind for good.

Yeah, and how bored would Carrie get then? Without the glitz, the fame, the buzz of her career…

She'd wanted to escape once, but that didn't mean she didn't want to go back.

"It's been a long time since I've hiked," she said, turning to face the track.

"This isn't a hike, it's a stroll."

She eyed him. "Not according to my memory. You had to give me a piggyback over the last stretch."

He shrugged on the backpack, his mind on that exact memory, and locked the car. "I figured you were just making excuses to get close to me. I never for a second thought you were tired."

She smiled, her lashes lowering flirtatiously. "Maybe I was."

He grinned and hooked his arm around her, encouraging her into step alongside him as they made for the trail. "In that case, feel free to do so again."

She laughed, the sound coming so often now he was practically addicted to it, living for the next time it erupted. She dropped her head to his shoulder, the moment brief, but an instinctive sign of affection that had hope swelling in his chest. This could be the future if they wanted it to be—if they could find a way to make it work.

They walked quietly for a bit, Dan's thoughts wrapped up in what their life could be like. He had no idea if she felt the same, or if he was reading too much into the time they'd spent together and her confession about the past. But every time she looked to him, squeezed his hand, wrapped her arms around him, he'd swear he felt it.

"It's so pretty here. It's just as I remember it."

"Yeah, some things don't change." He shrugged the backpack higher and pulled her around a particularly boggy patch that looked harmless enough if you didn't know it like he did.

A dog scampered up to them, striding straight through it, his legs sinking and coming up caked as his owners stepped readily around.

"You seem well versed in the terrain still?" She eyed him, her intense stare probing. "Do you come here much?"

"When I need to empty my head for a bit, get some fresh air—"

"Impress the ladies?"

She said it teasingly, but he could feel the genuine question there all the same. "No, no ladies. Not here."

"Just me then?"

"Just you."

The unsaid meaning hung in the air between them as they continued on, and eventually she spoke up. "Have there been many? You said there had been, well, you implied there had, but have there? I mean serious ones?"

"Good God, no. I don't go in for *serious* ladies."

She dug him in the ribs, her laugh gentle but awkward. "You know what I mean."

He met her eye, pausing on the crest of a hill. Their picnic spot was only a few meters away—the spot where he had kissed her that very first time—and any need to lie blew away with the wind that whistled around them. He curved his hand around her cheek and felt her hair whip around his fingers.

"I know what you mean," he murmured, closing the gap between them, "and my answer remains no."

He brought his other hand up, cupping her face in his hold as his thumb brushed across her perfect lips. "There has been no one serious, not since you."

Her eyes watered in the breeze, but she didn't break contact. "In ten years?" she whispered, her disbelief evident.

"In ten years." And then he bowed his head, his lips sealing his confession. She had been honest with him, and now he had done the same.

She curved into him, her sigh carried away on the wind. "Sounds lonely."

"About as lonely as you in Hollywood?"

"Yes." Her voice was soft, earnest, sad even.

And then she stiffened, the sound of her phone buzzing shattering their connection. *Goddamnit.*

"Isla," she gasped, breaking away from him to dig inside her jeans pocket and pull it out. She checked the screen. "It *is* Isla."

He nodded, trying to be supportive, it was the call she so desperately wanted after all. "You best get it."

But the disappointment was hard to shift. He'd felt they were close to something—close to carving out a path together.

Eagerly she swiped at the phone and turned away from him, raising it to her ear. "Hey you! How are you?"

He watched her walk away, back to the spot where they'd shared their moment all those years ago, and let her have her privacy. There would be time for them later.

He dropped the picnic bag to the ground and considered their options long term. There had to be a way to make it work. So long as they were together, surely the rest would fall into place.

He lay out the picnic blanket and took a seat, his sights on the view and ears tuning in to Carrie's growing excitement. He could hear his own name being thrown in, and he listened harder.

"I have never heard Brad say anything like what he has said to you," she was saying. "In all the time I've known him, I wouldn't have thought him capable of saying those things. That has to mean something."

A pause.

"I do, sis," she stressed. "And if he has fallen for you, then this lie, this deception, it shouldn't get in the way of that."

Another pause.

"You need to make him understand Isla, blame me for it all, it was my doing anyway, you were just being a loyal sister...absolutely! And don't you take any nonsense from him, let him rant at me."

He smiled at her insistence, at the hope in her voice.

"You promise me, you'll stand your ground, Isla, and send the shit my way? Don't just try, do it! You guys are clearly made for each other."

And were *they* made for each other too? Carrie and him? Did she feel as deeply as he did?

"If he turns you away, I'll fly out there myself and knock him silly."

The idea of Carrie knocking anyone silly would have been ludicrous if he hadn't seen her ability to pick up boxing so readily. And the idea of her smacking Bradley had him grinning.

"Make sure he understands it was all my idea, you hear? That *I* made you do this…look, it was me that told you to keep up the pretense…you told me we should tell him the truth and I begged you not to—remember?"

Now he could hear her guilt, her pain, and it had him rising to close the distance between them. He pulled her into his arms, trying to give her the reassurance she needed but hadn't asked for.

"So, there you go, you put the blame at my feet!" she exclaimed, turning into him. "When is he due back?"

He could hear a muttered response from Isla, and Carrie nodded. "Well, keep me posted, okay?" Then she looked up at him, her eyes so full of emotion that his throat closed over with the reciprocal surge. "I need to go."

Isla said something that had Carrie hesitating, and then she smiled softly. "Dan's waiting for me."

Whatever Isla said had Carrie's eyes flashing and her smile becoming a grin. "Don't you start, you sound like mum!" And then she hummed and gave a "Bye."

She slid the phone back into her pocket as he smoothed his hands down her body, hooking them into the rear pockets of her jeans and pulling her against him. "Not quite on her way home yet then?"

"Nuh-uh."

"You going to fill me in over food?"

"Yes—*crap*." Her expression shifted from happiness to horror so quick he felt whiplashed.

"Crap?"

"Food. Mum. She invited us. You. To dinner. Tonight."

"Ah, yes." He'd forgotten, as had she clearly. "Well, what time do you eat?"

"She used to do it for around five, no idea anymore."

"We can do that."

"But the lunch you've packed—the picnic."

"We can enjoy a little of it, and then I'll drive us over there."

"You sure?"

"Positive," he said, lowering his forehead to hers. "I get the best of both worlds: you here, with me, and then your mum's home cooking. Has to beat whatever Max has pulled together."

"Poor Max." She brushed her lips against his, her eyes softening and taking his chest with them. "But it'll make mum happy. Maybe we shouldn't tell him."

"I don't think he'll mind."

"No?"

"No, his wife and child have taught him well; always keep Mum happy."

"Ooo, I like that," she murmured approvingly. "Speaking of which, I'll just drop her a reply so she doesn't sock it to me for not getting in touch sooner."

"Good idea." He forced himself to release her and headed back to the picnic blanket, unable to wipe the smile from his face. Things were really falling into place. Isla in America, Carrie here. Now all he needed was to convince her to stay.

What, and give up on her dream? Could you do that to her?

But what was the alternative? Him in LA? He couldn't imagine it. His life was here.

And hadn't she fled LA? Wanted to get away? How happy was she really, living out her dream?

Maybe she was ready to come home. Maybe she was ready for a new dream...

Chapter Fourteen

HER MUM WAS IN HER ELEMENT FUSSING over the two of them, stuffing them both full and then loading up more. It was Carrie who broke first.

"Mum, I can't eat any more."

"Nonsense," her mother rebuked, tutting over her. "You need plumping up a little as it is—tell her, Dan."

Dan looked from her mum back to Carrie, and she glared at him as if daring him to even try.

"It's more than my life's worth getting involved with this one," he said. "But I'll take that extra slice of apple pie. It's the best I've ever tasted."

Her mum beamed at him, as did Carrie, and in one swift move he'd changed the subject and the situation was diffused.

Carrie relaxed back into her chair, admiring him as he took the extra helping her mum dished out. She could get used to this. Dinner at mum's, dinner at his place, dinner on a mountain. Anywhere so long as he was there, by her side.

"Is that your phone again, Carrie?"

"Hmm?"

Her mum was right; she could vaguely make out a buzzing coming from the sideboard where she'd left it, and for a second she wanted to ignore it. But there were only a few people whose numbers were set to divert to Isla's phone—the ones important enough to keep in touch with, and Isla herself. She had to get it. At least check who it was.

"It is, sorry, Mum, I best get it." She pushed back from her seat and stood, her brain racing over who it could be and stumbling when she saw it was her agent calling.

"Ann-Marie," she said, lifting it to her ear and trying not to sound as apprehensive as she felt. "What's up?"

"Ah, Carrie, darling, so glad I caught you," she sing-songed down the line. "How is the fabulous land of nod?"

She gave a disgruntled laugh. "It's England, Ann-Marie, not the middle of nowhere."

But even as she said it, she recognized her own view in Ann-Marie's words. It was an opinion she'd held for years, but not anymore. She glanced at Dan and her Mum, who were both looking to her expectantly, and mouthed, "My agent."

They nodded, but the strange unease she glimpsed in Dan's gaze caught at her.

"Well, whatever," Ann-Marie dismissed. "We need you wrapping up your business pronto."

Her hand tightened around the phone. "We do?"

"*Absolutely*, I have such exciting news."

She could feel the color draining from her face, and Dan's eyes narrowed in response. "You do?"

"Good Lord, you sound petrified. Is everything okay? I know you needed a break, but if this is what it's done to you, maybe you shouldn't have gone at all."

"Don't be crazy, it's just Sunday. Day of rest and all that."

"Sunday, Schmunday, since when has that ever bothered you?"

She had a point. It was a question she could answer all too readily; the answer was staring straight at her.

"Carrie? Are you there? I don't have all day and this is H-U-G-E, *huge*, you are going to be beside yourself when you hear."

She gave herself a shake. She was being ridiculous; this was her career they were discussing, and if Ann-Marie said it was huge then it sure would be. She looked away from Dan and grinned, her acting skills coming to her aid. "Lay it on me, honey."

"Ah, that's better, now you sound like you," she cooed. "You wouldn't *believe* who I've just had lunch with?"

"Wh—"

"Only Kimmy-Bloody-Diaz."

She knew Diaz mainly by reputation; the woman was at the top of her game. She was the filmmaker everyone wanted to work with, and just as hard to be cast by.

"And?" She could sense where this was going, and felt a spark of excitement even as she acknowledged it wasn't as powerful as it should have been.

"And she wants you! She's put in a special request, wants you out here ASAP to meet with you."

"How soon is ASAP?"

"Oh, does it matter, darling? She says jump, we just ask how high—right?"

"Right."

"Sorry, can't hear you, Carrie…are you sure you're feeling okay? I was expecting to have to hold the phone away from my ear to cope with your screaming. I mean it's a starring role, all about you—well, a girl called Henrietta to be exact, but still…"

Carrie forced a smile, injecting enthusiasm into her voice. She would have time to rationalize it all later and make herself realize how huge this was, but right now, all she could think was that it meant leaving. Leaving England. Leaving Mum. Leaving Dan.

"It's fabulous, honey, really pleased, I have a few things that need addressing and then I'll sort some flights out. Will be a few weeks at the earliest."

Whatever the case, she'd see Isla's club finished first.

"A few weeks? Goodness me, I'm not sure she's going to be all that impressed, can't you—"

"No."

"No…right…okay then, I'll see what she says."

"Thanks, Ann-Marie."

"Will call you when I hear back."

"That would be great, but make it tomorrow at the earliest. I'm having dinner with family tonight."

She was vaguely aware of her agent agreeing as she lowered the phone and cut the call, but her head was circumnavigating one single question: *now what?*

She had two weeks to get Isla's club back on track and somehow sort out her future with Dan. It was a future she really wanted, but would he come to LA? Would he even consider it? And if he wouldn't, could she consider staying here?

When you have Kimmy Diaz offering you the role of your career? Are you crazy?

She was beginning to think she was…

Dan watched Carrie replace the phone on the sideboard, aware of the shifting mood in the room. It was coming from her mother as much as him.

"So come on then, dear, what was all that about?" Helen's eyes sparkled, but there was a sadness in their depths, or maybe it was him projecting his own inner turmoil on her? He didn't know; he just knew he didn't want to hear what was coming.

Carrie walked back to her seat, lowering herself into it before looking to her mum with a smile that smacked of being artificial. "Well, you won't believe it."

"Try us?" His voice was hard; he hadn't wanted it to be, but he couldn't keep the edge out of it. Both Carrie and her mother's eyes swept to him, and he could feel Helen's sympathy already, could feel Carrie's defenses rise before she even spoke.

"It appears Kimmy Diaz has asked if I will appear in one of her films."

"Kimmy Diaz." Her mum frowned. "The same Kimmy who keeps sweeping up the Oscars year after year?"

"Yes, the very same," Carrie returned smoothly, her attention dropping to her plate as she picked up her spoon to fold and re-fold her apple pie. "She wants to meet with me as soon as she can to talk through it…back in LA."

"Of course," her mother said, taking up her wine glass for a considerable sip. He could practically feel her effort to control her emotions. Or was he still projecting? He wished he hadn't said he'd take the extra pie. The last thing he wanted now was to eat anything.

Kimmy Diaz. Like hell he could compete with that; he shouldn't even be trying. This was her—this was Carrie Evans, the actress, the star. This was her dream. It didn't matter that she'd run home—that probably had more to do with Bradley than her career. And he couldn't stand in the way of this, not if it's clearly what she still wanted.

"When will you go?" he asked, taking up his spoon and scooping up a large helping but tasting nothing as he waited for her confirmation.

She turned to him slowly, her head tilted as though considering what she was going to say next. "I'll take the flight I originally planned, the day after the launch party. I'd hoped to stay a bit longer and spend some time with…with Isla…but it gives me enough time to sort the club and also…"

She broke off, her eyes intent on him, like she was trying to find the right words and failing. Was she feeling guilty about having to leave all over again?

"That should be plenty of time," he said, coming to her aid. "The party will be the biggest demand on your time, I think."

"The party?"

"Yes. The foreman will have the rest in hand, you just need to make sure you're on hand for the odd query and get that party organized."

"What about you? Where will you be?"

Far enough away from here.

Far enough to get his head together and do the right thing when the time came.

To say goodbye.

He coughed and wiped his mouth with his napkin. "I have some work that needs tending to up North. I'll be back in time for the launch party. Sooner if I can manage it."

"Oh." Her throat bobbed, her lashes fluttering as her eyes returned to her plate. Was that guilt he'd seen in them? Sadness? Something else? "I see, of course. I understand."

He could feel Helen's perceptive stare as she took it all in, and he wished to God that he and Carrie were alone. He wanted to tell her he didn't blame her; that he'd loved every second of the time they had shared, but that he had to end it now, before…

Before what?

You're already in love with her.

He did, so much it hurt.

But that's why he had to give her up now. Free her to get back to the life she always dreamed of, the life she was destined for…

"Speaking of work, I do need to go, ladies." He pushed his chair back and stood, both sets of eyes following him. "I have packing to do, and I've kept Carrie from you enough already this weekend."

"Oh, nonsense, Dan." Helen stood. "You don't need to leave yet. In fact, you could stay if you wanted."

"*Mum.*" Carrie looked to her with open horror.

"Oh hush, darling, I merely meant he could take the sofa."

"Yes, I'm sure you did," Carrie muttered and Dan felt his cheeks heat through the sadness.

"That's really kind of you, but I do have to get home."

"Oh, very well. In that case, why don't you see Dan out, Carrie, and I'll clear up."

"Why don't I help with that?" he asked, guilt at not having offered in the first place setting in, his manners having been momentarily forgotten in the tide of pain .

"Not at all, you're our guest. Now come on, Carrie, don't keep Dan waiting." Helen dropped a hand to her shoulder and gave it a squeeze. "He has things to do."

"Sure," she said quietly, rising slowly. Her gaze flitted to him briefly before she made for the doorway and stepped out into the hall. He followed close behind, his mind racing with a million-and-one things to say and none of them feeling right. The thing he wanted to say most—I love you—was the worst one of all. He wouldn't hang that over her—not again.

She pulled open the door and turned to look up at him. Her eyes were so full of sadness that his chest squeezed, his lungs struggling for air.

"I guess I'll see you around," she murmured.

"See me around?" His brow raised. "You'll see me at the party, maybe before."

"I thought…" She lowered her lashes, her lower lip trembling and sending a shudder through him. "I thought, you and I, I thought…"

She broke off and he reached for her on instinct, his hands caressing her arms through her sweater. "Hey, we've had fun. We've made amends. I don't regret a second of it."

"Fun?" Her eyes lifted to his, their fire sudden and surprising.

"I certainly thought so." He stood his ground. He had to get through this. He could beat himself up later, but right now he had to put them on the right track. "Let's not pretend it's more than it is. It could never be more. Our lives are worlds apart; you know that, Carrie."

"But—"

"I know you said you left for Isla, and I believe you, but just think—if you hadn't, you never would have achieved the career you dreamed of. You never would have become the star you are."

Her eyes wavered, his words hitting home.

"You know I'm right," he pressed on. "So let's just see this for what it was: a chance to wipe the slate clean and start afresh...as friends."

"Friends?"

"Well, close friends."

"Friends with benefits?" She was joking, he could tell in the quirk to her lips, but her words were weak with tears that hadn't quite fallen.

He gave a small laugh. "I'll take all the benefits you throw my way whenever you are back in the UK."

"Why don't you come to LA?"

"I'm sure I could manage the occasional holiday."

"I meant—"

He cut her off with his mouth. He knew what she was going to say, and he couldn't give her the answer she wanted. Closing the geographical barrier didn't change the fact that they were two very different people—that she aspired to more than he could ever want or give. She'd told him as much when she'd left ten years ago...

But she's already explained that away, already told you it was just a lie to push you away.

But had it been, deep down?

She'd got it all in the end, just as she'd said she would. She had become the star, regardless of what her reasoning had been back then. And she needed someone who knew her world, who would revel in it alongside her. He could never be that man. And if she came to the UK, she would get bored eventually, tiring of the ordinary and wanting to return to the glitz-and-glamor. He couldn't hang around and wait for that to happen.

The more he thought on it, the harder his kiss became, possession born on instinct leading him to claim her mouth over and over. It was her moan of submission that brought him to his senses—the moan that told him she was wet and ready for him and had his cock only too eager to respond.

He tore his mouth away, and she blinked up at him. "Stay, *please?*"

He stroked his thumb across her swollen lips, his eyes fixed there. They were unable to meet the plea in her own. "I can't."

And then he turned and walked away, not daring to look back. Not even for a second.

He was doing what was right for her. And himself.

He only wished his brain would quit with its insistence that he was making the biggest mistake of his life.

Chapter Fifteen

HE'D GONE. HE'D TRULY GONE. SHE HADN'T believed it at first, but as the days had gone by—five and counting—and there'd been no sign of him, not even a text message to check in, she knew it for what it was: a reality check.

A reminder that it truly had just been a bit of fun for him.

No matter that they'd shared so much since her return; no matter that things had changed between them enough for her to be hopeful of a future together, one she'd believed he wanted too. It had clearly been just her and her own foolish imaginings.

And she was mad. Mad that she'd let herself get in too deep; let herself fall in love all over again. For not being excited over Kimmy-*bloody*-Diaz and her career-rocketing role.

But if not for the anger, she'd feel dead inside. Lost. It was Isla's club that kept her busy, stopped her from wallowing. And Carrie Evans didn't wallow; she got things done. Which was a timely reminder that she was supposed to be calling the electricians to shift some sockets.

Giving a sigh, she lifted her phone from the bar, and as if by magic it started to ring. *Isla.*

It was early stateside, and her heart fluttered inside her chest. *Please let it be good news. Let one of us be okay.*

She answered the call, raising it to her ear. "Hey honey." She cringed. The endearment was her superficial go-to, the one she used when putting a face on, and her sister would know she wasn't okay.

"Carrie."

She forgot her slip-up as soon as her Dad's voice registered and panic sent her words rushing out. "Dad? what's going on, where's Isla? How have you got her phone?"

"Hey, slow down sweetheart. Take a breath"

"Where is she? Dad, what's happened?"

"She's okay, she's here. We're at mine."

"Where's Brad?"

Her father's sigh was heavy, and it twisted at Carrie's heart. "Dad, tell me."

"He's at home, I guess. I don't know for sure, but he knows...he knows about your switch."

"Isla told him?" *Please let Isla have told him.*

"No, not intentionally...he overheard us talking."

"But how? Isla refused to speak to you, she wouldn't listen to me when I told her to see you—she wouldn't even contemplate it." She was trembling, her hand shaking over the phone, her mind running away with horror after horror of possibility. "She wouldn't come to you unless...oh God, how bad is it?"

"She didn't come to me. Brad did. He wanted me to be there when he proposed...to you."

Her ears started to ring, her vision blurring over. "Proposed?"

"Yes. On a yacht. He had it all planned out and had me flown in especially. He was going to deliver a grand proposal in front of his family, in front of me. He'd gone to a lot of effort, he really had..."

"Uh-huh." She could barely hear her own prompt as he fell silent, the blood ringing in her ears making it hard to hear.

"But when I arrived, it didn't take long to realize she wasn't you, her contempt was obvious, even after ten long years..." He sighed, the sound heavy even down the line. "And I couldn't keep quiet, as soon as he was out of earshot, I had it out with her. I was too stunned to keep my mouth shut."

Now he sounded guilty, like he was shouldering some of the blame. She knew where this was going, and she didn't want to hear it; didn't want the confirmation. But she knew she had to listen. There was no escaping the truth.

"What happened?"

"Brad came back while we were talking," he admitted softly. "He overheard enough to know what had happened, to know who Isla was."

"How did he take it?" she asked on auto-pilot.

"Like you'd expect. He kicked us off the yacht. Told your sister he never wanted to see her…you…any of us again. I can't blame him. What you did, what you both did…He wouldn't let Isla explain. He wouldn't hear any of it. Isla collapsed—"

"*Collapsed?*" Carrie croaked out.

"She took it badly. We've chatted some…I get that she loves him, that she believed he'd fallen in love with her too, thinking she was you, but it's so wrong Carrie. What were you even thinking pulling a stunt like that?"

"I know, Dad, I know, but I had to get away. Things were a mess and I felt suffocated. Brad was meant to be away filming—all Isla had to do was keep up appearances so that the press would stay off my back. Then Brad came home early and…and…"

"You asked her to keep up the pretense?"

"Yes, but I didn't know she'd fall in love with him, or that he would do the same."

"I don't know about that, love. It's clear Isla loves him, but Brad…he was real angry. When he asked me about proposing it was clear he loved you—*her*. But his face when we left…"

"I'm convinced he loves her. From all that she has said, all that I know of him, I can't believe he doesn't. I have to make this right. I have to speak to him."

"You can try sweetheart, but I'm not sure what good it will do."

"I don't care. I have to try."

"Well, in the meantime, she's staying with me—about the only good thing to come out of this is that she's at least talking to me now. It's a start. But she's going to want to come home soon. She's already talking about booking her flights."

"Okay, Dad, can you keep me posted? Get her to ring me even? When she feels up to it?"

"Of course."

"Thanks, Dad."

"Bye, sweetheart."

"Erm…Dad."

"Yes?"

She wanted to tell him about the club, all the great things she'd put in place for Isla's homecoming, but she couldn't do it. It all seemed so pointless now. If Isla felt as soulless as Carrie did without Dan, then the club would be the last thing on her mind.

She'd tell Dad later, when the dust had settled and she'd had time to apologize to Brad. She'd make him realize that she was to blame, that Isla was innocent and that he was free to love her; that he *should* love her. Isla deserved it.

"Nothing. It's nothing. I'll speak to you later."

She hung up the phone and immediately dialled Brad's mobile, fingers trembling as adrenalin fired through her system. It rang and rang, then went to voicemail.

She tried his work number. No luck. She tried his mobile again and left a voicemail begging him to call before giving him Isla's number and confessing her guilt.

She paced the bar, planning her words for when he did call. She went over and over it like she was rehearsing a part in a new movie. She couldn't get this wrong.

But she needn't have bothered.

Two days later and still no call from Brad, still no contact from

Dan. She was still pacing the same floor, wearing the same blue overalls and disposable shoe covers.

Her anger was going strong, and it was the only thing getting her through. Anger at herself for believing in a future with Dan. Anger at Dan for leaving. Anger at Brad for not giving her the chance to explain, to defend Isla. Anger at life for being so damn complicated.

And then there was the guilt. Even her sister hadn't spoken to her directly yet. She was too hurt, too messed up by it all.

The only thing she could do to stop herself going out of her mind with it was focus on the club. Isla was due back any day now and they needed all hands on deck, including hers, if they were to get it in a state for Isla to see.

She let go of a heavy breath and quit pacing. It was time she got down to work, too.

Taking up her paint roller, she slopped it into the tray at her feet, coating it in deep red. Stray hairs fell across her face, coming loose from her ponytail, and she brushed them back with her free arm. Christ, she looked like hell—felt like hell. She was tired, and her body ached. She wasn't used to manual labour, and two days of it had already started to take its toll. It had given her a newfound admiration for the people that did this day in and day out, especially those working with her and being kind enough not to take the piss when she made a rookie error.

"I never thought I'd live to see this day."

Dan's voice washed over her bent body, heat seeping into every pore. It couldn't be...

She schooled her expression, her emotions, before straightening up and turning.

And there he was. Dan. All in black: black leather jacket, black jeans, black T. So dark and sexy.

Not clad in blue overalls and looking a sight.

Color surged in her cheeks, embarrassment combusting with

frustrated anger. "I was beginning to think the same about seeing you again."

His grin was lazy and riled her blood further, not to mention what it did to her libido, her heart. "Sounds like you missed me?"

She raised her chin. "I wouldn't take it that way."

"Now you just sound angry."

She sucked in breath—*angry, excited, angry, excited…it was a dizzying mix.*

"I never realized that you in overalls could be so damn sexy."

Her lips parted to say something clever, anything, but her brain emptied with the hit of pleasure, the reassurance that he *still* desired her even in this state,.

But he left you, remember.

"Stop it, Dan."

He raised his brow in exaggerated innocence, his arms spread wide as he shrugged. "What?"

"Don't tease me."

"I wasn't teasing. I was speaking the truth."

He closed the gap between them and she stepped back, casting her eye over the others in their presence and noting how they were all finding someplace else to be. It wasn't just her that his presence had command over. He had them all disappearing just as he wanted. But what for? What did he want from her?

"Are you here to check on progress?" She injected ice into her tone. She didn't need him messing with her head—her heart—not when everything was already going wrong.

His brow lifted a little as he halted. "Sorry, I…" He shook his head and looked away, his hands planting into his pockets. "I couldn't stay away."

Her heart sang at the confession and at the way his shoulders softened, the words costing him. *But he still left, remember? Dismissed you as a bit of fun. It doesn't change anything. It doesn't give you what you want.*

"You mean, you missed our fun?" She hated the emotion straining her voice, hated the way her eyes hurt, but there'd been so much more in her request for him to stay, and he should have known it—should have seen it. He should've stayed and given them a chance.

His eyes snapped to her, their depths probing, and she couldn't bear it. She turned away and threw her focus into work, into rolling paint on the wall; the motion was far more aggressive than it needed to be, but it was helping. *It's not his fault you saw more in it. It's not his fault you wanted more.*

"I missed you."

Her eyes squeezed tight, the roller freezing in its progression. Inside, her heart soared; butterflies danced. But he only missed the fun. *Don't get sucked in. Not again.*

She forced her hand to move. "It was fun worth missing, but I don't have time for it right now. I have a club to sort and you're…" Her heart panged painfully in her chest. "You're a distraction, and I'd be grateful if you left."

She was pummelling the wall now, her roller leaving streaks of paint on either side as it slurped along, but she didn't care. She needed him gone. She needed the pain to stop.

The silence stretched out between them. Finally, she heard him move, the air seeping from her lungs in relief, in disappointment. What did she want? For him to just grab her and kiss the week away? Kiss her until all sense and anger were gone?

Yeah, like that's going to help with tomorrow and the day after, and the day after that, when he's had his fill of fun again.

She kept on rolling long after the door had clicked shut and the roller was bare, her hand aching from the constant motion and pressure. Then she dropped back and stared at the wall, refusing to let the tears fall.

You don't have a right to be angry with him.
You left him ten years ago. He left you a week ago. It's karma.
Well, karma fucking sucks.

She took a shaky breath and swept her free hand through her hair.

Pondering karma isn't going to help you get the club finished.

The door swung open behind her and her mutinous heart soared. She turned towards it—*Dan?*

It was just the foreman, plus, a couple of guys from the team. Her heart sunk into her belly.

"Looking good, Miss Evans," the foreman nodded to her.

"Thanks, Tom." She gave him a smile, although she knew it was watery and pathetic.

"We're all set to clean up in the other rooms," he said. "Just have these guys finishing the second fix."

"Great."

She turned back to the wall—second fix, electrics, she was learning. Isla would never believe it. She started towards the tray, ready to go again. Her focus was returning, and she felt stronger, more determined. She'd show Isla—she'd show herself. She could do this.

The door swung open. This time she didn't look, and her heart behaved as she bent to load up the roller.

"Right, put me to use."

Carrie froze in position, her derriere proffered towards him and sparking many enticing images, none of which helped his cause that second. He was there to help her get the club finished. Although, he couldn't deny he wanted the rest, too.

A week away, and the inner rant telling him he was screwing up had won out. He shouldn't have run; he should've made the most of every last second they'd had left together. But there would be time for regrets later—what he wouldn't regret was this time now, being there for her. The second Helen had called to tell him about the disaster stateside, he'd dropped everything. Carrie needed him, and whether she accepted it or not, he would be there for her.

Slowly she righted and turned towards him, roller in hand. "I wasn't kidding, Dan. Isla is on her way home and—" She broke off, her eyes landing on him and scanning top-to-toe. "Where did you get those?"

"You mean the overalls?" He looked himself over too and gestured to the doorway with his thumb. "Contractors have spares in the van. Same designer as yours, I'd guess."

He was trying to lighten the mood—anything to get back on good footing with her. But Carrie didn't look amused and his shoulders sagged. Perhaps he'd have better luck going for straight up honesty. "Look, I know you're running out of time and I know Isla's on her way home. Your mum called and told me everything."

She frowned, frustration, anger, and disbelief all blazing in her fiery blues. "She did? Well, fan-bloody-tastic! So, she doesn't think me capable of getting this done alone either?"

"It's nothing like that," he hurried out. Who else didn't think she was capable? *Him?* Hell, she'd proved her worth to him a thousand times over. Or was it just her own breaking resolve coming through? "She was worried about you—Christ, *I* was worried."

Her eyes narrowed as she gave a loaded laugh. "Well, how thoughtful of you."

"Please don't be like this, Carrie. Of course I was worried. I knew you'd be taking all this on yourself...blaming yourself. I had to come back and make sure you were okay."

"I'm fine." She sniffed, her free arm sweeping back over her forehead. She didn't look fine; she looked tired and clammy. He stepped forward and her eyes flashed dangerously. "No thanks to you."

He stilled, his blood running cold at her rejection. He got that she was stressed—under pressure—but this was more than that. This was about them.

He shook his head. "I just wanted what was best, all round."

"Well, what's best right now is for me not to get distracted again, by *you*, and get this club ready." Carrie's voice wobbled, her lower lip trembling, and Dan's fists clenched in tune with his heart. "It's the least I can do for fucking over her life."

He wanted to reach for her, to hold her close and tell her it would all be okay.

"And don't look at me all sympathetic and sorry," she blurted. "I know I deserve what's coming."

"Hey, I—"

"But Isla doesn't." She shook the paint roller at him, uncaring that it splattered its fresh load over the coverings as well as their clothes. "He won't even speak to her, let her anywhere near him, all because of me...and *you* said—" she thrust the roller forward, and he sidestepped the spray aimed directly at him, "—you said, that if he loved her, he'd see past it."

"I know. But it's a shock. He just needs time."

"Yeah, well, time isn't on our side anymore. I want this place cleaned up to show her tomorrow evening."

"And that's why you need me," he stressed. "Let me stay. Let me help."

She considered him, hesitation written on her face.

"Look I just want what's best for you both. Let me prove it to you...I have something outside for you to see."

She frowned, his change in tack clearly surprising her. He only hoped it would win her over. "Like what?"

"It's a surprise."

Her lashes fluttered. Was she thinking about his last surprise? Hell, he'd feasted on the memory all week. No matter how much he thought he was protecting himself—protecting her—from future pain, he couldn't deny this ingrained desire to be with her; to think on every second they had shared, and want more.

"Come," he said, offering out his hand. "I'll show you."

She moved, sidestepping him and his outstretched hand completely. "You best be quick about it."

At least she's coming, he told himself, following close behind her.

As they reached the doorway, he swept around her. "Let me."

She looked to him, daggers flying, but he ignored her to push the door open.

Outside, two men were hauling his surprise out of a van, hidden beneath a dust sheet. They looked to him as he approached.

"Can you give the lady a sneak peek?"

"Of course," one of them said as they maneuvered it to rest against the wall.

Nerves fluttered up his chest. Would she like it? Would she be pleased? Grateful?

"You ready for it?" he said, turning to look at her and seeing only curiosity in her gaze. It beat the cold hard look of seconds before.

"Yes."

The guys flipped the sheet up, his eyes staying fixed on her. And there it was: sheer joy. Heaven in her face as she inhaled sharply, her hand lifting to her mouth, her eyes wide and glittering. "Oh, my goodness, Dan, it's perfect."

He knew it was. As was she, and he couldn't take his eyes off her as she walked forward to trace her fingers over the twisted gold lettering that spelled out *Isla's Haven*.

"It fits Isla's drawings to the letter," she said softly.

"Lucky that, would hate to make a spelling mistake on the signage."

She laughed softly. "You *know* what I mean…it's beautiful…But when, how…"

She shook her head, her eyes meeting with his, before going back to the sign, not so quick that he missed the tears welling. *Christ, she is stunning.*

"Why didn't you say anything?" she asked, her voice shaking.

He closed the distance between them, pausing just behind her. "I figured with you being so busy with the interior, that this was something I could take care of."

She spun into him, surprising him by swinging her arms about his neck and hopping on her tiptoes to plant a kiss to his cheek. And then she dropped back, the moment broken just as swiftly.

"Thank you," she said to the floor, her arms wrapping around her middle.

He wanted to reach for her, but he didn't dare. He'd made her happy for a second, but he wasn't any better off—he still had no idea whether he was welcome or not.

"It's the least I could do."

"I hadn't even thought of it, you know." She raised her hands to her eyes, her fingers rubbing at them aggressively before releasing them red-rimmed. "I'd been so busy concentrating on the work in there that I'd missed this. Something so fundamental, so important...Mum was right to call you. I don't know what I was thinking."

"Don't be crazy, Carrie." He couldn't stop himself from reaching out and nudging her chin up so she'd meet his gaze, but she kept her lashes lowered. "Look at me."

Slowly she did as he asked, her eyes connecting with his and leaving him winded. He wished their audience away; wished the world away. Wanting only her and this moment, to convince her of just how wonderful, how capable she was. "You've achieved so much in such a short space of time. Many people would have failed where you have succeeded. How can you not see that and take pride in it?"

She took hold of his hand and pulled it away. "That may be, Dan, but it's not enough, and it doesn't take away the pain that I've caused."

She looked so tired, so unsure, so vulnerable. It was killing him. "We all make mistakes," he said. "The important thing is how we come back from them." He gave her a small smile. "And right now, you're going above and beyond, and I'm here to help. So let me. Please."

She looked from him to the sign, and back again. "You're really going to muck in."

"If you'll have me."

A small smile played about her lips. "In that case, okay, if only to see you work in overalls, I'll agree to your assistance…but I'm in charge," she said, fingering his chest.

And then she turned and headed back inside, her head held high. He followed behind her, his eyes on her back, his mind on the torrent of emotion whirling up inside.

The smidgen of Carrie Evans, the actress, that had come out at her mother's dinner table had vanished just as swiftly as it had appeared. The person she was when they were together was something else, now he understood her, now he knew what drove her: her love, her family, her heart.

And he would have known it all along, if not for that decade-old lie.

"Where do you want me?" he asked as they approached the area where she had been working.

"You can work with me here," she said without turning. "I'll just get you an extra set of tools."

She headed off into the room next door, and he turned his attention to her handiwork, appreciating the perfect lines, the even coverage, she could really paint—her work was as good as any professional's. And he should know, his late father had been one.

"Here." She came back into the room, a tray and roller in hand.

He took them from her before gesturing to where the ceiling met with the wall. "You do the cutting in yourself too?"

"If you mean the edging—yeah." She stood proud, her hands on her hips as she followed his gaze. Her mood seemed to have lifted. "You impressed?"

"I am." He dipped his head to her, his smile cheeky. "I never would have thought you had it in you."

She smiled, not rising to his gibe. "Truth be told, neither did I."

He saw the sincerity in her eyes and couldn't look away. Two weeks ago, he'd never have believed it possible that he and Carrie would be here like this; that he would feel so utterly caught up in her that she overtook his every thought.

"We should get on," she said softly.

"Yes, we should."

She lifted a brow as he failed to move. "I mean now."

"Yeah...I know."

She fluttered her hands at him, her eyes dancing a little. "Off you go."

He didn't move a muscle. "Sure thing, boss."

"Boss?" Now she smiled, a real, wholehearted smile that lifted him from the inside out. "I could get used to that...it beats princess." She winked at him and turned away, bending forward to lift the handle of her roller and nodding in the direction of a paint pot a couple of feet away. "There's the paint, off you go."

Off you go? All he could do was take in her proffered derriere once more, only now it was within arm's reach.

"Dan?"

"Yeah," he said absentmindedly.

"Stop staring at my arse."

"I'm not."

She sent him a look that had him chuckling. Sassy Carrie was back. "Yes, Princess."

She rolled her eyes at his deliberate use of the pet name she'd just rejected. But to hell with it; she was his princess, and he'd bloody well call her that.

Several hours later, Princess had morphed into Satan. She was a demonic boss lady that could go like a Duracell bunny. And he was wrecked.

Every time he thought she'd pack it in, she simply took up the paint pot and poured more into her tray. The place had long since emptied out when she finally turned to him, her eyes weary, and admitted defeat.

"I think we should call it a night."

"Thank God for that." He threw down his roller and flexed his aching fist. "I was beginning to think you'd have us going all night."

Her smile didn't reach her eyes. "You can head off, I'll lock up."

"Head off? I'm going nowhere without you."

Her brow furrowed, and he suppressed the urge to reach out and smooth it away.

"I said you could help. I didn't say we could pick up where we left off."

"I wasn't suggesting that." Or was he? Deep down, wasn't that exactly what he wanted—to spend the next few days in and out of bed with her before he had to say goodbye?

"No?"

"Okay, yes, I was, kind of." He ran his fingers through his hair, shaking it off as he tried to explain himself. "I don't know, Carrie. I just know that I want you. I can't be with you and not want you. I want you in any way I can have you, until you go back to your life, until you've had enough. I know how fucked up that sounds, I know it sounds masochistic and ridiculous and confusing as fuck."

"You're right there."

"But it's the truth."

She worried over her bottom lip, neither agreeing nor pushing him away, and he switched down a gear. "Well, we need to eat. We can at least do that together."

She nodded gently. "I guess we could do dinner together..." Her hand came up, her brow with it. "As friends."

"Friends." It was better than nothing.

She bent forward and winced, one hand lifting to press into her lower back as she took up a roll of cling film from the floor.

"Sore?"

"A little."

"Here, let me do that." He took the wrap from her and tore off a strip, using it to cover the sponge of her roller.

"You know that trick too?"

"Aye, Dad was a decorator. I used to help him when I was kid."

"I'd forgotten that." She smiled. "I remember your mum though. She used to give me the eye when I came around—she knew we were up to no good." Her cheeks flushed bright with the memory. "Think she felt the need to protect you even more after your dad passed."

He laughed. "Yeah, well, it was just the two of us, and she was no fool. She knew we weren't spending *that long* on homework…she liked you though."

Carrie's eyes narrowed and fell away. "Not so sure her feelings would have stayed that way."

"Hey, don't be like that." He reached for her, pulling her into him regardless of whether she wanted him to or not. He wouldn't have her beating herself up over the past anymore.

"If she'd lived long enough to see it all, she would have seen through it I reckon. Probably would have knocked some sense into me while she was at it."

She hummed into his chest, her sniffle giving away so much. Just how tired and strung out was she? She'd never been quick to cry. Worry over Isla must be taking its toll—*yeah, and what about your whole "it's been fun" spiel? Surely her reaction, her bitter resurrection of it when you arrived, tells you she wants it to be more?*

He closed his eyes and pressed his lips to the top of her hair, breathing in her scent. No, she couldn't be that caught up in him. He couldn't believe it. He wouldn't. It would give him too much hope for a future he didn't dare think possible.

But what if you are wrong? What if it is possible?

He raised his hand to her cheek, his fingers combing through her hair. When his thumb brushed against her skin, he heard her sigh.

"It's been a long day," he said quietly. "How about a takeaway and then I'll massage out those aches?"

She gave a soft snort, followed by another sniffle. "You're going to give me a massage—*as friends*?"

"Why not?"

She looked up at him. "Doesn't a massage involve being partially naked?"

"To do it properly," he said, very seriously. "I'd say so."

"And it wouldn't lead to any funny business?" she asked slowly, a little spark coming alive in her eyes that made him happier than she could ever realize.

"I don't know what massage parlors you've been to—" he raised his brow in mock horror, "—but they sound well dodgy to me."

She giggled, the sound perfect to his beating heart. "In that case, I'd love one."

Chapter Sixteen

SHE FOLLOWED DAN UP THE STAIRS, WISHING yet again that there was a lift and wondering why she was even here at all, especially when his arse was at eye level and far too appealing to her conflicted psyche.

Had he really meant it when he'd suggested their friends with benefits arrangement on Mum's doorstep? No strings; just plain old fun?

She stared at his rear, long and hard. Did she have the strength for that? Was it enough? Was it the perfect compromise?

It left her cold as much as it sent heat simmering down low. *He won't be yours, though. There'll be no commitment, no life together…he could just as easily have another girl in his bed the following week—the following day even.*

Her stomach twisted and she pressed her hand over it, forcing her attention on lifting one leg in front of the other as she huffed out a breath.

He turned to look at her over his shoulder. "Hey, nearly there."

"Yeah, I remember." She remembered alright. Too well. She'd spent far too long reliving their moments together, trying to work out how she could have got things so wrong—how she could have lost sight of their casual arrangement and ended up where she was now, in love and alone.

Well, not quite alone.
He still wants you.
You just want more, and he wasn't foolish enough to fall into that trap with you.
You've only got yourself to blame.

She forced her eyes off his behind, but they found their way back, the heat down low continuing to simmer regardless.

Just go with it.
Use this—the heat between you—and bury the rest.
At least for now.

They reached the landing, and her muscles sang their gratitude.

"I'll run you a hot bath," he said, pausing in front of his door.

A hot bath…it was just what she needed. That, and…she swallowed, waiting behind him as he unlocked his door. Would he join her?

"Thank you." She ran her teeth over her lip. "I'd love that."

"You can take a soak while I get food ordered." He swung the door open and headed inside, tossing his keys on the console table and hooking his jacket on the wall. She followed him and did the same with her own. They were so close she could smell his aftershave, could feel the warmth of his body seeping into her own.

"What do you fancy to eat?" he asked, looking to her. She flushed. Could he read her instinctive response: *you?*

She lowered her lashes and stepped away. "Anything."

Truth was, she was ravenous—for him *and* for food. She'd not had him in a week, and she'd not eaten since breakfast…even then, it had been a quickly-snatched piece of toast. "Why don't you surprise me?"

His eyes flashed. "I thought you weren't a fan?"

"Your surprises seem to work out fine." She gave him a small smile. The picnic, the sign—his surprises were perfect. What she couldn't cope with was the expectation that he would want more too, and having him put her straight. Breaking her heart in the process.

His eyes wavered over her, and then he nodded, his hands rubbing together as he seemed to motivate himself to move. "No worries. One hot bath coming up."

He swept past her towards the bathroom, calling back, "Why don't you grab yourself a glass of wine in the kitchen, and I'll come and find you when it's ready."

She watched him disappear off, a new warmth taking hold of her. He was looking after her. No one looked after her. She took care of herself.

Yes, Mum clucked around her now she was home. But it wasn't like this; it didn't feel like this.

Just don't get used to it.

She shook off the warning and headed to his kitchen, taking out her phone. She needed to text mum and let her know she wouldn't be home.

So you're staying, then?

She looked in the direction of where Dan was running her bath, and accepted it, she wasn't going back to Mum's tonight. She needed him; she wanted to be with him. Whatever the future held, she'd deal with it when the time came.

She raised her phone and sent her mum a message before placing it on the kitchen side and turning her attention to his impressive wine rack. There would be time to worry over her heart when she was back in the States. Right now, she had him, and that's all that mattered.

She plucked out a Shiraz and helped herself to a large glass. She was enjoying her first, warming sip when her phone buzzed. She looked at the screen and the reply from her mum:

Okay, love, Isla called, flight due in 05:30am, she's insisted on getting a cab from the airport back to her flat. Not sure what you want to do x

Like hell she is.

She swapped her glass for the phone. The last thing her sister needed was to be alone, not when Carrie could be with her. And there was no way she'd let Isla arrive in the UK to a blasted cab, whether she was speaking to her or not.

"Everything okay?"

She'd been so caught up in the message, she hadn't heard Dan approach. Now he came up behind her, his hands gentle on her shoulders, his presence radiating down her back and drawing her in.

"I've got a text from Mum," she said, turning her head to the side and leaning into his comforting warmth.

"And?"

"Isla lands at five-thirty in the morning. Mum says she's getting a cab to her place."

He squeezed her shoulders. "Let me guess, you want to meet her at the airport?"

"Yup." She rested her fingers over one of his hands. "I don't want her alone. Would you be able to take me back to the club early so I can collect my rental car?"

"Of course. I can come with you to the airport if—"

She shook her head. "Thanks, but I'd rather it was just us."

"Of course."

She pressed a kiss to his fingers to soften her refusal, to thank him. As she raised her head, she took in the flecks of paint still marring his skin and asked the question she'd been desperate to. "Take a bath with me?"

She felt him stiffen. "That wasn't my intention, I didn't—"

"You look like you need it just as much as I do," she interjected softly, her fingers trailing over the colorful spots adorning one of his hands.

"Are you sure?"

The rough edge to his voice teased over her skin, over the throbbing heart of her that couldn't get enough. She nodded gently and reached for another glass, pouring it without asking him first, knowing what she wanted more than anything and trying not to think on what tomorrow would bring, or the day after, or the day after that…

"For you."

His hand slipped around her fingers to take it, and she turned into him, lifting her gaze to his and warming in the softness she saw there. "But you need to get that food ordered first."

He grinned. "You're on."

He dropped his head, his lips brushing over hers and making them plead for more. "Now off you go," he ordered, curving his hand around her hip and encouraging her away.

"Yes, Boss."

"I thought you were the boss."

She laughed as she walked away, phone and glass in hand. The tension in her spine was already easing. There was something about this place that did that: made her relax, no matter what.

Or was it the man who owned it?

She paused on the threshold, her eyes returning to him. He had a menu in hand now, his gaze studious as he scanned the colorful sheet. She took a sip of wine as the answer thrummed through her veins: *it's all about the man.*

She gave a small sigh, her lashes lowering as she turned away and set off to the bathroom once more. The heady scent of lavender had already reached her, its relaxing essence permeating her nostrils and making her body ache with anticipation for the liquid warmth awaiting her.

She entered the dark-tiled room. It was so masculine and vast, yet the soft-lighting gave it a relaxing, cozy feel. She placed her glass next to the sunken tub and peeled away her layers. Her eyes on the rising steam, she inhaled deep and slow, letting the essential oil work its magic.

Dan and scented baths. Another one of his little surprises…

She took up her phone to send messages to Isla and Mum and tell them her intention. She didn't tell Isla about Dan, though. That would have to come later. She wasn't ready to deal with the questions that conversation would entail. But she told Isla she'd be at the airport, and since her sister wouldn't get the message until she'd landed, there'd be no chance for her to object.

She placed her phone a safe distance away and dipped her toe in the water, its pleasing warmth teasing up her leg and encouraging the rest of her in. A blissful sigh left her lips as she sank down into it, every muscle in her body singing Dan's praises.

Perfect. Just perfect.

She lay her head back over the curve designed to support the head, closing her eyes and emptying her mind of everything but the heavenly scent and the soothing cocoon of warmth.

If only life could always be as simple and blissful as this...

Dan had never been more impatient to ring a food order through, or more anxious over the selection. Both took him forever. Or at least, it felt that way when all he'd wanted was to follow Carrie and forgo food altogether. But he'd known she needed to eat.

He was fully aware of just how hard she'd worked this past week. Both the foreman and her mother had filled him in, giving him a sense of how little she had looked after herself in that time. And he wanted to change that. He wanted to take care of her, to make sure she got the rest she needed and the support she would need to deal with Isla's return. It was going to pull her apart—hell, it already was.

His chest tightened, his love for her driving his desire to be with her. Tossing both his phone and the menu down on the worktop, he grabbed his glass and made for the bathroom.

The steamy vapours hit him first, followed by the peak of her head as she rested it back over the bath edge. Her hair was slicked back from the water, her lashes fanning her flushed cheeks. She looked peaceful, almost sleep-like... *was* she asleep?

He edged closer, scared to disturb her. "Carrie?"

Her eyes drifted open and closed, her lips murmuring something.

"You can't sleep in the bath," he softly admonished, lowering his glass to the ground next to hers and pulling his top over his head.

"It's comfy." A small smile played about her lips as her eyes opened and fixed on his. "It's about time you joined me."

Something fluttered deep in his gut, and he returned her smile, knowing where the flutter came from and going with it. Enjoying it. Enjoying her. He stood to strip off his jeans and her eyes followed the move, their hungry flare pushing all thought away as his cock sprang free. She wet her lips, her hand shifting to stroke over her throat.

"Miss me?" he asked, his voice raw as his eyes trailed over her, penetrating the water and seeing everything he desired.

"More than you know." There was something about the way she said it that had his eyes soaring back to hers, his throat clamping shut and making any response impossible.

Slowly she sat up, water trailing across her shoulders and down to the gentle swell of her breasts as they broke the surface. Heat surged, his cock nagging for a long overdue release. And then she winced, her back arching and calling him to his senses.

"I promised you a massage."

She made a soft hum deep in her throat, her head rolling on her shoulders as she rubbed the back of her neck. "You did."

He climbed in behind her, careful not to send the water out as he bracketed her with his legs. Mentally, he urged his cock to stand down. He was hardly aware of the water, the heat, the tub—all his senses were honed in on where their bodies brushed against one another; the sight of her gleaming in the light; the water droplets forming on her golden skin.

He brushed his fingers over one shoulder, drawing her hair to the side and letting it fall over her front. "Be warned—I didn't say I was any good."

She gave a sleepy laugh. "I won't judge."

He circled his fingers and thumbs into her skin, savoring every little noise, every little movement she made; learning what she enjoyed and doing more of it. It was no use telling his body to stand down, not when she was giving herself over to him so completely, making heady little whimpers and rolling into his caress.

But she was tired; really tired. Even if she hadn't been dozing when he entered, he'd know it now for sure. Her body had turned to liquid under his caress, her upright position getting less and less so as she leaned back into him. Eventually she was too close to continue and he gave in, letting her fall into him, her head resting back against his chest on a heady sigh.

He looked down at her. Her eyes were closed once more, her face serenely at peace. "Nice?"

She made an appreciative sound that rumbled against his chest and buried her head beneath his chin.

His lips quirked. "Come on, I'm taking you to bed."

"Hmm?"

"Bed. Now."

He helped her upright and stepped out of the bath. Taking up his dressing gown from the back of the door, he hooked it around her. She snuggled into it, her smile tired but content.

He returned her smile and swung her up in his arms, uncaring that he was dripping wet and cold.

"You should get yourself dry."

"I will once I have you in bed."

She hooked her arms around his neck and nestled into his shoulder. She felt so right there. So perfect.

As he headed to his bedroom, a peace-like sensation filled every fiber of his being; save for his heart, which couldn't rest until he knew what the future held.

Chapter Seventeen

CARRIE WOKE TO THE BUZZ OF HER PHONE, the glare of the screen lighting behind her closed lids. She blinked, awareness spreading through her as she registered Dan's hard warmth against her, his arm hooked over her middle and head resting above her own.

She was in his bed. He'd carried her there. She remembered now. All of it—the massage, the comfort, the feeling of belonging.

And then there was Isla, and the fact that she would be back in a few hours, which meant this—whatever this was—would have to end. Not that it had restarted in any real way. She hadn't acknowledged any of it last night; she'd been too tired, too wound up, too conflicted to really consider what Isla's return meant for her and Dan.

It meant no more of this; not when her sister's own love-life was so messed up, and all because of her.

She swallowed back a rising swell of emotion, trying to snuggle deeper into Dan's hold. The clock on the side read half-past three; just another hour, one more hour like this and then reality could hit.

Her phone buzzed again, and she reached for it. Fearing the light would wake Dan, she shielded the screen with her hand as she peered beneath it.

It was Anne-Marie—a text and an email. Her stomach twisted as she opened the first:

Things moving fast. Kimmy's organized a dinner for Saturday evening, everyone will be there. Will be tight with your flight but doable. Emailing your flight details now.

She closed her eyes, wanting to unsee it. It wasn't Isla's return bringing an end to everything, it was this—her return to LA. Isla's return had just brought it closer, made it imminent. Their time was up.

Her throat clogged and her breath caught, pain wracking her ribs, and she couldn't stop the tears forming.

She returned the phone to the side and turned onto her back, rigid as she tried to hold them back.

"Hey, what's up?"

Dan's husky question startled her, and the press of his lips to her temple made her turn into him to find those lips with her own; bury the pain with this.

He groaned low in his throat, the press of his sleep-induced erection hot against her thigh.

"I want you," she whispered, grateful that the darkness hid her tears from sight.

She pressed him onto his back and lifted herself over him, his robe falling off her shoulders and its tie coming loose at her waist. His hands smoothed beneath the fabric and traced up her body, their gentle caress and the buck of his cock giving his silent approval.

She took hold of him, her hand moving over his length to coax his tip back over her clit, and she bit her lip at the spike of pleasure.

She rotated herself over him, pushing her own need higher and higher as she teased him too. He moaned beneath her, his fingers massaging into her skin and becoming harder, more demanding. Their silence filled the air, intensifying every sensation as they spoke with their hands; their touch.

Desire throbbed through her, her body answering the need in his, her heart seeking the intimacy that him being inside her would provide. She took him back to her entrance and she lowered herself slowly, relishing his entirety—her possession of him, and his of her.

She rode him with the same steady, savouring pace. If this was to be the last time they made love, she wanted it to last; wanted to draw it out.

He groaned beneath her, his body bucking, "Carrie."

His voice echoed through the silence, the strain in her name mirroring the torrent of emotion swelling uncontrollably within her.

She stroked her hands up his chest and felt his tension beneath her fingers, sensed his head pressing back into the pillow. He was close. So close. She kept her pace, her eyes burning through the darkness to take in his silhouette against the sheets. Oh, how she loved him. Her body ached with it.

Her muscles started to tense and fill with the pleasurable heat of her own budding climax. *Not yet. Not yet.*

His hands dropped to her upper thighs and spread them wide, his thumbs seeking out her aching clit. She would have stopped him, should have stopped him—she knew it would be her undoing—but she was ready. So ready.

He flicked over her with one thumb and she cried out, her head lolling back; then the other joined in. An intermittent rhythm built between the two, snapping her control. Her orgasm fired hard and fast, racking her body and squeezing him tight within her.

He erupted, his cry almost anguished as she shuddered over him and bliss-like warmth clashed with cold-hard reality as she fell forward, her face damp upon his chest.

She breathed through the surging pain, fighting to stop her body from giving her away. His arm came up around her, his fingers gently stroking over her skin. "Are you okay?"

She nodded against him, knowing she should say something—that a nod wouldn't suffice—but she couldn't trust herself, and he didn't push.

They lay in silence for a long time. She wondered if he slept, but when her alarm went off at four-thirty, she had the distinct impression he hadn't. He was too quick to release her when she moved to silence it.

"I can get a cab if you want to stay in bed," she muttered, pushing herself to sit up.

"No." He rolled to the opposite side and stood up. "I said I'll take you and I will."

He made for the bathroom and she watched him go, the words out before she really knew what she was going to say. "We need to talk."

He paused and looked at her over his shoulder. "If you mean about Isla and what it means for you and me, don't worry; I don't need it spelled out."

And off he went.

She didn't know whether to be relieved, or hurt, or angry that yet again he could dismiss her—*them*—so easily. Instead she just felt sad. And it was that sadness that filled the car as he took her to the club, that stopped her saying anything of substance. They talked plans: club clean-up, party arrangements, timing; anything to avoid any talk of them.

And it was as it should be. She had Isla to worry about, not her own selfish concerns.

He pulled up outside the club but didn't switch off the ignition. She undid her seatbelt, her teeth worrying over her lip as she braved the question on her mind: "Will you meet me at the club tonight to show Isla around?"

"Do you want me there?" He didn't turn to look at her, his eyes fixed ahead and his face lit by the orange glow of the street lighting. He looked hard and uncaring, nothing like the Dan she had become accustomed to.

"Of course I do." Her voice sounded small even to her own ears. "It wouldn't have been possible without you."

"Then I'll be there." He looked to her briefly, but his eyes were unreadable. "What time?"

"After dinner." She stepped out, ducking her head in to say, "Seven-ish?"

He nodded, and that was it. She closed the door and watched him drive away. Her body numb as she forced herself into her own car and made for the airport, her head trying to make sense of his detached demeanor and getting nowhere.

Did he truly not care? Or was he just closing himself off—protecting himself? And if that was the case, did he care for her more than he was letting on?

Dan was barely aware of the drive back to his place, but somehow he'd made it, he was here. Parked outside and staring into space.

Around him, the city had started to wake up, dog owners getting a walk in before work and early morning commuters hitting the streets, but he had no motivation for anything.

He should have expected it, of course; that Isla's return would mean a change for them. Even without their past history, the fact that Isla was heartbroken over Bradley meant that Carrie wouldn't want any hint of their relationship getting out. But damn, it hurt. Really hurt.

History was repeating itself. Just as he'd feared. Just as he'd known it would.

She'd left him to protect her sister once, and now she was pushing him out to do the same again. Soon, she would be gone. Out of his life all over again; back to her life of fame and fortune, where she belonged.

He couldn't stand it. The pain, the fear, the loss crushing him whole.

He'd survived her the first time around, but he'd had anger—hate, even—to help him through.

Now, he had nothing.

Chapter Eighteen

THE SECOND CARRIE SPIED ISLA IN ARRIVALS, she knew she had to get through to Brad somehow. She would beat his door down if it came to it—she had to make him see that *she* was to blame and get him to forgive Isla. She'd never seen her sister so withdrawn, so...so empty.

Isla's hair was scraped back, making her shadowed eyes all the more prominent, and her skin was pale—*well, paler than her usual pale*. Her smile barely touched her lips. It wasn't like Carrie had expected her to be happy, but some sign of her usual sisterly affection—ribbing, anger even—would have been better than this.

Carrie pulled Isla into her arms the instant she could and squeezed her so tight, Isla had to beg her way out. "Hey, easy sis, you're gonna break something."

Carrie couldn't help it; she couldn't let her go. Suddenly she was crying, the tears falling uncontrollably, and Isla stilled in her hold, her shock evident. Hell, Carrie was shocked.

"Shhh, love," her sister soothed. "It's okay."

Good God, Isla was comforting *her*.

Carrie straightened, wiping at her eyes with the back of her hand and shaking her head. "Like hell it is."

Isla looked away, her own eyes clouding over. "No, it's not, but it is what it is."

She sniffed, "I'm so sorry."

"I know you are."

"I'm just relieved you're here now."

"Me too." Isla gave her a small smile. "But you shouldn't have come, I just want to get home and get some sleep."

Carrie could see her sister meant it, her tiredness obvious amidst the pain. "There was no way I was letting you get a cab."

"You're impossible."

"I know." She gave a shrug. "But you still love me."

"I will if you'll drive me home and leave me be for a few hours," Isla insisted. "I just need to get some rest."

"I'd hoped we could go back to Mum's," she tried, wanting anything but to leave her alone. "We have some catching up to do."

Isla frowned at her. "Sounds good, but later, yeah?"

Carrie wanted to argue, but how could she? Not when her sister looked so tired and worn. And who was she really trying to look out for—Isla's best interests, or her own guilty ones?

She averted her eyes and made herself busy with Isla's trolley case, taking hold of the handle and hooking her free arm through her sister's. "Okay, come on, let's get you home."

She dropped Isla off and then drove to Mum's, guilt her constant companion.

For the next few hours she tried to busy herself with phone calls relating to the club—the party arrangements; the clean-up op; making sure everyone was doing what they should be—but her sister's appearance haunted her. She was counting down the seconds to sun-up stateside so she could hound Brad again. She had to get through to him. *She had to.*

She checked her watch, again.

"Will you please quit pacing, love? My living room carpet can't take it."

She looked to where her mum sat nursing a coffee in the bay

window—the perfect vantage point to spy Isla's car when it arrived. She wasn't the only one anxious to see her sister.

"I can't, Mum."

"Well, why don't you ring her?"

"I've tried." Her mum shot her a look then. Yes, she'd promised to give Isla space, but she hadn't started ringing until twelve, so it wasn't like she'd hounded her all morning.

"And?"

"She's not picking up."

She expected her mum to admonish her, but instead she looked to the window and frowned. "Then drive over there and bring her back here. Tell her I'm making dinner, and we'll distract her until you're ready to head to the club. Believe me, that place will be distraction enough once she's sees it."

"You think?"

Her mother smiled as she turned to her, confidence blooming and rubbing off on Carrie. "It'll blow her away."

Lord, she hoped so. Anxiety didn't suit her. And it wasn't just anxiety over Isla's reaction to the club—it was anxiety over how she'd left it with Dan; anxiety over how Brad would react when she eventually got hold of him. If she ever managed to.

But first, Isla…

Thankfully, she didn't have to resort to breaking her sister's door down. She came out eventually, probably more out of concern for her neighbors and the noise Carrie was generating trying to get her to open the damn door than anything else.

Regardless, it had worked.

And now they were back at Mum's, being cooed over and doted on, their mother going into parental overdrive making sure they were fed, watered, and looked after.

It became obvious it wasn't so much about distracting Isla from her heartbreak, but rather their Mum's genuine happiness at having both her daughters back under the same roof. It was nice. It would have been perfect, if not for the underlying sadness in the room.

But Carrie wasn't giving up—not where Brad and Isla were concerned. Every chance she got, she snuck off to call Brad's mobile, but each time it just rang; she'd even tried blocking her ID in the hope he would pick up, with no luck.

Now it was almost time to leave for the club, and they were clearing away the dinner dishes when she decided it was time to try his work number again instead.

"Are you guys okay clearing up while I make a call?"

They both turned to look at her, Isla giving her a teasing smile. "Anything to get out of the dirty work, hey?"

She laughed in response. If only Isla knew just how much she *had* worked this past week. But she'd know soon enough. A small bubble of excitement started. If she could just get this Brad mess fixed too...

She grabbed her phone from the side and headed upstairs. His office number was ringing before she'd even closed her bedroom door.

"Come on, come on, pick up."

It rang and rang, and her heart sank as the voicemail picked up. She tried again. And again. Time was pressing on, but she wasn't ready to give up. She was mentally drafting a voicemail message when finally, the phone clicked. "Hello?"

Her heart launched into her throat. It was Brad; hoarse, pissed off, but definitely him. "About time!"

"Isla?!"

She could hear his tormented joy, but she wasn't Isla...*oh God*. She squeezed her eyes tight. "It's Carrie, Brad."

She opened her eyes cautiously, ears straining down the phone line to hear his harsh exhale and his eventual, "Of course it is."

She gripped the phone tighter, beating back the fear alive in her belly. "Look, I'm sorry to call you at work, but you're not answering your mobile and..." She took a breath and went for it, "I can't sit back while you ruin your own and my sister's life."

"Me! Ruin my life!" She winced. "That's a bit rich coming from you!"

"Please," she croaked. "Brad, you need to listen to me."

"There's nothing you can say that I need to listen to, Carrie."

She sensed him hanging up the phone, panic rushing her veins as she blurted, "*Please*, Brad."

Nothing.

But he hadn't hung up, the line hadn't changed. What could she say? What would make him listen?

"Spill it, Carrie, and then be gone."

Her tummy fluttered, his begrudging tone not enough to dampen her relief. She had his ear, and she had the one thing he needed to hear: the absolute truth. "She loves you, Brad."

It had worked, she was sure in her gut; she could feel his attention burning down the line through the silence.

"And I screwed it all up for her," she continued, her vision starting to blur. "She would have told you ages ago if I had let her, but I preyed on her loyalty, I used it to stop her…" She shook her head, fighting back the tears. "Look, Brad, if I'd realized the two of you were made for each other, I never would have told her to lie to you in the first place."

"Made for one another." He scoffed. "I'm glad you think so highly of me that you consider a liar my perfect match."

"You don't mean that, Brad." She clenched her jaw, his disparagement of Isla pulling her apart. She couldn't stand it; she had to make him see the truth. "That girl is one of the kindest, most loving human beings I know, and if you buried your pride for long enough, you would realize that too."

"It's not just pride, Carrie." His breath shuddered down the line. "She hurt me."

"I know she did." Her shoulders slumped, her eyes closing over his pain. "But that was because of *me*. Surely, you must realize the reason you are suffering as much as you are is because you love her too?"

Nothing.

"You were the man that thought love wasn't for you—don't you remember that?"

"I *should* have remembered that."

"But she made you realize that wasn't true," she stressed softly. "She made you capable of love. How can you turn your back on that?"

"Enough, Carrie," he bit out. "You've caused enough pain. I don't need to listen to this."

No, no, no.

"Just give her a chance."

"So she can pull the wool over my eyes again? I don't think so!"

The phone cut dead and Carrie's tears fell, a sob breaking free. Had she just made it worse? Had she just made a huge mistake?

She sank onto the edge of her bed, clutching her phone in her lap and staring at it, wishing for him to call back. Wishing for anything but the mess she'd created.

"Hey, lazy-bones!" Her sister's call reached her from the downstairs hall. *Isla.* Oh, God, what had she done? "We're almost done if you've finished with your call?"

She took a breath and cleared her throat. "Yeah, just a sec."

She didn't move right away. She couldn't. His words revolved around her brain; his heartache, his anger. Surely, he had to love Isla? Surely, he would come to realize they had a future together?

Yeah, because life's one big fairy tale.

"Come on, Carrie."

She looked to the doorway and took another deep breath. *At least you tried. You really did—*

But you wouldn't need to try, if you hadn't caused it all in the first place.

She got to her feet and slid the phone into the pocket of her jeans.

Leave it tonight. Focus on the—

Her mobile started to ring and her heart gave a leap. *Brad?*

She slipped it back out, her eyes dropping to the screen. *Oh my God.* Her lips parted as her heart made it all the way to her throat.

"Sorry," she called downstairs, "just have another call coming in, won't be long!"

She rushed the phone to her ear, answering it at the same time. "Brad?"

There was nothing.

"Brad—are you there?" God, please don't say he'd pocket dialled her?

"Yeah…I'm here."

"Brad, thank goodness!" She didn't want to give her hope free rein, but she was already hopping from one foot to the other, her body positively vibrating with it.

"I'm still so angry with you for what you did…" She stilled; she could hear the *but* coming. Her breath was hanging in her lungs, her fist pressed to her mouth as she willed it. "But I do love her, Carrie…more than I ever thought possible."

She dropped her hand, her lips breaking into a smile as she pirouetted on the spot. "I knew it!"

"Yeah well, know-it-all, I think I'm going to need your help to fix it all."

"Anything, Brad, anything!"

"I don't even know where to start."

"I have the perfect plan." And she did. The most perfect, fairy-tale plan to sweep Isla off her feet. It was already playing out in her strung-out brain. "You ready to hear it?"

It was seven o'clock; Carrie was due to arrive any minute with Isla, and Dan was suffering. Not being able to hate her—to be angry—left him defenseless against his love for her, and if they only had a short time left, he didn't want to spend it in the shadows.

She could leave him again. That was already in the cards, but he didn't want to lose this between them now. He wasn't about to rub Isla's face in it, but he'd make sure Carrie knew he wasn't ready to end it.

"We're all done, Boss." He looked up from the main bar that he was propping up to see the foreman at the door with a group of contractors. "A couple of sparkies are just finishing up, but in the main, the place is good to go."

He gave him a nod. "Cheers, Tom."

The guy walked out, and Dan looked to the bottle of Scotch sitting pretty on the shelf behind him. *Just a small one before they arrive.* It might take his angst down a notch.

He poured a glass and replaced the bottle on the shelf, but he didn't hang around. He took the glass with him into the adjacent room, wanting to give Isla and Carrie their own private moment when they arrived.

He was about to settle into one of the deep red sofas when his phone buzzed with an incoming text. He lifted it out of his pocket—it was Carrie:

> *Been delayed, managed to reach Brad, I have so much to tell you! Can't wait! Upshot is he's coming to the party. A special guest! Shh, it's a surprise! See you in ten! C xx*

Well, I'll be…

His heart beat faster, Carrie's excitement reverberating off her words. It seemed everything was going to be okay after all. *Everything except*—he necked the scotch.

It was good news. It really was. And he needed to be happy for Isla. But where did this leave him and Carrie?

Did it change things?

It must do…

He was still pondering when he heard their voices in the main room twenty minutes later. He headed to the doorway, hanging back to get the lay of the land before he stepped out. Not that he was chicken, but if Isla wasn't taking it well…

Carrie sounded excited though, her words coming in a flurry: "When Dan showed me the vision you'd been mocking up, since like forever, I just knew we had to make it a reality. The different zones, the quirky features, the lot! It's quite simply brilliant…you're not mad then? So, I can tell Dan he's safe to come out now?"

His lips quirked at the implication. He *wasn't* chicken, he was being thoughtful.

"Dan's here?" he heard Isla ask.

"Oh, yes, he's just in hiding in case you completely flipped your lid." Carrie laughed, the sound reaching him and coaxing at his core even from the other room, burying all confusion with a far baser urge.

"Poor guy, he's been nagging me for years to let him do this."

That was no lie.

"And you should have bloody let him! Do you know how much I had to beg him to get involved?"

No lie either. She had begged alright, and he'd enjoyed taking all he could get.

"I can imagine."

Probably not the full picture…

"I had to promise that if you hated it, I was to say he had nothing to do with it. Now that you love it, he will of course want to take all the credit."

He grinned, their easy camaraderie drawing him out. He stepped into the room, seeing Carrie first, her face flushed and eyes bright with excitement.

"Of course I will," he teased, his eyes locked on hers. "It was all my idea after all."

She raised her chin at him, her eyes flashing in challenge, and his body stirred. She was just too much fun to goad.

He tore his eyes away, looking to her sister and seeing all that Carrie would have seen: the pale complexion, the shadowed eyes, the arms that hugged over her middle. Maybe the blonde hair, the change from fiery red, made her look far paler and worse than she was. He could hope.

He walked up to her, his smile softer. "It's good to have you back in the country."

"Hey, you!" She swept forward, her hands lifting to his shoulders as she raised herself up to plant a kiss on his cheek. "It's good to see you!"

He gripped her hips and set her back from him, his playful spirit taking hold. "So," he grinned at Carrie, "do I get the same greeting from you?"

She scowled at him, the gesture making him want to laugh before her eyes flitted to Isla and back again, her face lifting into a sickly-sweet smile.

Oh no.

She closed the distance between them, her hands curving over his shoulders soft and smooth.

He stilled, rigid with the frisson triggered by her touch. And then she was there, at his cheek, her lips brushing against his skin, her scent assailing his nostrils, the hint of lavender still in her hair. Christ, he even felt his lashes lower, his senses feasting off her nearness; and then a hand clap pierced the air.

"Well, come on then, you two!" Isla gushed, squeezing her hands together. "I want a tour."

He wanted to slap himself. He'd goaded Carrie, gotten what he wanted, and lost himself in her—in front of Isla. *Idiot.* He forced a grin and broke away from her. "Absolutely!"

He looked back to Carrie, a silent message passing between them. "Care to lead the way?"

"Sure." She swept up to Isla and grabbed hold of her hand, pulling her along. "Now regardless of what I said earlier, anything you don't like was all Dan's fault, *comprende?*"

Isla laughed and the mood was broken, but its effect lingered long past the tour of the premises.

Isla loved the place. Her reaction to every new feature, every modification, every teeny element had her exclaiming, and Carrie increasingly stoked—helped along, he was sure, by the fact that Carrie had the biggest surprise of all still to come: Brad.

They were back at the main entrance now, and Carrie was gushing over some dress she had picked out for her sister to wear to the launch party. "It's perfect for you," she was saying. "I figure we can head over to collect it now and I can fill you in on the incredible guest list we have sorted."

"You do remember that this is Isla's club, Carrie?" He couldn't help it, he was on edge, and all because of her. Yet she had her feelings under control now—on the surface at least—and it was pushing him to the brink. "Maybe she would like to choose her own outfit for the launch night?"

"I have exceptional taste," Carrie rebuked, a frown pinching between her brows. "It's what I do."

But you're also taking over, he wanted to tell her, *like you always do, whether you mean to or not.*

Just like she'd taken him over—*heart, mind and soul.*

She was watching him intently, and then she blinked, her brow lifting as she cleared her throat and turned back to her sister. "Of course, if you don't like it, Isla…" She cocked her head demurely to one side. "We have time to sort something else."

Wow. Had she really just bowed down?

Isla looked just as surprised. "I'm sure it will be perfect, Carrie."

"See!" Carrie all but combusted on the word as she looked to him triumphantly.

He shook his head, his blood rushing with heat; Carrie-with-attitude was back. He wanted to laugh, high on amusement, desire, frustration, love—all for this maddening woman who he couldn't keep.

And she must have seen it in his face, because she wasn't looking so full of glory any more. Her smile had softened, her eyes dark with a look he now knew so well. She dropped her fingers to the hair at the base of her neck, twining a curl around and around and making his own fingers itch to join in.

"I just need to get some air, I'll meet you outside, Carrie." Their attention snapped to Isla as she spoke. *Shit.* She looked fit to vomit.

"Hey, I'm fine," she hurried out, clearly reading their concern. "It's just a lot to take on board."

"I'll come with you," Carrie said, moving to follow her.

Her sister raised a hand to stop her. "I'm fine, you guys finish up and find me when you're done."

Dan nodded, he could see she needed space, and she definitely didn't need them on her heel. That worked for him too; he had something more pressing he wished to do, and he didn't want Isla bearing witness to it.

He took up Carrie's elbow to hold her steady. "Come on, I need to speak to you about one of the guests you mentioned."

Carrie's eyes flicked hesitantly between them, but he'd hoped his reminder of Brad's arrival would make her agree. Not that he wanted to discuss him, Isla, the party, any of it…

"What are you like, sis?" Isla gave her sister an easy smile. "When will you just do as you're told?"

"Oh, don't you start too!" Carrie complained, her eyes rolling as Isla simply laughed and headed for the door.

Dan chuckled as Carrie tried to shrug off his hold.

She was so close, so tempting. She parted her lips to say something and he swiftly cut her off, his own lips crushing hers with a pent-up need that he couldn't control. He was drowning in her; in her taste, her scent, the heat of her body pressed up against him.

The door clicked shut and she shoved at him, tearing her mouth away. "What was that for?"

"To shut you up. Can't you see she needs some space?"

She shoved against his chest again. "All thanks to you!"

He pulled her against him hard. "What's that supposed to mean?"

"You know exactly what that means. I told you we weren't to be like...*like this*...in front of her."

"That was before you fixed everything." He shrugged. "Seems to me Isla's life will be just perfect shortly, and I'm not letting you choose her over me—not this time."

She stilled, her eyes hesitant, questioning, looking for answers. He'd said too much.

"But if it's air you want..." He stepped back, creating some much-needed space for him now—he wouldn't beg—and gestured to the door: "After you."

She wavered on the spot. "It's not like that."

"No?"

She closed the gap between them. "What is it you want from me?" she whispered, her eyes searching. "One minute you tell me we don't have a future, and the next you kiss me so hard I think you're never going to let me go."

"That's just it, I have no choice; I have to let you go."

"Why?"

"You know why."

She shook her head. "I don't, Dan, I don't know why at all."

And then she turned and walked away.

Because I love you, he wanted to scream, his eyes boring into her back.

Because I love you, and you have another life to live in a world where I don't belong, and I can't risk going through it all again.

Chapter Nineteen

SHE BARELY SAW DAN OVER THE NEXT TWO days. It turned out organizing a red-carpet affair at the eleventh hour was just as challenging as renovating a club in less than a month. If Carrie wasn't on her phone to suppliers or reaching out to prospective guests, she was in a meeting with someone discussing some other aspect of it.

But being busy was good. It meant not dwelling on Dan; it meant keeping Brad's return a secret; and it meant sweeping Isla up in the excited buzz.

It also meant forgetting to sort her own outfit. And *that* had been a crisis she didn't need.

She smoothed out the midi skirt of the strapless black dress she now wore, and her mum tutted at her.

"It looks gorgeous darling, far better than it ever did on me," she said, taking a sip of her Champagne. "Don't you think so, Dicky?"

Her father started. Whether it was because of Mum's use of his age-old nickname, being put on the spot, or the fact that he'd been in some trance-like state over her mother since the moment he'd arrived, she wasn't sure. Probably all of the above.

"In truth, you always looked amazing in whatever you wore," he said smoothly, his recovery swift and sure. "It's easy to see where our daughters get their beauty from."

Carrie looked at her mother and smiled. She was so glad Dad had come; not just for Isla, but for Mum too. The flush to her cheeks since he'd walked in that afternoon seemed to take years off her. She looked vibrant and happy, like a shadow had been lifted. Yes, there was a little awkwardness, more of the teenage first love variety, which was hilarious. But her Mum's ribbing and her father's retorts were flowing like an easy stream of consciousness. Like they'd never been apart…

"Still the smooth-talker, hey?" Her mum swept her gaze over the steady flow of party guests, purposefully avoiding her father, but that light was still there—the spark of enjoyment, humour, fun.

"Only for you."

"Oh, Dad." Carrie rolled her eyes. "I am here you know."

He just grinned. He was clearly having far too much fun. He'd already announced his flight was open-ended; he intended to stay around a while, his reasoning being to spend more time with Isla, but Carrie couldn't help wondering if it had more to do with Mum.

Not that she'd be around to see it—her flight was imminent. In just fifteen hours she'd be airborne, and this would all be behind her. Subconsciously, her hand went to her belly, the lead-weight beneath getting heavier by the second.

Like her mother could sense the direction of her thoughts, she piped up, "Where's Dan? I thought he would be here by now?"

You and me both, she wanted to say, but the snappy retort was too close to how she felt inside; too vulnerable. And letting that out wouldn't help keep her focused on the night, on Isla and the surprise to come.

"I think he's been held up." She opened her clutch and took out her phone, checking for the umpteenth time whether he'd called. Nothing.

Seemed he wasn't so keen to see her as she was him.

Or had her parting question freaked him out so much he thought it best to stay out of her way?

She'd been foolish to push, but she'd been so caught up in his kiss, in its meaning and the blaze to his eyes, that she'd been convinced they were on the precipice of the truth. A truth that would have had her confessing her feelings and fighting for an *us*.

And now here they were, an hour into the party, and he hadn't even arrived.

Should she call him?

No, too desperate.

But...

"Oh look, honey," her mum exclaimed. "Isn't that him catching up with Isla by the door? Oh my, doesn't he scrub up well."

Carrie turned on her heel, her heart fluttering in her chest.

Oh...my...God.

She felt her lips part, her hold over her Champagne glass weakening.

"Don't lose your drink, sweetheart."

It was her father who spoke and righted her fingers, but she was hardly aware of it. Every sense was on Dan and the vision he made. His hair, its devilish length, was him all over, but she'd never seen him in black tie. Never seen his muscular frame encased in a well-cut suit. And as for the pristine white shirt and slim black tie...

Oh...my...God, she mentally repeated.

"Why don't you head over and greet him?" her mother suggested.

She would if she could make her legs work. If she wasn't paralyzed with a desire so intense and a love so fierce she could scarcely breathe through them.

"You might want to close your mouth, though." Her father chuckled. "You'll start catching flies."

She heard a rustle and he gave a grunt—had Mum just elbowed him?

"Go on, love," she encouraged. "We'll come with you."

Carrie nodded; it was about all she could manage as she started towards him, but as soon as his eyes found hers, she stilled.

She felt the rake of his gaze as it travelled over her, burning her through in its wake. Isla said something that drew his eye and he spoke back, pulling her into his embrace as he kissed her cheek, and then his attention was back to Carrie. His stride, his sight, his pull.

She couldn't swallow; the world stood still as he closed the distance between them, and then he was before her. His fresh masculine scent swept over her, her eyes lifting into his as her body swayed forward. She went with the move, lifting up to touch her lips to his cheek as she inhaled softly.

"I'm so happy you're here," she said, dropping back.

"Aren't we all," her father declared, getting their attention. "What time do you call this? I thought it was women who went in for the fashionably-late thing."

"My apologies, Mr Evans" He offered out his hand. "It's good to see you again."

"Oh, Lord, Richard, please." Her father said, shaking his hand. "Or Dicky if you want to follow my wi—Helen's lead." He coughed out the last, the slip-up so very telling and making her mother's eyes land on him with questioning force.

Dan grinned. "Very well, Dicky." Then he looked to her mother. "Helen, you look beautiful."

"Oh, thank you, Dan." She flushed crimson as she leant forward for an air kiss. "But I think you'll be forced to admit my daughters have stolen the show tonight…"

She stepped back, freeing his focus to return once more to Carrie, and there was that look in his eye again. The one that had her pleading with him to be honest with her. The one that gave her hope. "Where have you been?"

He suddenly looked sheepish, the look at total odds with his sheer masculine appeal and making her want him all the more. "I may have forgotten I needed something appropriate to wear."

Her lips twitched. "You and me both."

His brow raised. "You're kidding."

"No." She threw her mother a grateful look. "Mum came to the rescue with this number."

His eyes grazed over her, penetrating her clothing, her skin. "Your mum has good taste."

"Seems someone you know does too. You look..." Her voice failed her, her lips and throat parched. *Ravishing*, she wanted to say. Hardly appropriate in company, especially *this* company. "Lovely."

She wanted to cringe—*lovely*, it didn't even come close, and he cocked a grin at her. "Lovely?"

"Very," she added with a teasing smile.

"As much as I'm loving this mutual appreciation," her father piped up, "shouldn't you be announcing Mr You-Know-Who soon?"

He gestured to the empty mic and the mill of people starting to gather around the stage. Goodness, he was right! Poor Brad was hiding out upstairs waiting for his cue to arrive. Waiting for her.

"Yes, absolutely," she hurried out. "Why don't you guys head over to Isla? Make sure she doesn't collapse when she catches sight of him."

Her father gave a soft chuckle. "Will do."

Then she turned to Dan. "Can you just double check everything is working, then come and get us?"

Last minute nerves were getting the better of her. She wanted this to be perfect.

"Sure." He slipped his fingers around the stem of her glass to take it from her, his eyes piercing her own. "You've got this."

She gave him a small smile. "I hope so."

"I know so." He raised his hand to her hair, stroking back a loose curl designed to fall from her up-do. "You're about to make a couple very, very happy."

Emotion clogged at her throat. Happiness, sadness colliding in one. She wanted Isla and Brad to be happy. She did. But she also wanted them to be happy. Her and Dan. She wanted this for them, too.

She blinked, her eyes hurting as she forced herself away and cleared her throat. "See you soon."

Focus on Isla. Focus on Brad. That's what you're here to fix. That's what matters right now. Then tomorrow you'll be gone, and you can focus on fixing your heart.

Dan watched Carrie leave. Her figure swayed evocatively in the tight-fitting black dress, her bare shoulders giving much away with their slight tremor. She really was nervous. Or was it something else?

"You know," her father said alongside him. "There was a time I thought Carrie would only ever have eyes for the limelight; it seems I was wrong."

He looked at her father and caught the speculation in his eye.

"Come on now, Dicky, leave the man be, he has a job to do," Helen said, hooking her arm through her ex-husband's and starting to lead him away. Her eyes came back to him briefly as she smiled. "He's not wrong though. It's such a shame she has to fly home tomorrow morning."

Fly? His chest squeezed tight. "She has her flights booked?"

Helen paused to frown at him. "Sorry, I thought you knew; she flies just after eleven."

He shook his head, fighting back a wave of nausea. "Of course. She said she was leaving the day after the party." But she'd said that a fortnight ago. She hadn't mentioned it since. It hadn't been real. Fixed. Set in stone.

She was going. She was leaving him.

Helen was still frowning, likely seeing the whole episode play out on his face. "But perhaps if she had a reason to stay…?"

She broke off, her eyes saying the rest, and his brain saying even more. To ask Carrie to stay was wrong. But for him to go with her…he shook his head, fighting for reason, for clarity, for the same judgement he'd held all those days ago when he'd told her there could be no future. It was all so vague now, so impossible, the idea of a life with her; the idea of a life without her.

"You best start moving, son, or I have a feeling Brad is going to come legging it down those stairs, grand announcement or not."

Her father was right, he had a job to do. He could worry on them later.

He checked the mic before clearing the space and heading upstairs to the old apartment that resided on the top floor: Bradley's hiding place. He took a breath and rapped on the door.

Carrie pulled it open, face flushed and eyes bright, and his heart soared. "You ready for us?"

"I'm always ready for you," he said, doing what he'd wanted from the moment he'd seen her in the skimpy black number. He pulled her into his arms and kissed her full on the mouth.

She folded into him, her sigh trapped in his mouth and her body like liquid heat in his arms. Oh God, he didn't want to stop, didn't want to return; he wanted to stay in this moment where everything felt crystal clear and perfect.

Someone cleared their throat. Loudly. "If you guys don't break this up, I'm going to go and introduce myself, I can't stay up here any longer."

Carrie's hands froze either side of his face, her mouth breaking away with an impish grin. He looked over her head, and there he was, the man of the moment: Bradley King. The man who had slept with Carrie and the man who had stolen Isla's heart. A weird sense of jealousy and protectiveness came over him.

He tried to smile—it was polite to—but he knew his eyes probably looked like he would break the man.

"Sorry, mate, this girl's checking out of my life soon…" *Far too soon.* He kept an arm around her, pulling her in tight and forcing his voice to remain jovial. "Gotta take it while I still can."

Bradley looked between them, his surprise clear. This had to be weird for him—the last time he and Carrie were together properly, Carrie would have been his. Dan swallowed uncomfortably.

"Hey, I get it," Bradley said, the guy's American twang reminding him of Carrie's and upping his possessiveness. "But I'm going to break something if I don't see Isla soon."

He could see the desperation in his face, the same need to be with the woman that he loved, and took pity. He got it. He pounded him on the back. "It's good Isla has finally found a man worthy of her—that's if you *are* truly worthy of her?"

"Look, I love her, okay?" Bradley had visibly paled. Maybe he'd overdone the big brother act. "But if there is some weird thing you have going on with her and Carrie, then it ends here. Isla's all mine."

Haha. He gave him lopsided grin, his arm squeezing around Carrie's hips. "That's good to know." He dropped his eyes to Carrie and back at him. "Believe me, this one is enough trouble on her own."

Carrie tensed in his hold, throwing him a look that made him want to laugh. "Let's go before you say something you can't come back from, *Dan.*"

She pushed out of his hold and stomped off down the corridor. He chuckled after her, and so did Bradley. Not that he was really aware of the guy; he only had eyes for her.

Turned out everyone else had eyes for the pair of them—Carrie and Brad. The excited ripple that surrounded them as they broke through the crowd to head to the stage was palpable. It was easy to see them together as a couple—hell, they had been, unbeknownst to everyone—and it made sense; they lived in the same world.

He thrust his hands in his pockets as he took up position alongside Carrie, allowing Bradley to hang back in their shadow while she took hold of the mic.

He looked out to the crowd as she spoke, his mouth a hard line, his body and jaw tense. This is what she was used to. People hanging on her every word. She demanded attention, was comfortable in it. Lived for it.

But if she loved him, even half as much as he loved her, did it matter that he wasn't part of this world? Did it matter where they lived? Weren't Bradley and Isla about to *prove* it didn't matter?

He found Isla in the crowd, her eyes reflecting the lights of the club as she looked past them to Bradley. Her lips parted in disbelief.

"And here he is," Carrie was saying. "Our very special guest this evening, all the way from LA, Bradley King."

Carrie turned away from him to gesture to Bradley. "You want to come up here and tell us all what has you so excited about this new joint?"

He stepped up to the mic, scanning the crowd. "Would you believe I'm actually nervous?" He looked to Carrie briefly as the crowd gave a chuckle. "It's not like I don't get up and do these things often. Talking in a public place is simple, but this, this is different. I'm not just here to tell you how great this place is and insist you all give it a try…I am, of course, telling you that too! But I am also here to make a public confession of something I never thought possible."

The crowd murmured, someone yelled, "You been a naughty boy?" And a group howled. His grin grew. He was in his stride now. Hell, even Dan was getting sucked in. And he didn't like it. Didn't want to be jealous of the way Bradley was so at ease in this.

"So, I, Bradley King…" He gave a crowd-pleasing flourish of a bow, and as his head came up, his eyes locked with Isla's. Their moment hung in the air like weighted magic and then he straightened. "I confess to all of you here, that I am one hundred percent, head-over-heels, crazy-in-love with the lady behind this business."

The crowd gave an audible gasp, a cheer quick on its tail, and Carrie's hand dropped to Dan's, her touch breaking him out of the weird dance inside. She squeezed his fingers and looked up at him, her eyes glittering with happiness and making his own prick. *What the hell.* He didn't do tears.

"And if she would do me the honor of getting up on stage with me now," Bradley was saying, "I will introduce you to the true guest of honor tonight, the woman who stole my heart—Isla Evans!"

Carrie's gaze swept to Isla, her bottom lip trapped in her teeth as she watched her sister walk through the parting crowd. But he could only watch Carrie, captivated by her joy, her love.

She backed up and he stepped with her, making room for Isla to stand with Bradley.

"Say you'll be mine, Isla," he heard him whisper. "Please say it."

Carrie's breath caught, her fingers gripping his own. At any moment she would squeal, he was sure.

"Always," Isla whispered back, her voice breaking, and Dan looked to her, saw her locked in Bradley's embrace, their faces so full of emotion. "I love you so much."

And then they were kissing. Crazy, passionate, eating-each-other deep.

"Do you think we should step in?" he murmured in Carrie's ear. "I don't think this—"

She squealed over him and the crowd roared. Any second now the happy couple were going to be naked on the floor, or Dan was going to grab Carrie and deliver exactly the same treatment.

And would she let him? With all the press in attendance, the public, would she let him kiss her? He didn't know. If she was just anyone, just someone normal, he wouldn't think twice; he'd pull her into his arms and kiss her with every bit of the love he felt.

It was so easy to forget—to think of her as just Carrie; *his* Carrie.

He ran a finger under his collar, his discomfort mounting by the second. He couldn't do what he wanted, and he couldn't stand there and watch while another couple did.

He coughed and stepped forward, releasing Carrie's hand to reach into the curve of Isla's back as he leant close to her ear. "Sorry to be terribly British about this," he said, "but you may want to take that upstairs."

They parted, barely, and he continued, ignoring the scowl Carrie was sending him. "I mean, hell, I couldn't care less if you get yourselves off on this stage, but the press in attendance may have a field day."

The camera flashes had been incessant and now that Brad and Isla had separated, Isla seemed to get it, her cheeks flushing red. "He has a point," she whispered up at Bradley.

The man gave her a devilish smile. "In that case, upstairs looked to be pretty private—you up for it?"

Too much information...

"You're on," she said, slipping her hand in his and looking to Dan, then Carrie. "You guys got this covered?"

They gave her a nod and she smiled, moving to leave. The crowd applauded, and she looked to them with a small smile. She hesitated, then grabbed the mic as Bradley tried to pass it back to Carrie.

"Sorry, folks," she said. "I've not seen this man in a fortnight and we're long overdue to catch up, but I promise you now, this club will be the place to be seen. Hopefully, tonight has given you a taste of that." She gestured around the building, her face lit up in genuine wonder as she took it all in once more, and then she looked back to her sister, giving her a smile of heartfelt gratitude. "And now, I'll leave you with my fabulous and gorgeous counterpart, Carrie, and her equally gorgeous guy, Dan. They will ensure your evening ends on a high. Over to you guys!"

Her equally gorgeous guy.

He froze, his eyes finding Carrie's as she hung back, her hand taking the mic from Isla on autopilot. The crowd started to talk, the camera's flashing anew. The excited buzz was back, only now it was on them. Now it was on *their* relationship.

Had Isla guessed at it all? Had they been that obvious?

Carrie looked at him, almost fearful, and he couldn't react; didn't know what to do. This was it. How she played this would tell him so much.

He wanted to fall back into the shadows, as much as he wanted to step forward and stand by her side. But this had to be driven by her. It had to be her decision.

And so he stood there.

She raised the mic to her lips, her smile sweeping over the crowd. "Trust my sister to stir it all up, hey?"

She threw him a look, and his heart dropped in his chest. Whatever was coming, it wasn't what he wanted.

"This is our childhood friend, Dan, the man who helped make tonight possible and managed to survive growing up with sisters as demanding as us. Hey, Dan, come take a bow."

She grinned at him, but it didn't reach her eyes; her eyes said so much more.

Was it an apology? Was it a question? He didn't know.

All eyes were on him now, and he stepped forward, hanging by her side until she moved onto her speech of thanks. And then he drifted into the background as the press representatives came forward, huddling around her and firing more questions. He heard Kimmy Diaz mentioned, talk of her new film taking center stage.

"It is a fabulous opportunity, you know." Her father came up alongside him, offering out a glass of whisky, which he took far too eagerly; he needed it. "It'll catapult her to the top, that movie."

He nodded, murmured some sort of agreement, but he wasn't really listening. His eyes were on Carrie, but she was lost to him now. Doing her job. Doing what she did best and playing Carrie Evans—the great actress. He recognized her, and yet he didn't; a strange contradiction that messed with his head. With his heart.

"She has a dinner lined up tomorrow night with Diaz and some cohorts."

Dan nodded, quietly sipping at his drink and nursing its warmth.

"Something tells me if not for that, she'd be sticking around longer."

Sod a sip, he took a swig. He felt her father's eyes on him, probing and reading into his silence.

"Of course she would," he forced out. "She'd love to spend more time with you, with Isla and Helen. It's been a long time."

"True." Her father nodded, his brow raised. "But I was thinking more of you."

He coughed, the harsh hit of alcohol getting caught in his throat.

"Don't act so surprised, Dan, it's obvious how much you love one another. One would have to be blind not to see it. Even the press here tonight will have *you* all over the paper tomorrow."

"What? Carrie and her childhood chum, yeah, I can just see the headlines." He gave an empty laugh, but her father didn't return it.

"She said what she had to. Why would she publicly proclaim something that you two don't seem to want to acknowledge to one another?"

He was speechless, her father's words full of truth and messing with his head all the more.

"But we're worlds apart, her and I," he said eventually.

Richard shook his head, his eyes spying Helen in the mix and coming back to him damp at the corners. "Don't make the same mistake we did. I lost ten years with the woman I loved because we let our paths separate down the ordinary and the celebrity. Seems to me Isla and Brad have realized their lives can converge. You and Carrie need to see the same."

"I'll only hold her back. We don't belong together, she needs someone more like…"

"Like Brad?" her father supplied for him. "By your logic, they would be made for each other, but look what happened there. It's Isla and Brad that work."

"But she doesn't love me, not like…" *I love her*, he wanted to say but he couldn't get it out. "Not like they love one another."

"Don't you think she should tell you that?"

He gave a soft laugh. "I'm not a masochist, I don't need to hear her say it."

"You've not even given her the chance."

He swallowed past the lump forming deep in his throat. Her father was right, wasn't he?

Carrie's eyes found his through the crowd and she stilled, her lips curving in a gentle smile. She said something to her companions and then she was heading towards him, her stride slow and purposeful.

"Just think about it," her father said, walking away as he spied her approach. He didn't respond. He was lost in her coming towards him. Her beauty. Her perfection. How could he ever be good enough?

"Well, you did it," he said when she stopped before him.

"*We* did it."

"Okay." He accepted her correction with a smile. "We."

She turned to scan the people milling around them. "I wish we could get out of here."

"Why don't we?" He had so many ideas about what they could do instead, ways to make the most of their remaining hours...

"What? And have both hostesses out of action? Hardly." She gave a soft laugh, but as her eyes came back to him, they were strange; haunted almost.

"What is it?"

"The truth?"

He itched to reach for her, to pull her into him, and he probably would have if not for their audience and the further speculation it would cause—speculation he wasn't all that sure she was happy to encourage following her statement to the press, despite what her father had said.

"Yes, the truth."

"I don't want to get on that plane tomorrow."

His heart leapt. "Then don't."

"You make it sound so simple." Her eyes locked with his.

"Isn't it?" he said, his fingers reaching to curve around her hip. The movement was subtle enough not to be seen amid the crowd. She looked to where he touched her, her lower lip catching in her teeth. "You can do whatever it is you want."

She let go of a small breath. "Not according to my agent. If you listen to her, my career lives or dies on that dinner tomorrow night." He saw the hesitation deep in her eyes, the uncertainty.

"That sounds more like you doing what *she* wants."

She shrugged. "She got me where I am today."

"No." He lifted her chin, uncaring for the masses now. "You got where you are today because of you. No one else."

She dropped her lips to his hand, her kiss gentle. "Perhaps."

Now. Ask her now. Ask her to stay.

She took hold of his hand and lowered it from her face, her eyes discretely scanning the crowd. Was she worried they'd been seen? A tiny shard pierced his heart, but he ignored it, focusing on the end game.

Slowly she came back to him, her eyes wide and unguarded. "I'd stay," she said softly, her tongue wetting her lips. "If you asked me…you only have to say the words, and I'll stay."

Oh, Christ.

He looked to where their fingers still touched, the truth searing home even as she offered it to him on a platter. He couldn't do it to her. He couldn't ask that of her. Demand it of her.

When he raised his lashes to meet her gaze, he knew she saw it coming—could see it in the way her eyes glistened back at him.

"If I did that, I'd be just as bad as your agent."

He stepped away from her, breaking their contact, conscious that they were drawing more and more attention. He needed to leave. Now, before his heart drove him to do exactly as she said, and not only ask, but beg. To confess the true extent of his feelings and to hell with all else—her career, her future, the world she dreamed of.

"I need to go."

"Go?" She frowned, her eyes widening into pools of blue that he could so easily get lost in, if he let himself…

He looked away, placing his glass on the nearest surface and taking another breath as he stared into the golden liquid. "Max has messaged." He couldn't look at her as he delivered the lie. "There's a problem at the club that I need to check out."

"But..." She touched her fingers upon his shoulder. "But I leave tomorrow...first thing in the morning."

"I know." He mustered his strength and turned to face her, but it wasn't enough. The urge to take her in his arms for one last hug, one last kiss was too much to resist. He reached out and a flash of light illuminated them both, a photographer honing in. *Fuck.*

Her lashes barely flickered in reaction. *Of course, she's used to this, the paparazzi, the intrusion on normality, the constant attention.*

His hands fell back to his sides in fists. "I'll try and swing by your mum's before you leave."

She shook her head. "But my taxi's at eight."

"I'll try."

And then he walked as fast as he could through the crowd around them, feeling her eyes on him every step of the way. He wished for her to run, to chase him down. To tell him he was fool. Tell him she loved him. Tell him she would stay, not because he'd asked but because she wanted to.

He was still hoping the next morning, sitting in his office and staring at his phone, willing it to ring, to buzz—any indication that she was coming back to him. Every knock at his door took him back to the first time she had reappeared; her insistence to gain entry and the hold she immediately had over him.

But...nothing.

He picked up his phone and stared at it long and hard, the truth eating away at him, begging to be outed.

You can't do it. You really can't...but...

Chapter Twenty

SHE WAS STANDING, STARING AT NOTHING. Around her people milled and talked. Now that they knew she was here, people were far more aware of her presence and no amount of disguise could detract from the cameras that followed. She stood out, but she couldn't care.

She looked to the departures board and tried to read it, but she couldn't focus through the tears, her sunglasses making it impossible to make out the text on the screen. This was ridiculous.

She took a steadying breath and slipped them off, praying the tears wouldn't fall. The speculation that would cause would be too much to bear. She felt like the world already knew her pain; was certain Brad and Isla could see it even through their loved-up haze.

She lowered her bag from her shoulder to extract her sunglasses case when her phone started to ring. *Could it be…?*

She couldn't help the flutter of excitement in her belly, although it was getting far less forceful with every passing second as her hope diminished. Ever since Dan had walked out at the party, she'd prayed that every buzz of her phone, every knock on her door would be him. And then when he hadn't turned up to say goodbye, she'd *known* her hope was a waste of time, a waste of emotion…but still it hung on in there like a foolish moth to a flame.

She pulled her phone out and her tummy slumped again, her lips trembling. She clenched her jaw and took another breath. *You can do this.*

She lifted the phone to her ear and answered it. "Ann-Marie."

"Ah, Carrie, just making sure there's no last-minute glitches. I have a car ready to collect you from the airport. I'll be there too of course, we'll head straight to Kimmy's from there—she's positively buzzing about the whole thing, you know?"

The woman hadn't even paused to breathe.

"Carrie? You there?"

"Is she?" she said dumbly. She just couldn't feel excited.

"It's not ideal, of course. You'll have to freshen up on the plane, change if you need to…she's invited several influential characters, some of whom I've not even had the luck to meet as yet. This is huge, absolutely—"

Her phone vibrated against her ear, the arrival of a message temporarily cutting Ann-Marie's incessant trill.

She pulled it away from her ear to check the screen, and there was Dan's name blazing, a text that was too long to preview appearing.

Oh my God. Oh my God. Oh my God.

Fingers shaking, eyes disbelieving, she opened it.

I'm sorry I didn't say goodbye, I couldn't do it, turns out I'm too selfish. If I'd been in front of you, I would have held onto you and never let you go. I love you Carrie, I always have, I always will. Now go and shine, Princess, be the star you were always destined to be, I don't regret a second of what we've shared.

She stopped breathing, her throat closing up as her eyes overflowed. *I love you, Carrie.* It was all she could see; all she could think.

And he'd got it so wrong.

It all made sense now. The pushing her away. Not telling her how he felt. He was protecting her, her career, her life, her dream as he saw it.

But how could he not see that *he* was her life now? Her dream? That without him, everything else became meaningless?

"Carrie...Carrie...are you still there? Blasted cell phones..."

Ann-Marie's wittering called her back to the phone, and she brought it to her ear as she spun on her heel and headed to the exit, suitcase in tow.

"I'm sorry, Ann-Marie, I can't make it. I have some place else I need to be."

"Carrie, what are you saying? Don't be silly now, don't do anything rash. Just get yourself on that plane and then we can talk thr—"

"Please give my apologies to Kimmy. I totally understand if she wants to cast someone else in my place."

"But Carrie..."

"But nothing Ann-Marie, I need to go and win the love of my life. Everything else comes second."

"Really? Are you quite well?"

"I'm better than well. I'm in love."

She cut the call, her smile growing, her step light and her determination palpable. The crowds seemed to part for her, even the photographers seemed to get out of her way, a curious buzz building around her. She headed to the taxi rank, her destination clear.

And if Kimmy wanted her that much, she could bloody well wait. This was far more important.

He was pacing, wishing that he'd just gotten in the car and driven like an idiot to get to her in time.

She should have got the message before she'd boarded the plane, so why hadn't she replied? *And said what exactly?*

"I don't know," he erupted to himself.

What the hell had he been thinking? Had he totally screwed up walking out last night? Had his confession hurt her somehow? Had he insulted her by calling her Princess? Would she never speak to him again?

Christ, he was going out of his mind.

A rap on the door stopped him mid-step, and he stared at it as if he would somehow see through it. "Yes?"

Max entered, his face oddly cautious.

"What is it?"

"You have a vis—"

"Dan, you bloody idiot."

In she stormed, her confident stride so like that first time she'd walked into his office. He couldn't believe she was real. Was it some twisted joke? Was it actually Isla come to bollock him?

"Carrie?"

"Who else? The bleeding tooth fairy?"

"Err, I'm just going to leave you to it," Max said slowly, backing all the way out the door and swinging it closed.

His lips twitched; joy, hope, surprise all making him want to laugh.

"How could you wait until the very last second to tell me you loved me?"

He shook his head. "Didn't my message make that clear?"

"That you're selfish?" she blustered, her cheeks pink and eyes wild with unshed tears. "It also missed that you're pig-headed, annoyingly contradictory, and loveable beyond all reason."

His heart swelled, his ribs fit to burst; did he dare to believe? "Is that how you tell me you love me?"

She stilled, her lips parting, her head shaking. "Haven't I been showing you how much I love you ever since I returned?"

He gave a soft laugh. Hadn't she tried? Didn't he see that now?

"I couldn't let myself believe it," he admitted. "I wouldn't force you down a path with my own feelings, I had to be sure you were doing what you wanted. I was too scared of being responsible for the way the future panned out."

"You mean my future career."

"Yes...partly."

She smiled as she walked towards him, her hands reaching up to cup his jaw and rasping over his stubble. "I loved you all those years ago, and I still love you now. Only this time I'm older and wiser. I know my life will never be complete without you in it. That it's you I've been missing, you that I've been searching for—not my next big role, or the next big move in my career—"

"Oh God, Kimmy Diaz!" His eyes widened as he took hold of her hips. "Your dinner, tonight—"

She pressed her thumb to his lips, silencing him. "If she wants me that much, she'll wait. And if she doesn't..." she shrugged, "...I don't care. I only care that you want me."

She lifted up on her tip toes, her lips replacing her thumb as she brushed over his mouth with her words. "I love you, Dan."

The air swept from his lungs, his arms wrapping around her tight. "I love you too, Princess."

He bent to kiss her, and she arched back to evade him, her eyes alive and sparking into his. "Boss. I prefer Boss."

He chuckled, and she laughed, the melodic sound filling his ears, his heart. He swallowed it with his lips, breaking their kiss just long enough to say: "Yes, Boss."

Epilogue

One Year Later

THE REGISTRAR'S SMILE SWEPT THE ROOM. Fairy lights adorned the rich, wooden beams of the barn in which they stood, reflecting in her eyes as they came back to settle on the couples at the altar. "You may now kiss the brides."

Carrie turned to Dan. Isla turned to Brad. Mum turned to Dad. The crowd cheered around them.

It was so funny, so magical, Carrie giggled as she pressed her lips to Dan's.

"You shouldn't laugh, you know," he murmured against her. "They'll think it's a joke."

"You can't say it's not unusual."

"Everything about you is unusual."

She erupted again, and then slowly raised herself up on tip toes, her lips beside his ear. "Not *all* of me I hope."

She dropped back, her eyes staring into his questioning gaze. Was she talking sexual innuendo during their wedding ceremony? His lips quirked. But then she took his hand, and dropped it to her belly, the move so subtle—so meaningful.

No—they couldn't be.

He raised his brow. The registrar spoke, but all he heard were Carrie's silent words as she pressed his hand just there…

Yes. A baby. Their baby.

His eyes glistened, happiness catching in his throat. When she'd told him she loved him, he hadn't thought it possible to be happier. She'd proved him wrong when she'd moved in with him. Proved him wrong again, when she agreed to marry him.

And now, here he was, the happiest man alive all over again.

It seemed happiness knew no bounds when it came to the love of his life.

Carrie leaned to her right, her eyes gesturing to Isla, and he followed her gaze to see the couple's mirrored pose.

You have to be kidding.

It could only happen with twins. With Carrie and Isla.

His eyes swept to the other couple taking up center stage, and there they were staring right back at them all, a look of realization and sheer joy in their doting gaze.

"Now if you will all be seated, while the happy couples sign the register…"

He shook his head in amazement, his eyes coming back to hers. "I love you," he mouthed.

She smiled, her lips mirroring his. "I love you too."

About Rachael Stewart

Rachael Stewart writes love stories, from the heartwarmingly romantic to the wildly erotic! Despite a degree in Business Studies and spending many years in the corporate world, the desire to become an author never waned and it's now her fulltime pleasure, a dream come true. A Welsh lass at heart, she now lives in Yorkshire with her husband and three children, and if she's not glued to her laptop, she's wrapped up in them or enjoying the great outdoors seeking out inspiration.

You can reach her via:
Twitter @rach_b52
Facebook rachaelstewartauthor
Website rachaelstewartauthor.com

Also by Rachael Stewart

Unshackled
The Good Sister
The Bad Sister

Dear Reader,

Thank you for reading *The Bad Sister*! Many books thrive or perish based on reviews or a lack thereof. Please consider posting an honest review on the site you purchased this book from and/or on Goodreads. If you're new to writing reviews or wouldn't know how to write one, you could start by sharing what you found most enjoyable about this book.

Also, be sure to sign up for the Deep Desires Press newsletter. This is the best way to stay on top of new releases, meet the authors, and take advantage of coupons and deals. Please visit our website at www.deepdesirespress.com and look for the newsletter sign-up box at the bottom of the page.

Thanks again,
Deep Desires Press

WIN FREE BOOKS!

Our email newsletter is the best way to stay on top of all of our new releases, sales, and fantastic giveaways. All you have to do is visit deepdesirespress.com/newsletter and sign up today!

SUBSCRIBE TO OUR PODCASTS!

Deep Desires Podcast releases monthly episodes where we talk to your favorite authors—or authors who will soon become your favorite!

Deep Desires After Dark features sexy excerpts read by our fabulous authors!

Find both podcasts on Apple Podcasts, Google Podcasts, Stitcher, Listen Notes, and our website (deepdesirespress.com/podcast/). Subscribe today!

Support the Deep Desires Podcast on Patreon and you can receive free ebooks every month! Find out more at patreon.com/deepdesirespodcast!

Don't Miss These Great Titles From Deep Desires Press

The Good Sister
Rachael Stewart

When girl-next-door Isla switches lives with her celebrity twin sister, she expects a temporary escape from her troubles back home—not to become girlfriend to her teenage celebrity heartthrob, a man who's falling as hard for her as she is for him. But can their love survive her big secret?

Available now in ebook and paperback!

Unshackled
Rachael Stewart

On a thrilling ride of sexual awakening, love, money, and corruption, 22-year-old Abigail becomes a player in a wildly debauched world where her chance at love might just mean losing everything.

A scorching tale of love, money, corruption, and sex—available in paperback and ebook!

To Love This Woman
Patricia Pellicane

She wants him. She doesn't have to love him to love the things he can do to her. He insists she must, but what has love to do with want?

Available now in paperback and ebook!

The Weeping Forest
James Missaglia

When Julieta is captured by her enemies, she is handed over to a sadistic countess with one aim—to use pleasure and pain to turn the demure princess into a pleasure slave for the sadistic warlord who burned her city.

A very erotic romance in ebook and paperback!

Finding A Keeper
Michelle Geel

When PA Brenna Palmer meets millionaire and sexually unquenchable Gabriel Burke, her search for Mr. Right gets a lot more complicated when he makes her an offer she can't resist.

A scorching hot love story, available in paperback and ebook!

Kinksters at Play
Sonni de Soto

When Kat and Peter's marriage starts to fall apart, a community of kinksters brings them back together again in these interwoven stories about how, with trust, communication, and the right partners, play can make life and love so much better.

A hot, kinky bundle in ebook and paperback!

Stealing Beauty
Fairy Tales After Dark #1
Jessica Collins

This time, it's the Beast who's going to attempt to tame the Beauty. The only thing he can't protect her from...is himself.

A modern and sexy re-telling of Beauty and the Beast! Available now in ebook and paperback!

Finders Keepers
Fairy Tales After Dark #2
Jessica Collins

When a sexy-as-sin Dominant shows her a whole new world of whips and restraints, Jayla wants to trust him, but the scars of her abusive past are in the way.

An almost-too-hot retelling of Aladdin! Available now in ebook and paperback!

Body Language
Tim Bartholomew

In this fast-paced tale of beauty and three beasts, an irresistible hero is locked in deadly conflict with a craven older woman out for carnal revenge. Can Andrew's manhood survive in the teeth of her demands?

A comedic, sexy romp in paperback and ebook!

Going Solo
The Complete "Casual Car Sex" Series Bundle
Storm Stone

When a sexy Las Vegas bad boy finds out that his sex experiences with a mysterious Englishwoman are being used for her blog, he decides to extract his revenge, but it becomes a gateway into their deepest, darkest desires, where there is no turning back...

Available now in ebook and paperback!

Heathens
Britt Collins

Murder, drugs, revenge, along with an overbearing family of criminals; JB and Amina will need each other to stay alive.

Available now in ebook and paperback!

Power To Love
Power Brothers #1
J. Margot Critch

The Key West vacation Cash Power had planned—a chance to clear his head of the memories of his time as a conflict photographer—takes a turn for the steamyw hen he meets Karen Gallagher, an environmental lawyer who needed a break from her stressful worklife.

Available now in ebook and paperback!